CROSSED WIRES

CLOSSED WIRES

CROSSED WIRES

John E. Simpson

Carroll & Graf Publishers, Inc.
New York

First Carroll & Graf edition 1992

Carroll & Graf Publishers, Inc.
260 Fifth Avenue
New York, NY 10001

Library of Congress Cataloging-in-Publication Data is available.

ISBN: 0-88184-800-X

Manufactured in the United States of America

This novel is a work of fiction. Names, characters and incidents are
either the product of the author's imagination or are used fictitiously.
Any resemblance to actual events or to persons, living or dead, "real" or
on-line, is entirely coincidental. Actual locales referred to in the text
may be recognizable to readers familiar with central New Jersey, New
York City, and Philadelphia, but are manipulated for purposes of this
fictional narrative; no suggestion is made that they have ever accommo-
dated or could actually accommodate the events described herein.

To the memory of my father:
first and foremost of puzzlers.

Acknowledgments

A number of people on the CompuServe Information Service provided invaluable (albeit sometimes unwitting) assistance in the preparation of *Crossed Wires*. Chief among these were the members of MedSig, Disabilities Forum, and the Literary Forum; thanks very much for your help and continued friendship and encouragement, folks.

In particular, I'd like to thank LitForum members G.G. Brame, Alex Krislov, and Toni Whitfield, for help with a variety of technical and stylistic questions; John L. Myers, for his ongoing fulfillment of the cheerleading function; and my agent Virginia Kidd, for helping me make my faltering, neurotic way through the maze of my first book's publication. Special debts are owed to LitForum's two "DGs": David Gerrold, for showing me the way to my characters; and Diana Gabaldon, for showing me the way to my confidence.

My management at AT&T made it possible for me to take the leave of absence during which *Crossed Wires* was written. Thanks to Al Grorud, Cindy Pedersen, and Dale Riebold for that; and to others (notably Iona Kerr, the two Claires, and Lydia) who ensured that the paperwork and other bureaucratic requirements were fulfilled without a hitch.

Thanks, finally, to Margaret J. Campbell, for Ashland. Thought I'd forget, didn't you?

Prologue

Traffic shishes past on a darkening street, early in an autumn evening; the streets are slick with wet brown leaves; overhead, a thin scimitar of a crescent moon is just poking through the clouds, barely illuminating the tumbled-blocks structures of an apartment complex in the suburbs of a large city. Telephone lines shiver and gleam in the wet; death is perched there at first, then effortlessly soars aloft for a moment, stoops, and comes to rest, silently, on the landing outside the door of one apartment.

Through the curtains in the window of this apartment seeps a pale yellow light, echoing the moonlight above, and on the other side of the window, at a desk in a corner of her bedroom, sits a young woman. If we could peek inside her mind, we might observe that she is both young enough and old enough to be both always confident with men and always surprised by them; that she has in fact loved many men, with just this mixture of pleasure and confusion, been head over heels with a few, even; but that she has never loved any of them in quite the way that she loves what she sees on the glowing green screen of the computer parked on her desk.

Across the surface of this screen, two, three, or more times a day, dances an ensemble of words written by people whom she has never met and never will meet (none of them, that is, except for one: very briefly, and very soon), people who, like her, sit as though hypnotized before an unblinking glowing rectangle, a green or white or multicolored eye, their thousand fingers clicking across their keyboards like the chattering of teeth. Meanwhile, spouses and lovers go ignored, children and pets unfed, jobs uncompleted—all put on hold, for now, all for the sake of faraway, invisible friends.

Invisible, yes, but neither nameless nor without substance. Some of her friends' names are real (a John, a Liz, a Sharon, and others) and a handful are patently fictitious (Butterfly, AntMan, and so on). One friend makes a joke out of everything; another is always ill-tempered and discourteous unless you need advice; yet another seems always caught helplessly in an endless succession of life-tangles, and can suffocate you with his dependence if you let him. Minnesota, New Mexico, Georgia, Japan, Hawaii, Illinois, Vermont, California, England, New York, Virginia, France, Saudi Arabia: yes, they reside in all these places and many more. But they sense one another only through their machines, as if only there do they truly *live,* inhaling and exhaling—taking life in and expelling it—through a little box attached to each machine, a little box from which snakes a wire umbilicus to the telephone network.

You might say it is love that the little box and the wire deliver: the young woman loves all these friends as revealed in their words that whisper across her screen. She loves their playfulness, their occasional spite, all the shifting emotional chiaroscuro of their tangled webs of relationships and electrons. Sitting there in the twilight in her room, the only sound the whir of the computer's fan, the click of its keys, a rare *beep,* she can sense the love running out and the love running back in, endlessly, in a silent electronic tide.

She sits there reading their words and smiling, or sometimes with her brow furrowed in perplexity or her eyes flashing with the intensity of her feeling. Once, she laughs out loud, covering the sound of a faint *click* from the other room. She presses a button on the keyboard and the screen flashes clear, then refills with new words, and the flashing on the screen obscures from her the reflection of a shadowy form in the doorway behind her. She chuckles again, and then types out a few more words; she sips from a can of diet soda, sighs, and presses a final, very special key. She places the can back on the desktop.

Then there is a thump, and a soft, slow scraping sound, and the bubbling away of her life onto the carpet is obscured by the faintest of noises coming from the little box attached to her machine: a buzz and a series of seven *beeps* followed, as always, by a click and a brief, high-pitched cartoon scream. And her final message goes flying out over the wire, that more-than-eloquent message which will flash across the screens and into the hearts of all her dear, distant friends when next they check:

Good night, everybody!!!

Chapter One

In her dream, Finley was skipping from stone to stone across a brook. The little islands of rock seemed connected somehow, tied together, was it, by string? Suddenly a hand shot up out of the water, frighteningly soundless, the arm clad in black, gleaming and wet, and it seized her by the ankle. But she slipped free and continued to hop across from rock to rock. Giggling crazily.

She'd awakened, giggling aloud, before the first alarm clock sounded—the one with the clamorous jangling bell from hell—so she was able to stifle it before being yanked noisily from sleep. When the second alarm went off a few minutes later—the clock-radio, tuned to the local oldies station—she was *thrilled* to be nudged playfully out of bed by a morning Motown special; Finley wasn't old enough to have heard them when they first came out, but she *loved* Motown oldies. . . . She remembered to remove both her hearing aids before entering the shower (not always a given, you know, not always something to be counted on); she sang, with the music, of hearing a symphony there under the delicious warmth of the water drumming on her skin, the walls of the shower stall vibrating in joyful sympathy with her voice and mood.

She'd gone then to her bedroom closet to select the day's wardrobe, and laughed softly to herself. The shelf in the closet, victim of her landlord's colossal ineptitude, was fastened to the drywall not with anchors, but with simple screws; it was always threatening to collapse on her—she could see the white-dusty threads protruding from the wall—but, miraculously, hadn't yet done so.

And today it held, too, on this beautiful morning on which nothing could go wrong. Indeed, all her landlord's "repairs," from the closet shelf, to the barrel-bolt on the *inside* of the closet door, to the kitchen tap handles that you had to turn in the wrong direction and the lumpy ill-spackled spots on the walls—all of this just made her laugh today.

She could feel the day's very goodness in the soft scratchiness of the knit cotton shirt when she pulled it down over her head, in the cotton hug of her jeans when she tugged them up over her legs and rubbed them smooth over her fanny and hips.

Her teakettle of water, on the portable burner by the computer workstation in the bedroom, began to whistle just when she was ready for it, a second after she'd finished feeding her parakeet, Stupid. She pulled up the window shade and the fall morning was beautiful, bright oranges and golds standing out starkly against a blue blue sky; Stupid seemed to agree, and began to chirp maniacally and in apparent ecstasy. And as Finley sat before her computer screen, sipping at her tea, and checked her electronic mail from the night before, every single message made her smile, from whatzisname's dopey puns all the way down through the stack to the giddy exuberance of her friend Tracy's closing message of the previous night:

Good night, everybody!!!

So Finley just knew that, yes, it was going to be a wonderful day.

But it didn't turn out that way.

To begin with, when she boarded the bus that took her a few miles from her apartment in New Brunswick, New Jersey, out of the city to the former farmlands now rehabilitated as office buildings, shopping centers, parking lots, out to the computer center where she worked, she managed somehow to step on the lace of one of her sneakers. She fell headlong against the bus driver, breaking the strap of her favorite handbag; worse, when her head hit the man's shoulder one hearing aid fell out.

She didn't at first realize this had happened, not until she righted herself and said, "Oh! I'm sorry!" when her voice thudded, muffled, inside her head as though she were speaking into a pillow—then of course she knew, but where did it fall . . . ? It was there, in the man's lap. Instinctively, she began to reach for it; then, reddening, caught herself. "Can I have . . . *that?*" she asked him, and pointed at his lap. Several passengers erupted into laughter.

"There you go!" said the driver, grinning, as he plucked the hearing aid from his crotch delicately between thumb and forefinger and handed it back to her. "The family jewel!" he added. Her face burning, Finley moved up the aisle. Great, she thought, now she'd have to put the damned thing back in her ear in public. She *hated* to do that—it still, after all these years, made her feel self-conscious, like screwing in a wooden leg or something. . . .

"Finley!" bawled a voice six rows back, a voice that was always recognizable even without hearing aids. What the hell, she thought, was the always-insufferable William Lord doing on the bus? And, oh God, there's an empty seat next to him—!

"Finley!" he called again. "C'mon, sit over here!"

Resigning herself to an interminable half-hour ride next to this donkey, Finley sat. She reached up with one hand to pull her hair out of the way in order to insert the hearing aid. "Hi, Bill," she began, "what're you doing on—"

"Here, let me help," Lord interrupted, and he reached up with one of his *pink clammy hands* and, yecch! *started to touch her hair* . . . !

Finley lunged away from him, her head thrusting out into the aisle and ramming into the unfortunate abdomen of an elderly man shuffling to the front of the bus. "Ooooo," the man said, doubling over, and Finley's other hearing aid plopped to the floor.

"Ha ha! Oh-for-two, Finley!" Lord brayed.

So no, it hadn't turned out to be the best of mornings after all—and it got even worse shortly after she arrived at work. She stopped in first to chat with Ray Daniels; but he was on the phone, early though it was, and he merely waved her away, with a shrug that wasn't quite apologetic enough for Finley's mood. Her buddy Monica Van Ness wasn't even in yet. Then finally she'd just sat down at her own desk with another cup of tea, had just tapped the power switch beneath her table; the computer as always had just presented her with the day's wakeup message (this one said,

"In two words: im possible. —Samuel Goldwyn");

the day's event list, including the names of the previous day's crime victims, had just begun to scroll slowly by on the screen, and the words

"HOMICIDE: WILLIAMS, TRACY CHRISTINE . . .
incision . . . computer . . ."

had just begun to nibble at the corner of Finley's mind—" 'Tracy'? *TRACY?"*—when the power blacked out.

Power blackouts were not supposed to happen at large government computer centers: information was supposed to gallop without pause or failure up and through and around the circuitry, landing at last onto the screen of the person who summoned it, whether law clerk, senator, military attaché, or—like Finley herself—researcher here at CIAC, the National Crime Information and Analysis Center. There were battery backups and generators by the dozen, all to ensure the uninterrupted show of data.

So Finley knew, in the abstract, that this was not a good thing, this blackout. But from her perspective it wasn't too bad, in itself; she actually enjoyed a little the sensation of sitting in sudden silent darkness—who'd think to have a candle handy?—instead of the ever-present vague white light from the overhead fluorescent panels and the constant flickering glow and buzz and whirring of dozens of terminals, computer screens, and printers. She'd even had to suppress a giggle when Morris, her normally never-funny boss, fell over a box of printer paper a few seconds into the blackout, crashing against a metal desk somewhere out there on the darkened floor, dragging a telephone to the floor with him, *bang* and *ding*, cursing a deep blue streak.

But the problem, for Finley the damned nuisance, was that when the power did come on, it just trickled. Overhead, a smattering of ceiling lights blinked and came on, preselected for their proximity to what were supposedly the most critical projects; Finley's own two projects did not fit this description, so she still was sitting in her cubicle in no better than a dim gray reflected light. Worst of all, the power to noncritical desktops was similarly restricted—so the screen of Finley's computer had remained, for yet another wasted half hour of frustration, blank and cold. Stalled.

Eventually, it was true, the building services people restored full power, and Finley could return to her work. But she had just begun to get her mind back to its interrupted groove, the event list was just rolling past again, when Bill Lord shambled in and sat in the spare chair by the doorway.

As usual, he had a huge styrofoam cup of lukewarm coffee in his hand. As usual, he was, within moments, past the office small-talk stage and into the leering, suggestive stage—this time, about the prospect of being in Finley's cubicle the next time the power went off. This had been almost an appealing routine in the beginning, when she first came to CIAC, before she knew him, before she heard it the first five or six or twenty-eight times. But Finley was no longer feeling playful this morning—especially for this nitwit—and she cut him off soon after he started. "Bill, the *power* just came on. I just can't make myself be polite enough to listen to you right now."

His watery eyes registered theatrically excruciating pain. "Okay, Jeez, no *problem,*" he said, and he stood up. The burly Morris chose that moment to veer around the corner into Finley's cube. He began, "Finl—" but didn't immediately get to finish, as he and Lord collided with a grunt; a plume of the latter's coffee arced the short distance across the table, down the front of Finley's pullover, onto her jeans, and—most painfully—across the keyboard of her computer. As she feared, after Lord had ducked out, squeezing without apology past Morris in the doorway, and after Morris himself had drawn her attention to whatever new little bureaucratic curlicue he'd dreamt up and then backed out of her cubicle, absently touching the fresh Band-Aid on his forehead as though saluting her—after all this, when she touched the keys of her keyboard nothing happened on-screen. Nothing.

She sighed in exasperation. She wanted to fly to Morris's office and demand Lord's immediate evisceration. Or even better: she would insist that the Center turn its clocks back and let her start the whole day over; let her stand, swaying, beneath the shower again, her voice blending with Diana Ross's in sweet muffled harmony. But no, get a grip, Finley; the world does not work that way. Compose yourself. Sit down in the cafeteria for a few minutes. *Then* meekly approach Morris and submit your humble but nonetheless heartfelt request (using, of course, the appropriate three-part form) that Lord be drawn and quartered.

Sitting in the cafeteria over by the window which looked out onto the treed courtyard, Finley at first continued to fume over the day's progress while she sipped at another cup of tea but gradually, with the tea, drifted down toward room temperature. She looked out the window. It was actually a mosaic of windows, made of some kind of lenticular glass block; the wall of glass taken as a whole showed you hundreds of miniature replicas of the courtyard scene, like the window of an electronics store full of television sets all tuned to the same channel. The interstices between the blocks were themselves narrow strips of mirror glass, so that the outdoor scene was webbed with slivers of the indoor. And in one of these narrow mirrors, a quarter-inch strip at a time, Finley's gaze moved from the glass block to examine herself.

She was disgusted about her shirt. She'd mopped at it first with wet paper towels, then dry ones, with little effect; the coffee stains would never wash out, she imagined. The pullover had a crew neck and it buttoned halfway down, almost like the top half of a union suit. She guessed she'd be able to wear it while painting walls or something, but not much more. Ruined. The jeans—well, jeans were jeans, they accumulated over their long lifetimes all sorts of spots and scars; these hadn't been splattered too badly so they'd be okay after a washing or two. And she always wore jeans, God knew she had lots of others to choose from.

Then she looked up at her face. Once she pushed aside an unruly lock of sandy brown hair, she could see, in the metallic ribbon that cross-hatched the window, the center of one brown eye; a few inches down was one corner of her mouth, slightly turned up in the beginning of a smile. She turned her head a few inches to the side, and the strip of reflection swept over to the other eye and the other corner of her mouth. And when she split the difference and turned back again just so, there was her narrow nose, not quite narrow enough to be viewed entirely in this slip of a mirror, but close. And there, too, was the slight ridge at the center of her mouth and her thin lips, and when she drew back her upper lip, flattening it tightly against her upper teeth, there was that damned incisor with the damned chip in the corner. . . . She reached up to touch the tooth, and then suddenly there was the braying voice of Lord himself across the table from her: "Well, if it isn't Bucky Beaver! Not so busy now, are we?"

He was just sitting down, as usual uninvited but, also as usual, not at all deterred. Finley drained her cup, then stood. "Yeah, Jeez, yeah, I do have to get some things done. Thanks for reminding me, Bill. 'Bye again." Her astringent civility amazed even her sometimes. She strode away, the slight curl at the end of her straight hair brushing against her shoulders as she walked. Just once, she sneaked a look back; behind her, Lord himself had turned to the mirror, and was exploring his own teeth with a fingertip.

But despite all the "things" she allegedly had to get done, Finley did not go to her desk; instead, she went directly to Morris's office.

"Morris, I can't use my keyboard anymore, not since Bill Lord and you"—taking a chance with that, Finley—"spilled coffee all over it. I'd like permission to switch it either with yours or his until it can be replaced."

Morris looked up, ponderously, from his own keyboard. He stared at Finley for a few seconds, not speaking; then he became aware that she was prepared to immobilize him for her own sake. "No, Finley," he said, "not mine. Bill's."

"I can take Bill's keyboard?" she asked. This was turning out to be easier than she'd hoped.

"No. You can use his PC. In his office."

"What? But—" But her remonstrances were in vain. Morris was a nice man, authoritative and good at his job, but frustratingly limited sometimes. Once she'd reduced him to a choice between Bill Lord's convenience and his own, she'd lost her case; that was the only dilemma he needed to resolve.

Her shoulders slumping in defeat, then, Finley returned to her cube and gathered up the materials she'd need for her current projects. Logbooks, blank diskettes, manuals, and the project files themselves. She trudged, arms full, across the corridor to Lord's office, trying, and failing, to come to grips with the prospect of spending an undetermined number of further horrible days in his execrable presence.

Chapter Two

Not more than a few hours later, on the way home, Finley shuddered as she recalled the rest of the so-called beautiful day. Lord had taken advantage of every opportunity to "just need to get a book on that shelf back there, no don't bother to get up, Finley," or sometimes a calculator, or a pen—brushing up against her stiffened back every time, once even placing a hand on her shoulder when he moved around behind the chair she occupied. She'd eaten lunch with Ray and Monica, but even their sympathy and laughter hadn't helped much.

But while moving in with Lord was a repellent nuisance, Finley carefully reminded herself, her job really was a pretty good one.

She was not a field agent with CIAC (which everyone pronounced "kayak")—not one of the lucky folks working behind the scenes with their counterparts in the FBI or state and local police, helping to crack difficult cases, occasionally there at the scene as a suspect was handcuffed for the cameras and reporters. No, Finley herself was just a researcher, a "searcher": she fed those agents, morsel of information by morsel.

The requested morsel might be a mouthful, like, "What has been the trend in cars stolen (by make, model, and model year) for the last twenty years?" Or it might be bite-size: "What times did nonstop passenger trains leave Boston for New York on December 12, 1978?" Finley seldom knew the purpose of these questions, nor did she need to; she just needed to get the answers.

But she didn't get the answers the traditional way, by plodding through books and magazines and face-to-face interviews with people who might eventually become expert witnesses. She used a computer, and seldom left her desk.

Somewhere out there, on at least one other computer, was the answer to just about any question you could imagine. Much of this information was stored in computerized databases of facts—over four thousand such databases the last time she'd seen a count—organized by subject matter; their data kept on huge magnetic platters stacked one atop the other and wired cunningly to the computers which hosted them; all this hardware residing in vast concrete-and-steel, air-conditioned buildings, just sitting there, dormant, waiting for the user to ask the right question in the right way.

More thrillingly, when the specific fact wasn't out there or when Finley didn't know how to get to it, there was always an expert out there who *did* know.

She still remembered the little buzz she'd felt in college when she first learned of this flickering, electronic web of expertise. She wasn't a computer jock or electronics whiz, just an undirected liberal arts undergrad, bumping from topic to topic like an oversized canoe in a narrow stream. In the course of researching a paper on the pronunciation of Old English, Finley had run out of resources: she couldn't account for all the vowels. Apparently puzzled that she hadn't thought of this herself, her professor suggested getting the information "by going on-line and—"

"Going *where?*" she had interrupted.

"On-line. You know, with a PC?"

Finley did not know, and the professor spent the better part of an afternoon showing her. You needed a computer, a little electronic device attached to it, called a "modem," and a telephone line. That was it. You pressed the right keys on the PC's keyboard and even Finley could actually hear it working—first the buzz of a dial tone, then beep, boop, beep—as the modem dialed a telephone number. Down at the other end, connected to the telephone number it was calling, was another modem which after a few rings actually answered, you could hear the clicks and then a high-pitched sort of whistle. Attached to this other modem was another, usually bigger computer—a computer not with just one, but several or perhaps hundreds, even thousands of other computer users accessing it, all tied to it through modems and telephone lines. Finley remembered reading somewhere that there were over fifty thousand of these larger computers around the country; assume one for almost every imaginable topic of knowledge—nursing, baseball cards, physics, library science, comic books, psychology, foreign languages, quilting—and even allowing for some duplication, the amount of information available to you and your computer and its little electronic wonder-box was almost unlimited.

To this day, she shivered a little with excitement whenever she "logged in," as the saying went, to one of these storehouses of knowledge, and posted a question there. They were called "electronic bulletin board systems," or "BBSs," and that was exactly right: you tacked up a note for everyone to read, or sometimes just for a particular someone, and a reply always came back. She had once asked, for example, "Why is it that latex paint is water-soluble, but oil-based paint isn't?" Everyone else who logged in to that BBS over the next few days found Finley's question there, and since she'd chosen the BBS carefully—its users were industrial chemists—she promptly got an answer. She knew she would; she *always* got an answer. People were just unbelievably generous with information and advice. Even if no one there knew the answer, someone would suggest a different BBS where she could post the question. Every question she'd yet asked in the course of her work was answered, somehow, within just a few tries.

She'd loved her job with CIAC from the start. And of her two current projects, one even had a little extra intellectual seasoning: she was seeking not a specific answer to a specific question, but a pattern. As the field agent had framed the question, it sounded simple enough: "How has the number of armed robberies over the last five years," he'd typed on the data request form, "varied with changes in the weather?" The question was too vague in that form, so she'd kicked it back to the agent: the number of armed robberies *where*? changes in the weather over how short an interval of time? He was only interested in Indiana, it turned out, but Finley had wandered through a dozen new databases and BBSs for this one. Getting, for example, the incidence of armed robberies was simple enough on an annual basis, but she'd had to dig more deeply to get information almost day by day. And what was a "change in the weather"? Was a fluctuation of a few degrees significant enough to be a "change"? When a barometer's gauge read, "Changeable," what did that *mean*? A puzzle, really, of philosophy, of linguistics, almost as much as statistics.

As for her other current project, she knew almost nothing about it; she'd gotten the first data request forms for it only a few days ago. A couple of homicides, maybe related and maybe not. The only searching she'd had to do for this project so far was some boring motor-vehicle checks on the victims' cars; she didn't even know their names.

But with the other one, her main project, Finley was learning about weather patterns, and she was just beginning to visualize superimposing a graph of the incidence of armed robbery in each major city on a graph, say, of precipitation. So this was *interesting,* she kept insisting to Morris. But she longed, just once, to work on a project the point of which she really understood, a project that engaged her imagination, her *soul,* as well as her *mind.*

She knew what that really meant, all right: she wanted to be a field agent. She'd even approached Morris with this once. He looked a little skeptical; field agents, after all, were generally former detectives, people with some first-hand knowledge of police and FBI procedure. But he said nothing to discourage her, just put her in touch with a woman he knew in Personnel. The interview was humiliating; the woman with whom she met had an extremely soft voice, and even with her hearing aids turned up to their full near-whistling maximum volume, Finley had had to struggle to hear. The woman had finally pursed her lips and paused and, for once speaking slowly and distinctly and loudly enough so that Finley could not mistake the words, said, "I'm sorry. Your credentials and your abilities are wonderful, but . . ." And, smiling ruefully, the woman had gestured at her ears. Finley remained a searcher.

Bill Lord, thank God for small favors, wasn't an on-line searcher like Finley, Monica, and Ray, huddled like them in one of the smallish gray cubicles running the length of the corridor. Otherwise, she'd have to deal with him more often. A daily barf. No, Lord was one of the dwindling minority of paper searchers, plodding dinosaurs as Finley couldn't help thinking of them, most of whom were located in Washington, convenient to the Library of Congress and other documentary sources. For some reason, the few paper searchers here at the computer center in New Jersey had offices instead of cubicles, offices with real doors—some sort of atavistic hierarchy, it seemed to Finley, as if a fact's black-and-white appearance on paper made it more "true," less arguable and hence more important, than its flickering across a computer screen. So Lord didn't make much use of his PC (she secretly doubted that he knew how)—and that was why, Finley accepted with a sigh, it made sense for Morris to move her there. That, and the fact that Lord's office was directly across the corridor from her cubicle.

But if this went on too long, she promised herself, if it took the tech-support people too long to replace her keyboard—well, hey, maybe Morris would let her work at home . . . ! She stepped from the bus at the corner by her apartment after an uneventful ride home, humming softly. On that hopeful note, she could almost hear a symphony again.

Stupid chattered and chirped at Finley as she read through the day's stack of bills and junk mail, then as she moved on to prepare dinner. As usual, when she pressed the beeping buttons on her microwave oven, Stupid sang out, "Cheep! Cheep! Chirp!" in reply. The parakeet would talk to anything that chattered inhumanly, the microwave oven and modem included. Even when Finley so much as opened a cabinet door, he might echo from his cage, "Creek?" Furthermore, if she then let the cabinet door slam shut, Stupid would go insane, screeching as though he'd been shot. Maybe *his* hearing was too acute.

She thumbed through the newspaper as she ate, looking for news of a Tracy Williams's killing. But there was nothing. Even if it was the same Tracy, she knew, her Tracy of the "Good night, everybody!!!" message, even then there wouldn't necessarily be any news of it here in Finley's own local paper; "her" Tracy could be anywhere in the country. Overseas, even.

That was one of the frustrations of communicating on-line: you never really knew the people at the other end of the wire—never any more than they chose to tell you. You didn't know where they lived, or what they did for a living, or whether they were married or single, or whether they had pets. If they were bedridden you couldn't tell; they could just as easily be convicts as high-school students; for all Finley knew, the elderly man whom she'd crippled on the bus this morning might be one of them. Many of them didn't even use real names, preferring imaginative monikers—aliases or "handles"—in the same way that CB radio users did. Finley herself, for that matter, just went by "Finley," leaving her correspondents to guess whether that was a first name or last; indeed, she'd so much liked the anonymity it engendered that she'd carried the habit over into real life. Now no one, on-line or off-, called her anything else.

Still, Finley reflected for the umpteenth time as she sat down before the PC, for as little as you knew about them you could get remarkably close to some of these people. "Her" Tracy, for example. They'd met on a library-and-research BBS called STACKS about four months ago; hit it right off, they did, and developed a near-daily exchange of private messages, sometimes about work, yes, how to go about finding some niggling little fact or other, but also about the most *intimate* damned matters. Tracy had an almost unimaginably wild life-style, which seemed completely at odds with the stereotype of her position as head librarian in a small town; she seemed to sleep with more men on a regular basis than Finley thought she herself had even *met*.

Also on STACKS were her friends Jon Little-Olden and Uri. Jon lived in Oklahoma or Kansas somewhere, and worked in a city library. Nice guy at heart, he perhaps was, but he insisted on maintaining a rigid misogynistic demeanor on-line that really grated on Finley's nerves. In the few months that she'd known him, she must have had at least six on-line battles with him, all triggered by some stupid generalization or other that he'd made. "But he's been pretty well-behaved lately," she said to herself, grinning—ever since she'd pointed out to him that being a librarian was a "woman's job."

Uri was something of a mystery. For one thing, it wasn't even his name; it was an acronym for "University of Rhode Island," where he worked in the library. He said he couldn't go by his real name because his use of the STACKS BBS was paid for by the college and was therefore not really "his." For another thing, Uri never revealed any personality or anything of his personal life. This, too, was intentional, he'd told Finley once in a private message. He just didn't feel right using the BBS for personal conversations.

Elsewhere, on a bulletin board called FORENSIC, there was a guy, Japanese, who went by the improbable name "Flokati Sostenuto." She and Flokati had known each other for a couple of years now; he'd become almost a big brother to her, she felt almost guiltily, thinking of Warren, her real big brother. But Flokati was different—certainly a heck of a lot less judgmental than Warren, for one thing. And it helped that she'd met Flokati on FORENSIC, which was used by criminologists and forensic specialists such as coroners. Finley wasn't sure exactly what Flokati did for a living, only that it had something to do with the department of forensic medicine at a university in a city called Hokkaido. So as with Tracy, Finley could "talk" with Flokati every now and then about work. With rare exceptions, Flokati was the only person with whom she communicated on FORENSIC, although she scanned the others' public messages from time to time.

Most of Finley's personal BBS usage, though, took place on a board called ABLE, for people with physical or neurological impairments of one kind or another.

She had a little over a half-dozen regular ABLE correspondents who, like her, were hearing-impaired. Collectively, they called themselves the Earwigs. It was like a club, the only requirements for belonging to which were that you had to have (a) something "wrong" with one or both ears and (b) a healthy attitude about it: you needed to be getting along pretty well in spite (or maybe even because) of it. The first letters of the Earwigs's names ran through the first seven letters of the alphabet, from Andrea through George.

And her new ABLE friend Jane—well, what could you say about Jane? She was as down-to-earth a person as you could imagine, not as shockingly open and confidential as Tracy but somehow just as honest, more solid, more stable. Finley knew this instinctively, right from the start, even though she'd only known Jane for about a month. Two months, tops. And it appealed greatly to Finley that Jane's own disability was that she could not speak: mute from birth with a malformed larynx. She loved Jane for the poignant symmetry of being there for Finley, unable to speak but "speaking" with precision into Finley's own perfectly "hearing" on-line consciousness. She saw Jane, in her mind's eye, as an older woman, hair now more gray than not, wearing reading glasses which she'd remove, lost in thought, chewing absentmindedly on the frames as she composed a reply. For whatever reasons of her own, Jane had not for some time corresponded with anyone on ABLE other than Finley.

Tonight, she decided, she would contact all three of her regular BBSs. STACKS first, to try dissolving the uncertain nagging pellet of fear about Tracy which had become lodged in the pit of her stomach. She logged in to STACKS, and typed:

```
To:        Tracy
From:      Finley
Re:        Knock, knock, knock!
Message:
```

She paused. The thought that Tracy might never read this message protruded into Finley's mind like a guilty secret. She went on, carefully:

```
Message:  Yoo-hoo . . . Hey, you out there? Haven't
heard from you for a few days. Drop me a line!
                    Finley
```

That was true. Finley had gotten the blanket message addressed to "All," but nothing to her, personally, since—when was it? Friday? She sent the message on its way with the press of a key.

Next, it was on to ABLE. When she logged in, Finley saw that there were two messages for her, one from Jane and one from Charlotte, one of the Earwigs. The message from Jane said:

```
To:        Finley
From:      <jane>
Re:        Funny story
Message:  Finley, dear, I have to tell you this story. It made
me laugh out loud—well, you know what I mean. I was in
the supermarket today and . . .
```

Jane went on to tell a riotous story about trying to communicate with a butcher about a particular cut of meat she needed—an extremely difficult message to get across, she said, because she'd left her pen and her "talking notepad" out in the car. So she'd taken a steak from the refrigerated rack in the store, placed it in the butcher's hands, and proceeded to karate-chop at it until he got the idea. Finley chuckled at the message, and was warmed as always by Jane's habitual sign-off:

> . . . Love you, dear. <jane>

Even her "<jane>" alias, Finley thought, bespoke in some strange typographic way Jane's daily struggle—and paradoxical success—with voiced language. She composed a reply to Jane's story, about the horrors of the bus ride this morning, and sent it on its way.

Charlotte's message was a reply to the previous day's message from Finley, part of a continuing series of droll Earwiggery about the design specs for something they'd been referring to as "punk hearing aids":

> To: Finley
> From: Charlotte Mittelman
> Re: Punk hearing aids
> Message: Yes, Finley, that's true. <grin> But I think the true distinguishing feature of the punk aid should not be the rusty metal from which it's made or its color or other super-ficial aspects, but its SOUND QUALITY. Just think, for once all the fuzzy wah-wah and feedback could be INTENTIONAL!

Finley laughed out loud at that, and posted a brief appreciative reply to Charlotte, which said, simply:

> . . . Ha ha ha! All right, you win, you can have the con-tract! Sex Pistols in your ear!

Finally, she checked FORENSIC. Nothing tonight from Flokati or from her other acquaintances there, and that was actually a little bit of a relief; her shoulders were stiff, her wrists ached, and she thought what she really wanted was to get out and away from the computer for a little while. She'd head over to McGarrity's, have one beer, tops, then come home and hit the sack. She wanted to catch an early bus to the Center tomorrow (just in case Lord's car was still in the shop and he was taking the bus). Maybe at work, from Lord's office, if Lord would just leave her alone there for a few minutes—maybe there she'd have a chance to write to Flokati sometime tomorrow.

She shut off the PC, stopped briefly before her bedroom mirror to run a hand through her hair—not likely to catch anyone's eye tonight, Finley, but not a disaster, either—and was out the door a few minutes later.

The midautumn air was sharp and clear tonight. McGarrity's Pub, only about five or six blocks away, in the center of New Brunswick, would be an easy fifteen-minute walk. No cab or bus needed tonight.

Crossing the street out front of the apartment complex . . . Mrs. Falco was still on duty behind the counter of the coffee shop —should be closing up soon, though—and she and Finley waved to each other. If the shop was still open on the way back from McGarrity's, maybe she'd stop in to pick up one of those rum-cake things, something sweet for breakfast. . . .

She'd lived in New Brunswick since getting the job with CIAC three years ago. Not at all how she'd pictured a city in New Jersey: clean streets, decent places to eat; accessible by train and bus to almost anywhere, Philadelphia and New York about equally, but far enough away from everywhere not to be tainted (yet) with the urban blues; big companies funneling big money into a variety of urban-renewal projects; the main Rutgers campus, beautiful in Georgian-style (even Georgian-*era*) brick. . . .

It really was a beautiful night. Something about it reminded her of another night she'd walked to McGarrity's, last March, before spring had really laid claim to the air—a night when she walked to the pub not by herself but with one arm linked in someone else's; there had been a hint of frost in the air on that night, too, and a crescent moon like tonight's, but there had also been laughter in the air. Frowning a bit, she again shut a heavy door on that memory, and walked on.

McGarrity's itself was now just a half block or so away. Incongruously, the owners had opted in this Georgian town for a Tudor exterior. Approach it for the first time and you might be fooled into thinking that herein lay a stuffy tourist-trap chain restaurant, where the bartenders were perhaps attired in Beefeater outfits, where ladies with lavender-tinged hair shared cottage-cheese platters for lunch.

But approach it like Finley, now, with foreknowledge, and even before you opened the door you'd know it for what it really was, at least by night: a dim-lit grotto whose bar and oaken dining booths were filled with loud, laughing, boisterous patrons, natives as well as newcomers, university faculty and university students, many of them like Finley herself sweatered, blue-jeaned, sneakered. All smart. All, for the most part, happy. Always at night, from a corner within these four bogus-Tudor walls, boomed the loud loud loud strains of an apparently inexhaustible collection of classic oldies, pumped out of a jukebox the size of a small bank vault. And as a final touch, just below ceiling level, ran a wide-gauge electric train track on which at random intervals the bartender unleashed a genuine Lionel train.

Finley opened the heavy wooden door, as usual being knocked backward a half step at first by the music. Hearing aids in McGarrity's were a bit superfluous. She reached up, turned off the aid in her right ear; "Close the goddam *door!*" she heard someone yell; she grinned, and then was inside.

"Finley!" called three or four voices from the bar. Bodies jostled a little one way then a little the other, making a small space for her at her usual spot, down at the right end of the bar so she'd have the left ear facing any conversation coming her way. Already grinning—you couldn't help it here—she hung up her coat on one of the empty wooden pegs and took her place. "Born to be Wild" gonged from the jukebox.

Colleen was the bartender tonight, as on most nights. She winked as she set before Finley a mug of Bass ale, but was unable to say anything because of the good-natured vociferous argument taking place just to Finley's left.

"Finley!" yelled one of the combatants, a guy with black hair whom she knew only as Tommy. "You work with computers, right?" She nodded and sipped at the beer, grinning a little at the general sort of question he was about to ask her even though she didn't yet know its precise contents. "Me and Patti here"—he pointed with a thumb at his opponent—"we were just discussing, y'know, PCs versus Macintoshes—"

Grinning more broadly now, Finley held up a hand in interruption. "Sorry!" she yelled over something by the Rascals, "I don't talk religion!" Patti laughed, and Tommy rolled his eyes in mock frustration.

She was back in the apartment not even an hour later, sleepy in spite of the brisk walk—and yes, Falco's had been closed, so she'd have to do without any pastry for the morning. She draped Stupid's "Garfield" hood over his cage. He chirped once, groggily. She went to her bedroom, undressed, and shrugged her way into her favorite nightshirt, the red flannel. She set both alarms, then turned out the light. She got into bed and began to drift off to sleep, thinking just once the single word, "Tracy" and nearly coming fully awake again. For a moment, across an otherwise blank screen on the inside of her drowsing eyelids, over and over, scrolled the word HOMICIDE, line by buzzing line. Then, finally, she was asleep.

Chapter Three

She dreamt, again, of a quiet but intense man with whom she was sitting in a dimly lit room, straining to hear his voice. Always unexpected, the dream came back to touch her sleep from time to time; it didn't disturb her, not really, but she'd once described it to a psychologist she'd met on-line, and asked him if it meant anything to him. Well, he couldn't say for sure, he replied; could she answer a few background questions for him? As she was composing her answers to his questions, that's when she had first thought to herself: of course, there's no mystery about it at all. It has to be tied to the events which started on that one day. . . .

Here is Finley, age twelve, sitting in her seventh-grade English class. Mr. Stefanowicz, the teacher, is stalking up and down the aisles in the classroom, barking out the questions for the pop quiz.

As usual, Finley knows most of the answers, and she transcribes them mechanically, without thought, onto the half sheet of lined paper on her desk. When she doesn't know an answer right away, she pencils in, lightly, an abbreviated form of the question: "Hero's friend's name? What country?" She'll give the page a once-over just before turning it in at the conclusion of the quiz, see if any of the missing answers reveal themselves.

But she's not really paying attention to the quiz. Outside the classroom window are the browns-turning-green of early spring. The sun is just shy of its noon zenith. On the soundtrack, if one were available, would be the tumescent creaks and groans of nature straining against its winter straitjacket, echoing the fainter sounds of borderline-adolescent hormones in the bodies of Finley and her classmates, fainter creaks and groanings which manifest themselves in disguised form as the sudden squeak of her friend Maryann's chrome chair, and as the nervous tap-tap-tapping of Jeff Wilkins's pencil on his desktop.

The casement windows along one wall of the classroom are angled inward. With the occasional sound of a passing car outside on Brown Street, slipping in through the open windows are not only the sounds of spring but also its air: that first warm loamy scent that had always made Finley—and always would make her, even after today—think of romping in a meadow somewhere and then lying down on a grassy hillside, looking up and speculating on the shapes of clouds while a friend tickled her chin with a dandelion. . . .

As usual, she is wearing jeans today, and sneakers. Also as usual, Mom isn't crazy about this, but what can she do about it? The school says it's okay with them. And Finley has donned, as a sort of consolation prize for her mother, a light cotton pullover, pale blue, one of Mom's favorites, a pullover that shows off the beginnings of a lithe figure-to-be without unduly accenting the residue of baby fat around Finley's waist. She had jammed the tail of the pullover into her jeans, put on her sneakers, then hopped from foot to foot down the stairs, the hard rubber soles rapping out a noisome tattoo, and danced, more or less, to the breakfast table. Orange juice as always, and tea, and Grape Nuts this morning.

"Now don't forget," Mom said to her as Finley crunched a mouthful of the hard little granules, "your father and I won't be here when you get home from school today. But we won't be too late, either, just let yourself in and read or watch TV or whatever." She escorted Finley to the door. "You won't need a jacket today, honey," Mom said, and kissed her on the forehead. "Got your spare batteries?" Finley reflexively reached up to touch the hearing aid, then down to pat the left pocket of her jeans. She nodded. "Okay? Be a good girl today." As Finley took her seat on the bus, mentally adjusting her energy level to deal with the kids now surrounding her, laughing, gossiping, rattling last-minute homework papers, she looked once out the window at her house. Mom was standing there in the picture window as though in a frame;

she waved, once, just a slight movement of an upraised hand, then was lost in the reflections in the plate glass.

Now, here in fourth-period English, Mr. Stefanowicz suddenly is not barking any longer. Now he is huddled over by the door with Mrs. Olson, the receptionist at the main office, whispering. He looks once in Finley's direction, then calls her name and waves her over. "There's a message for you down in the main office," he explains, his voice low. "Go with Mrs. Olson."

Finley thinks, "Well, why doesn't she just *give* me the message?" But she says aloud only, "My quiz—the paper is on my—"

"Yes, that's all right," Mr. Stefanowicz interrupts. "I'll pick it up. Go with Mrs. Olson now." Finley looks back over her shoulder, once; Maryann's luminous blue eyes are watching her.

Her sneakers squeak back and forth to one another on the tile as she walks along the empty hallway, like chatty mice. Mrs. Olson twitters ceaselessly about nothing at all, as usual, and Finley ignores her. There are no sounds of spring here in this dimly lit corridor; no earthy aromas. Just mute lockers, dry water fountains, the dull sheen and waxy fragrance of the recently polished squeaky floor. Through the narrow vertical rectangles of wire-reinforced glass in the classroom doors, Finley can see, as she passes, teachers mouthing their lessons in silence, silent, attentive students in the front rows, silent, distracted students in the back rows staring out the open windows; every now and then one of them glimpses through his or her side of the glass the sudden transient passing of gray forms in the hallway. From both sides of the glass, it is like a dream.

They arrive at the office, and Mrs. Olson abruptly ceases twittering. "Come on in," says Mr. Bellini, the principal. "Come on in, sit down."

What is this? Mr. Bellini closes the door. On the other side, although Finley can no longer see her, Mrs. Olson purses her lips in mild disappointment and returns, muttering under her breath, to her desk.

Mr. Bellini sits behind his own desk. The shade is drawn in this room; there is no overhead light. There is only the green-shaded brass lamp on his desk, leaving nearly all of his office's contents and indeed most of his face in shadow. He folds his hands on the blotter as though in prayer. "We, we have a message for you," he says quietly.

Finley leans forward to hear. "Uh-huh, I know. What is it? Who from?"

"It's your parents. Your mother and father, they've, they've . . . had an accident. In their car."

A little bubble of hysteria rises at the back of her throat. Now she strains to see the man's face, his eyes, in the dim light. "Are they all right?"

The principal looks down at his hands. These hands were not made for bearing and presenting such things, he thinks; these hands were made for wielding chalk, and dusty erasers, and lavatory passes. "No, they're not all right." Say it, say *the word*. "They're—they're dead. I'm sorry."

Dead? They can't be dead, something too weird about it, some mistake, wrong car, somebody else's parents maybe? The bubble swells, threatens to burst. "Are you sure it's my parents?"

"Yes. Your brother is on his way here for you. This is going to be a tough time for you, but I hope you know . . ."

He drones on. But Finley is no longer there, in that place, in that office and that side chair. Her mind and senses are twittering nervously like Mrs. Olson's voice; her knees are bumping up and down, frenetically, in hyper-animation. She is thinking of the morning bus; she is watching as a shadowy, waving figure passes from reality into silvered memory; above all, she is feeling, on the smooth warm plane of her forehead, above her now-trembling eyebrows, the delicate evaporation of a small and precious oval of moisture.

So then off Finley went, to live with her brother Warren and his wife Nancy in their little home in a suburb of Lancaster, Pennsylvania.

Tree-of-Life it was called, a quiet town with the highest per-capita number of Pennsylvania-Dutch-motif restaurants and gift shops in the world. While professing sickness unto death of the term "Pennsylvania Dutch," most residents continued to derive an enthusiastic income from it—whether directly (for example, working in a "handicrafts" factory that churned out tens of thousands of glossy red-cedar trinkets and knickknacks every year) or indirectly (pumping diesel fuel, say, out on the turnpike, from a pump emblazoned not with the oil company's logo but with a hex sign).

But Finley's memories of the six-year stay in Tree-of-Life were dominated not by hex signs, miniature cast-iron horse-and-buggy replicas, and all-day showings of "Witness," but by her brother Warren.

A police detective in Lancaster, Warren chafed under the burden of a word that had dogged him since childhood. The word was "almost." When he was a kid, for instance, he was consistently almost one of the first chosen for pickup football teams. He almost made the honor roll on every report card, laboring to correct each "C" only at the expense of a "B" in another subject. And he was almost an only child, being surprised, a little disappointed, and almost embarrassed by the birth of a baby sister while he was almost ready to graduate from *high school,* for crying out loud.

He'd almost decided to seek employment with the FBI after college, but feared that he'd almost but not quite make the cut. Nonetheless, although it had been his own near-decision it had become transformed in his mind into a near-employment; "I almost got into the FBI, didn't I?" he'd ask himself, wistfully at first and ultimately bitterly, each time he almost received an important promotion which went instead to one of a steady stream of increasingly younger men and women. Now, while Finley lived with him and Nancy through her high-school years, he was almost forty—too old to reconsider the FBI. Just as well, he told himself; in his opinion, the Bureau was almost too involved in local law enforcement anyhow—almost intrusive.

And then there was the other thing about being almost forty. At that age, he was almost but not quite young enough to sign up for training in all the new computer technology that was worming its way into the professional hearts of his colleagues and superiors. He'd missed it all. Well, all right: almost all. He'd had to take a couple of word-processing classes when all the typewriters were junked and replaced by desktop computers. But use a computer for real police work? Come on. It was silly, it was lazy, it was, well, *blasphemous.* Almost, anyhow.

Warren's succession of disappointments, of experiences almost but not quite undergone, had driven him into uncertainty, apparently, about everything under the sun. This came out in an odd little verbal tic that Finley had never noticed until moving in with him: he spoke in questions. Even when making a flatly declarative statement, his voice rose a little at the end, as though trying (and failing) to lift its content into the realm of fact and certainty. To talk to him at length could be exhausting; even his small talk felt like an interrogation. (Maybe it helped him in his work.)

Finley remembered the day Warren learned about the establishment of a new federal bureau or agency or something whose sole *purpose,* for crying out loud, was to use computers to catch criminals. He'd sat, brooding and sullen, through most of dinner. Nancy and Finley had no idea what was eating him, but it was clear enough that something was. The symptoms were all there: the knotted manner in which his jaw clenched with each bite, the furious blinking of his small, close-set eyes, the terse monosyllabic form of his usual questions. The women whispered back and forth across the table to each other, wary of his ever more volatile disposition, and almost made it through the meal without learning what the problem was.

But then Finley mentioned, in a timid murmur, that she'd used a PC in school for the first time that day. Something, a near-sound or -gesture from him, made her turn in Warren's direction. He was gripping his glass of iced tea, trembling almost, and then he cried out, "Are they *crazy* or something?" and then he threw the glass at the dining-room wall, almost as hard as he could. Fortunately, it almost but not quite cleared the upholstered wing chair in the corner, spilling tea all over the fabric but at least not shattering, and robbing the moment of a great deal of the drama it would otherwise have had. Of course, this infuriated him even more.

"A goddam whole federal *bureaucracy,* goddam it," he was shouting, punctuating each word with a bang of his fist on the tabletop almost hard enough to make the dishes jump, "what in the *hell* do they think they're going to accomplish with *more* federals and *more* goddamned computers . . . ?"

Four years later, on a holiday visit from college back to Tree-of-Life, Finley one night approached the door of Warren's study there in the same house. (He and Nancy had almost moved several times, but had always decided against it for one reason or another.) She knocked on the door. "Warren?" she asked.

"Sis? Why don't you come on in?"

She opened the door. He was seated behind his desk, leaning back in his chair, his fingers laced together behind his head. A single desk lamp illumined the room, and the shadows on his face accented his smile, making him seem—well, almost happy. And why shouldn't he be? After years of indecision, of almost wanting and almost having children, he and Nancy were now expectant parents.

"Come on in, what's up, how's college treating you, any football heroes in the picture?"

She smiled. "No, no football heroes." This was going to be tricky; she'd already talked to Nancy about it and Nancy had said, Do it now while he's in a good mood. "Uh, Warren, I wanted to tell you, I finally chose a major."

"Hey, that's great, Sis, what'd you settle on, psychology, English, you want to teach maybe?"

Well, no, she explained—gulping mentally—actually this was a new major, sort of an experiment, the government was even helping to pay for it, law enforcement—he started to interrupt at this point, simultaneously confused (new major? *he'd* majored in that, hadn't he?) and proud (wasn't that neat, she wanted to follow in his footsteps maybe?)—when she added the word that changed everything: "systems."

He rocked forward in his chair, placing the palms of both hands flat upon the desktop. *"Systems?* Law-enforcement *systems?* Does that mean what I think it means?"

She swallowed, nodded, and began, "Uh, like I said, it's—"

"It's *new,* I know, you said that already, didn't you? New and experimental, right? The wave of the future, am I correct?" He paused for a moment, almost as though expecting answers. "Haven't you understood *anything* I've said about all this crap for the last four years?" Another pause, scorn cascading from his eyes. "You are my sister and you are in my house at a time when a family is supposed to be together but I am *disgusted,* you understand, *disgusted,* got that? And I want right now for you to get away from me, I think I'm going to be sick, tell Nancy I'm not hungry, you understand? Get *away?"*

She backed out of the study. And it was a long time before she'd mustered the courage to tell him also the single source of the government funding for the new program: CIAC, her future employer, the special target of his most righteous anger.

Chapter Four

It was not quite so pleasant waking up to the oldies the next morning. Neil Diamond and "Cherry, Cherry." Bleech, ptui. Even Finley had her limits. Why would anyone have ever paid for such a single? let alone sufficient *thousands* of singles to make it a hit? On the other hand, Finley *did* succeed in missing Bill Lord on the bus and beating him to his office. She had just seated herself there with a cup of tea, had just begun to undo the night cleaning crew's careful straightening up, to rearrange the desktop for her convenience (keyboard over this way, mouse trailing off over here, weather maps to the right), when the phone rang. At this hour of the morning? She turned on the speakerphone and pushed its volume control up.

"William Lord's office. Finley speaking."

"Finley, this is Morris. Come on over to my office ASAP. You're going to have to drop the armed-robbery project, something else has come up."

She squeezed her eyes shut and counted all the way to two. "*Drop* it? Morris, I'm just about done with it! Can't I—"

"No, you can't. You can give it to, I don't know, Helen Walker maybe. This is more important. And it's just right for you."

Helen Walker, Finley thought, vacant-eyed Helen Walker. She began, "Come on, Morris, what could be so important—"

"*Now,* Finley. Bring a notebook. Forget armed robbery and wind direction. I've got something *interesting* for you." Finley smiled; she knew Morris was teasing her. But she also knew better than to imagine she really had an alternative.

She picked up her logbook and trudged the short distance up the corridor to Morris's office. From his desk, he waved her inside. "Finley. C'mon in, have a seat." Already occupying the other chair was a middle-aged man in an ugly brown polyester suit. "This is August Merrill, Finley. 'Gus.' He's one of our field agents."

Finley looked the agent over. Funny; in her three years with CIAC she had never actually met an agent—just dealt with them on paper or over the phone. She had fancied that they all looked like Brian Dennehy, even the women—gruff and rugged, a little too large for the FBI's physique requirement. But this guy, this Gus Merrill, looked like somebody's forgotten uncle. What was left of his brown hair was thinning, although his mustache still seemed to have some fight in it; he had pouches under his eyes, and both the eyes themselves and his mouth sloped down and out as though aggrieved. And that suit . . . ! Uncle Gus. She suddenly realized that the man was speaking to her. In a practiced flourish of movement, Finley simultaneously reached up and increased the volume of the hearing aid on one side, leaned forward, and said, "Excuse me?"

Like most people, Merrill's instinctive response—as though she were striving not for audibility but for confidentiality—was to lean forward himself, and then not to repeat his words more loudly but to *lower* his voice. Out of the corner of her eye, Finley saw Morris moving his mouth exaggeratedly as he waved a hand behind one ear, pantomiming to Merrill, "She can't hear you!"

"Oh! *Whoops,* sorry," Merrill said, and reddened a little. "I was just asking, is Finley your first name or is it, y'know, Miss—Ms.—Finley, or what?"

"None of the above. My name's just Finley, everybody around here calls me Finley. Pleased to meet you." They shook hands without rising from their seats.

Merrill's lips moved again in near-silence, then he caught himself. "Damn—I said, okay, Finley, and you call me Gus."

The voice thing was definitely going to be a problem, Finley thought. But she said only, to Morris, "So. What's this extremely *interesting* project you've got?"

Morris's mouth twitched in what was almost a grin. "It's the one you're already working on, Finley. The new one. Not the armed robberies, the homicides. The project that Gus here has also been assigned to." He gestured at Merrill—Gus—to indicate that Gus should provide the details of the project of which Finley, so far, knew otherwise almost nothing.

A little over a month ago, the field agent began, a young woman in New York City had failed to report to work for several days, without calling in. Her name was Aggie Bristol; police found her in her apartment, slumped in a chair near her computer. The computer was still on. Bruises on the back of the head indicated she'd been knocked unconscious, and her throat had been cut, ear to ear, with almost surgical precision.

Finley interrupted, "What was on the screen?"

Gus looked puzzled. "Well, some blood—"

"No no—I mean what program was on the screen, what software, were there any words or pictures on the screen?"

"Oh. Nah, nothing like that, it was blank. Except for the blood, I mean. Why'd you ask?"

She paused. "Umm, well, probably not important. Might help if we knew whether she used any boards."

" 'Boards'?"

"Never mind about it for now," Finley said, sighing inwardly to herself: Uncle Gus. Field agents had almost no idea what on-line searchers did. "Please go on, Gus."

A few days after this first killing, he continued with a shrug, another like it had occurred. Another young woman, also in New York, but this time out in Queens instead of Manhattan; again with the bruises on the back of her head, and like Aggie Bristol's her throat was also neatly incised. This victim, whose name was Dorothy Taylor, had been found in a stairway of her apartment building; upstairs in her apartment, her computer was on. As in the first case, the screen was blank. "But so far," Gus said, "the Evsee was still pretty low."

Like most of the on-line searchers, Finley was involved in retrieving information to support criminal investigations. In this respect, CIAC functioned simply as a clearinghouse of information.

The "event-victim correlation index," or EVCI—hence, "Evsee" —was a cornerstone of the other side of CIAC's work and reputation: information *analysis*. The principle was that crimes committed by the same person tended to share common features: they were likely to occur within a limited distance, within a fairly short period of time, and they shared the same *modus operandi*. A kidnapping in Illinois was probably not connected with an embezzlement, two years later, in San Francisco; this was common sense, and if it was all the Evsee quantified, it wouldn't be worth computing.

But CIAC had had its greatest success by factoring into the Evsee equations characteristics of the victims of crimes, as well as of the crimes themselves. Hair color, place of employment, mother's maiden name, hobbies, number and type of credit cards —all of it was possibly significant. (Occasionally a new crime provided a new characteristic to be checked for in later crimes. For example, the victims of a string of burglaries, otherwise apparently unconnected with one another, all used the same highway toll plaza on the way to and from work every day.)

All this information was kept in a database of staggering size here in CIAC's main computer center; the algorithms for processing it, reported the rumor mill, were as complex as those for controlling the flight of a space shuttle. When you sifted through the marvelous output of this marvelous parade of plain old algebraic and mathematical symbols, and came upon high correlations among crimes and their victims, you then could guess that the crimes were committed by the same person. The common characteristics of the *victims,* not of the crimes per se, began to outline for you a possible motive. In a way, you formed a picture of the criminal by forming, and analyzing, a composite picture of his victims.

"The Evsee was low," Gus was explaining. "I mean the murder weapon was apparently the same in both cases, but it didn't seem likely that there was any significance to the computers. Especially in New York, I mean, must be a million computer users there, right? And another thing, these two unfortunate young ladies apparently didn't know each other, and the New York police haven't turned up any friends they had in common. So like usual, just two crimes with some superficial similarities do not a pattern make."

He cleared his throat and glanced down at some information in one of the folders in his lap. "Then, two nights ago, that'd be Sunday night, a third woman was killed. Same general setup, I'm afraid: same kind of neck wound, plus the blank computer in her room, she was lying on the floor by the desk—that all tended to jack up the Evsee a bit. So we're *probably* dealing with the same guy—"

"You said, 'same setup, I'm afraid,' " Finley interrupted again. "Why 'I'm afraid'?"

"Oh—well, like I started to say, the third one occurred in Atlanta instead of New York. The location of a crime is a pretty big component of the Evsee, y'know, and when we factor that in, the Evsee goes back down quite a bit. So it turns out we're not really sure if it's coincidence or the same guy or what."

A next question pushed its way to the front of Finley's mind, a question she did not want to ask but could not ignore. "Gus—was the name of this third victim, by any chance—was it . . . Tracy?"

Gus started and his eyes widened. "Yeah, it was. How the hell'd you know that? Tracy Williams, she lived in an apartment complex just outside Atlanta."

But Finley missed all but the confirmation of the cold fact. Tracy. *Tracy.* Those dumb exclamation points of hers. . . .

"Finley, are you all right?" Morris asked.

"Huh? Oh—yes, yes, Morris—I just . . . I think I knew her. I saw the name in the event list yesterday. . . . She was an on-line buddy of mine, I think. I—what is it you want me to do?"

Her boss smiled grimly. "Finley, well . . . we think this is an unusual project. So far, nothing else seems to tie the victims together except their computer usage. Maybe something else will turn up later, but that's all we've got to go on for now."

"There's something specific about their computer usage that they had in common?" Finley asked, her voice seeming to take over of its own accord from her still-dazed mind.

"Well, yeah, they all had modems, we know that. So they were going on-line for something. But all their hard disks"—where, Finley knew, the computers' data and programs are stored— "were scrubbed clean, all the files erased, so we don't know for sure. That's where you come in, Finley."

He paused, then gestured in Gus's direction. "Gus here will help you out however he can, and he'll continue to deal with the local police and get the FBI involved if it really does turn out to be the same guy jumping from one state to the next. But for the time being, all the legwork on this project—it's all yours, Finley. At least to start with." He smiled. "I know it's a departure from standard operating procedure, but I didn't think you'd mind too much."

He stopped for a moment and looked at his watch. "I've got to get to a briefing on another project. Why don't the two of you sit down and start to work out a plan of attack? You can keep using Bill Lord's office for now, Finley. I'll tell him to move into your cube until your keyboard's fixed.

"And that reminds me, one other thing: you are to discuss this project with *nobody,* Finley, not even anybody here. Not Monica, not Ray, not Lord. We're pretty sure the killer is a computer user; if he turns out to be a BBS user as well, it won't take long for word to leak to him. You know how folks blab their guts out on-line. And the same goes for your on-line buddies *outside* work, too, I'm afraid."

Finley nodded. She understood at some level what was being asked of her. But she was also beginning to feel something feathery and tentative brushing up against her spine; there was grief for Tracy there, certainly, but also the first, oh so light touch of fingertips of fear.

Chapter Five

Now, Finley didn't think much about it any longer, but all this bobbing and weaving in her chair, all these requests to have conversation repeated, even her oft-recurring dream—they were all just components of her everyday cross to bear: her hearing.

"Parents' Back-to-School Night" of Finley's first-grade year: Mom and Dad sitting up at the front of the room engaged in who-knows-what kind of talk with Mrs. Tropp, her teacher, adult talk she guessed, while Finley herself sat at her little desk doodling on cheap lined paper. Her feet did not reach the floor, and she was kicking them, repeatedly and unconsciously, against the desk's chrome legs. Laboriously, she was erasing the picture of a telephone—it was too lumpy over on that one side, see?—when she became suddenly aware that the conversation by Mrs. Tropp's desk had ceased. She looked up; Mrs. Tropp and Dad were watching her; Mom still sat with her back to Finley. She resumed drawing, kicking, erasing, kicking, kicking. . . . Then she heard Mom's voice, "Honey, please stop kicking the desk." She looked up again: all three adults facing her now. "Sorry, Mom," she replied.

It had been a test, her first hearing test. Aged, long-widowed Mrs. Tropp—she of the quavery brittle voice, the wobbly sticklike legs, she of the fading eyesight—she had seen something no one else had: that Finley heard and understood speech significantly better when the speaker faced her. And that night, at the school, she'd demonstrated it to Finley's parents; Mom had asked her twice to stop kicking at the desk, but Finley had heard only the second request.

Clinically, the doctors would dub her problem with that ear "sensorineural loss," or, more plainly, "nerve deafness." What an arcane battery of tests led them to this conclusion! Finley would sit in a wooden chair, wearing a pair of hard, hard plastic headphones, in a carpeted, soundproof room, its wall and ceiling covered with acoustic tiles, a room that for some reason was always dimly lit. Outside, on the other side of a glass panel, sat a technician—an audiologist—twiddling the knobs of some mammoth electronic contraption.

"When you hear a sound," the audiologist's voice would say into her ears, through the headphones, "raise your right index finger." Sometimes instead of raising a finger, she was supposed to press a button attached to a wire that ran from the booth to another machine out there by the audiologist, and at other times she was to repeat into a microphone whatever words she heard muttered, at various volumes and pitches, into her ear.

Regardless of the mechanical specifics, these tests seemed to her in retrospect to have less to do with hearing and sensitivity to sound than with psychology and, it sometimes seemed, even ESP.

Audibility was important, of course, but Finley had somehow become adept at reading visual cues as well. "Lip reading"? Well, it included that, yes, but it also went far beyond watching and interpreting the curls, distensions, and flutters of people's lips. Somehow, it involved making an instantaneous judgment call from the whole of a speaker's demeanor: the way he lidded his eyes; the way her mouth drooped at one corner; the tilt of his head; the mini-shrug of her shoulders. It all meant something, and the harder you listened and the more attention you paid, the more it meant.

So there's Finley, then, a little girl awed by all this electronic apparatus, a wee bit frightened by the soundless and ill-lit chamber into which she has been inserted and in which she is now sitting, but determined to score well so she'll have to do it again as seldom as possible. She's kicking the leg of her chair, yes, right up to the point when the technician says, through the heavy discs clamped to her ears, that the test is starting . . . *now.* Then she stops kicking. Stops breathing, nearly. She's straining, now, to sense the merest whisper through the headset of what the technician might be up to. But she's also straining with all her *mind's* resources, straining to see the technician's face over there and to guess what it means: that little flick of the eyebrows, did he just raise the volume, or lower the pitch? that sudden glance in Finley's direction, had she just repeated a word exactly, or had she "repeated" a word when none had been offered in the first place?

In ways that Finley could never make clear to anyone, no matter how she tried, hearing what people said was only secondarily an after-the-fact *sense*. It was, more critically, a feat of anticipation, of guessing what other people were likely to say before (and while) they said it. Indeed, at least a third of everyday conversation seemed to Finley to consist of things that she needn't hear anyway —remarks to which she could reply (depending on the look on the speaker's face) either by saying, "Oh, *yeah!*" or by merely raising her own eyebrows in an ambiguous way.

Conversations, one-on-one, were in this respect exhilarating. Each one successfully negotiated was a triumph of intellect and intuition, of mind over matter. Parties and large meetings were much less satisfying: too much going on at once, too many stray sounds and voices and, yes, *faces* strove for her attention. Except for places like McGarrity's, where the people knew of and understood her problem and could compensate accordingly, she avoided these clamorous settings whenever she could.

She'd gotten along all right, nonetheless, for some time. Mom and Dad had bought her a hearing aid for the bad ear, which helped a little; at least, it had amplified sounds sufficiently that she then had had a sense of how much she was still missing.

But then later, in high school, after Mom and Dad had died and she'd gone to live with her brother Warren and his wife Nancy, she'd foolishly ignored an earache in the other ear. Now, years later, she still couldn't tell you why; maybe she was still reacting, in a teenager's go-to-hell way, to her parents' death.

Whatever the reason, she ignored the earache until she could no longer concentrate. They drained the ear, and with the fluid went most of her hearing there, as well. More soundproof rooms; more fidgety audiologists; and, finally, another hearing aid.

During this round of tests, they learned that since her earlier visits she'd picked up a new skill: "listening," odd though the idea seemed, with her skeleton, and especially with her shoulder blades. "Scapular conductivity," one especially pretentious audiologist had called it, and it wasn't all that uncommon; the principle was that sound vibrations could be transmitted by way of solid objects, like chairs, through her skin and into her bones and, finally, to her brain.

"It's common enough," one doctor said. "I've never seen anyone take it to such an unnatural degree, though." Depending on the quality of a person's voice, its pitch and timbre and volume, Finley would find herself leaning forward, away from the chair back, or leaning back, to pick up the reverberations. Her family and a few of her close friends knew about this, and while speaking to her they might place a hand on her back to help. But she didn't make a point of telling people about it at work; the thought of a Bill Lord, for example, placing a sweaty palm on her shoulder gave her the heebie-jeebies.

Socially in general, with guys? Well, she just wasn't comfortable. It was hard to choose dates on the basis of how well you heard them, too weird or something; too demeaning. And even when she could hear their voices easily enough, she had experienced few embarrassments to match that caused by the *plop* of a hearing aid onto a lover's chest at precisely the wrong moment. She had remained, since college, mostly a loner: insulated by a bubble of silence that surrounded her on all sides.

Even, then, with her big bag of body language and psychological tricks, and even with her hearing aids, Finley still had to concentrate pretty hard in order to hold a conversation. It could be exhausting. And so she had another reason for loving her job: when she was on-line, she had a perfect ear.

She loved the sensation of communicating free of ambiguity and tentativeness. If someone typed the word "cheese," it was absolutely and without a doubt not the word "cheats." "Button your fly" was not "butterfly." Oh yes: some of her on-line correspondents spelled atrociously, which created problems sometimes, and it amazed her how many intelligent, well-educated people couldn't compose a grammatically correct sentence. But on the whole, she could *see* exactly what they'd typed, and her sense of what they'd said was unfailing.

Small wonder that she preferred this manner of "speaking" to the normal, punctuated as the latter was with little pauses as she stopped to consider what the other person might have said or as she fiddled with a volume-control dial on one of the hearing aids. Small wonder that she'd latched onto this electronic form of "gabbing" with dozens of friends at once as better than attending a party with them. Small wonder, since she loved the medium so much, that she might be blind to its dangers.

Chapter Six

Silent and shaken by the news, so it now seemed, about "her" Tracy, Finley accompanied Gus to the cafeteria. She sat, glumly, and chewed on the little double-barreled plastic stirrer that came with her tea. Awkward, Gus placed to one side the folders he'd brought with him from Morris's office, and then asked if he could smoke here; Finley didn't reply, just pointed at the "Smoking Permitted" sign on a nearby wall.

He lit a cigarette and took a smoker's characteristic first deep drag, being careful to exhale the smoke away from the table. He said something which Finley couldn't hear.

"Excuse me, Gus?"

"Damn, I'm sorry, I've gotta remember about the—I said, I'm sorry about your friend. About Tracy Williams. And then I asked how long you knew her."

Finley thought before replying. "It seemed like a long time. Months, anyhow. Doesn't take long to feel close to someone when you, y'know, 'talk' to them every day." If only Tracy hadn't been so damned likable. You could find people similar to Tracy anywhere, people obsessed with falling in love, and perhaps just a touch obsessed with falling out of it as well, obsessed with chronic martyrdom or something. But people like that usually just grew tiresome after a while. Tracy was—had been—so energetic and enthusiastic and lively. . . . She had fallen in love with her computer and her BBSs, too, and now, apparently, they'd hurt her worst of all.

Gus was nodding. "Uh-huh, right, I *think* I get it. . . . Afraid I really don't understand computers or how you meet people this way. Isn't it a little—well, *strange*?"

In spite of herself, Finley chuckled. "Yes, it *is* strange. Funny. When you get close to people in real life, Gus, sometimes they get bored and leave you behind. But there's always a conclusion of some kind, a last—I don't know, confrontation or parting words or something. So you know it's over. But on-line that almost never happens; instead, new people drop in all of a sudden, and the old ones just disappear. Like Cheshire cats, you know, their last messages are the last anyone hears from them. You don't know if they got angry or bored or had their computer repossessed or they're sick or on vacation or . . . dead."

Gus tipped the long ash of his cigarette into his coffee cup, and only then looked around for an ashtray. He found one at the next table and brought it over. "You have any ideas how you, we, how we should start on this, Finley?" He tapped the folders on the table and pushed them a little in her direction. "Maybe you want to look through what's in the folders first?"

She mechanically picked up the folder on top. Its typewritten label contained the project number, the name "BRISTOL," and the date on which Aggie Bristol had apparently died. Finley opened it, looked through the contents. A picture of Bristol taken before she died, a set of pictures taken at the scene of the killing, a printed inventory of the contents of her apartment. . . . Finley looked over this last item with interest. One section was headed, "COMPUTER SOFTWARE."

"Hmm," she said, and opened up the folder about the Taylor case as well.

"You got an idea already?" Gus asked.

"Umm. No, not really. But look at this, Gus. This gives me an idea where we might start checking." She turned the two women's software inventories so Gus could read them, side by side, and ran a finger alongside each list. "See? It's just a list of the software they owned. There's a word processor here in Bristol's list, and also over here in Taylor's . . . and there are a few games over on this one. . . ."

"Waitaminnit," Gus interrupted. "How'd the police even come up with these two lists if the computers were blanked out, erased, whatever you call it?"

"There are a couple ways," Finley replied. "Most software comes with its own user manuals, so maybe they found the manuals in the apartments and just concluded that the victims had the software. Or more likely, the police just found the original floppy disks that the software came on."

"Yeah, okay. So what else? Anything important in the two lists?"

"Well, they both had the same communications program, called 'BoardWalk.' "

"What do you mean, 'communications program'? Is that significant, something I oughta worry about?"

Finley smiled to herself. "Well, not necessarily significant, no. BoardWalk is the best-selling communications software, and communications software is what you use to access BBSs—"

"Whoa, wait! You lost me already! BoardWalk, communications software, BBSs . . . is there some way you could, you know, *show* me how this stuff works? And skip the technical details?"

Not a bad idea, Finley thought, picturing Gus and herself occupying the only two chairs in Bill Lord's office. She couldn't think of anyone she'd rather not talk to today than Bill Lord. "Sure, that's a great idea. Why don't we go do that now?"

They rose from the table, and Gus stubbed his cigarette out. As she shepherded him from the cafeteria, she saw Bill Lord just coming through the checkout line. He looked at Finley and began to smile, then over at Gus. The smile faded. Sleazeball, Finley thought.

It didn't take long at all to outline the basics for Gus. As he'd said, he really didn't understand computers very well, but nearly everyone understands how a telephone call works.

"So," he was saying, "so instead of two people at the ends of the phone line, there are two computers? With a person sitting at each one? Why don't you just call each other on the phone?"

"For one thing, because each BBS has *many* people who use it," Finley explained. "And you don't always know which one is the 'right' person to talk to. So to talk to all of them, you'd need to arrange a conference call for everybody at the same time. Then you'd get them on the phone, and some of them would turn out to know nothing at all about the topic, so you just wasted their time and your own. And you know what it's like trying to schedule a conference call when everybody's in different cities, different time zones—forget it!

"This way, with BBSs, people can check messages at their convenience, decide if any of it applies to them, and answer whenever they feel like. It's like—"

"Like a conference call with answering machines instead of people?" Gus interrupted.

"Well, yeah. Something like that." Uncle Gus: the answering machine as the apex of technology.

"But then," Gus said, "doesn't that mean you don't get an answer right away? Suppose somebody doesn't check his messages right away?"

"Uh-huh, that's right—you do have to wait. Hours is usually the best turnaround you can get. Sometimes, just by chance, you might be lucky enough to get a couple answers a few minutes after you drop off the question—but then you yourself don't usually check back for the answer for a few hours. So yeah, it takes time, but it's always complete. And in the meantime, you can be picking up and verifying the answers to the dozen questions you left yesterday."

She waved him over. "Come on, pull your chair over here, I'll show you." As he pushed a wastebasket off to the side of the room and rolled his chair around to Finley's side of the desk, she moved the mouse across the rubber pad on the desktop. She clicked a button on the mouse a couple of times, and her BBS directory came up on the screen just as Gus settled himself. She swiveled the monitor on its base so they could both see it.

"Jesus!" Gus exclaimed. "Don't tell me we're on a—a 'board' already? They all look this complicated?"

Finley suppressed a giggle. "No, Gus, this is just a—well, it's like a phone book. See? Here's the name of the board in this column, here's a description of the main subject that it relates to, here's the phone number to call. . . ."

"What's '8N1'?"

"That's just tech-talk. It stands for 'eight bits, no parity, one stop bit.'" She saw the cloud of unknowing descending again onto Gus's brow, and hastened to repeat, "Just some technical stuff. Don't worry about it, my computer and my modem need to care about it, but I—we—don't. Here, watch, let me just show you something." She moved the mouse a little, and a black line moved down the directory.

"What's that?" he asked, and pointed at the mouse.

"It's called a mouse—see the long gray wire here, looks like a tail?" She turned the mouse over. "See, when I slide the mouse across the rubber pad on the desk here, this little ball here turns and—"

"Whoa! Please, Finley; computer talk."

Finley smiled, she hoped reassuringly. "Okay—let's skip the details of how to operate a computer; I'll just show you what a bulletin board looks like." Teasing a little, she added, "So save the tough questions for later!"

Gus's ears turned pink, but he didn't acknowledge the teasing. "What's this line on the screen here, it's darker than the others?"

She looked at the line currently highlighted. "NJBBS," it said in one column, and in another, "New Jersey Tourism." Finley was surprised there was such a thing; might not be a bad one to start Gus with.

"That," she ventured, "is apparently a bulletin board where you can drop questions about this lovely state we're currently sitting in. Is this your first visit to New Jersey?"

"Yeah, afraid so. Don't live that far away, just up in Connecticut, and I always wanted to come to the computer center here but— you know. Always too busy."

Finley nodded; field agents never came here, they were *always* "too busy." But she said only, "Okay, no problem. I'll get on the board now, and you think of a question you want to ask it. Any question about New Jersey at all."

Gus closed his eyes while he thought. Finley clicked a mouse button; the screen cleared, and the modem started to chatter, buzz, and beep. Fortunately, she'd prepared Gus to expect the noises. She completed the log-in, and turned to him. "Well? What do you want to ask this all-seeing all-knowing wizard of New Jersey information?"

Gus smiled and opened his eyes. "Ask it," he said, staring raptly first at the mouse, then at the modem, "ask it what's the best place to get hardware in New Jersey."

Hardware, Finley asked herself, *hardware*? But she just typed:

```
To:          All
From:        Finley
Re:          Hardware
Message:   Hi, all. Can anyone out there suggest the best
place in NJ to buy PCs and peripherals? Thanks!
                    Finley
```

She sent the message off, and turned to Gus. Once again, he was reddening.

"I didn't mean PCs," he said, "just hardware: hammers and saws. You know. Drill bits."

Finley did laugh out loud then. "Oh, Gus, I'm *sorry*! I just saw you looking at the modem and I thought . . ." She cracked up again.

"No, no," Gus said, grinning himself despite his embarrassment. "I wasn't very clear, I guess. Can you cancel the message?"

Finley thought about it for a moment. "Yeah, let me see. . . ." She logged in again and typed:

```
delete to: all from: finley re: hardware
```

The action on the screen paused for a few seconds, then said:

```
Working. . . .
Deleted To: All From: Finley Re: Hardware
```

"There!" said Finley, satisfied. "That should do it! You want to try again, with the real question this time?"

Gus nodded. "Yeah, if it's not too much trouble, could we? I'd like to get a feeling for how the replies come back."

As Finley created the new message and sent it along, he asked, "Can you delete *any* messages, the way you did just now?"

"No, not unless you created it yourself or unless it was addressed to you personally. Well, no," she amended, "now that I think about it—sometimes, if you're a sysop you can."

"A *what*?"

"A sysop." Sysops, or "system operators," were the BBSs traffic cops. Each board had at least one, some had two or more. They kept the stream of messages flowing smoothly around the bulletin boards; kept the boards themselves from getting cluttered up, by deleting old messages; and made sure that their boards' users stayed civil to one another. "Lots of other stuff, too," Finley added. "They can do just about anything—making new rules or, well, sometimes selectively breaking old ones."

"So these, these 'sysops' might be a good place to ask questions about the three victims?" Gus asked.

Finley eyed him approvingly. "That's right," she said. "But we probably don't need to bother. We don't even know whether any of the victims were BBS users, let alone which BBSs. I think we should take a look at the other software first, just to get it out of the way. Maybe after lunch, or tomorrow morning? I've got to pull together all the stuff from my other project so I can turn it over to Helen." Ye gods, Helen Walker, Morris must be *crazy*. . . .

Gus nodded again. "Sure. I've got to make some calls myself this afternoon, check with the local police to see if anything new has turned up. Anything special you want me to ask them about?"

After pausing to think a moment, Finley said, "Yeah. Find out if there were any floppy disks by the victim's computers, or in their apartments, their closets, whatever. Not floppies with software on them; the ones I'm after will probably look almost like they're blank, like this." She showed him a floppy from her own desk, with a blank self-adhesive label across the top. "And if so, see if you can get them for me. That's it, I guess."

"Okay, I'll do that. So, till tomorrow morning. Oh, and Finley? Tomorrow morning, can we check for messages about the hardware stores, too?"

She smiled; it never took anyone long to get the bug. "Sure, Gus."

He'd been gone not even a minute when Ray stuck his head inside the door of Lord's office. "I think we're alone now?" he said, grinning; he knew of Finley's fondness for oldies. "What the heck is going *on* with you, anyhow—moving into an *office* for crying out loud, meeting with strangers . . . ?"

He kept his tone light, but Finley could tell that he really wanted to know. Criminal information wasn't the only sort that her colleagues thrived on. "Well, Mr. Daniels, I'm not really at liberty to say at the moment. Now, if you offered to bribe me—"

"Ha ha! So okay then, tell me, what's your busy personal calendar look like for the next few nights?"

"Get out, you!" she yelled in mock annoyance, and threw a paper clip at his retreating form. He'd been teasing her, of course, he knew darned well that her personal calendar was open—and had been, since Spencer. . . .

Finley had first met Spencer Mann a year after moving to New Brunswick for her CIAC job, just a couple of years ago.

There'd been boys in high school, of course, and certainly in college: a parade of fresh eager faces reflecting various proportions of interest in Finley's intelligence and wit, patience with her hearing difficulties, and the usual adolescent preoccupation with sex. For her part, Finley had negotiated through their ranks with more curiosity than real romantic interest, watching their eyes for the first hint of a true spark's ignition. But she hadn't seen or felt the spark until meeting Spencer.

They'd met in an adult school class at a local community college, a class in elementary fencing. Ironically, Spencer had already donned his protective wire-mesh mask at that first meeting, so Finley at first could not see his eyes at all, let alone a spark in them. The instructor, trying to match opponents as evenly as possible, had paired off all his students, man-man and woman-woman, and been left at the end with an odd one of each: Spencer, and Finley.

"No, uh-uh, this won't do," he said, eyeing Spencer's six-three frame and Finley's five-two, and he was preparing to juggle the pairings again when Finley interrupted him.

"It's okay with me," she said. "I'm only here for fun anyhow."

The instructor looked doubtful. "How about you—you mind?" he asked Spencer's masked form.

A slight bit of hesitation, then a mellifluous baritone: "Nope. Fine with me." So the match was made.

The instructor first demonstrated some basic thrusts and lunges, showed them the importance of knowing their own center of gravity, and pointed out with his foil the proper placement of one's feet, which in his case were tiny and ballerinalike. Just like in the movies, he barked out *"En garde!"* then something that sounded to Finley like "Alley!" He feinted, dodged, and parried the attacks of an imaginary opponent, giving little grunts and cries of triumph and surprise, all alone by himself there in the center of the rubber mat.

Throughout this weird one-man performance, Finley stole furtive sidelong glances at her assigned opponent. Towering over her, with broad shoulders and long, strong arms and fingers. Dark curly brown hair pressed down in a crisscross pattern by the mask's head strap. A shadow of whiskers showing around his neck, where the mask did not cover. And most apparent, not disguised at all by the mask or by his loose sweatsuit: an easy athletic grace even while standing still. The apprehension began to grow in Finley's mind that perhaps their matchup would be unjust after all.

But then the instructor said that he wanted all five teams to take a turn on the mat. "Not for real," he assured them. "I just want you to get a feel for moving about on the mat, wielding your foil, facing an opponent, and so on. You two first." And he pointed, first at Finley and then at Spencer, with the tip of his sword.

Nervous, Finley stepped onto the mat, Spencer stepping forward a few seconds behind her. But he hooked the toe of one sneaker under the edge of the mat and sprawled suddenly forward, arms pinwheeling frantically, utterly devoid of grace, and somehow contrived to get the tipped fencing foil under him. The sword bent crazily and *sproing*ed out from under him like a pogo stick fleeing for its life. *WHUMP* went his large frame, loud and hard, and that was very convenient because it masked Finley's uncontrolled giggling. Clumsily, Spencer staggered to his feet and retrieved the foil from the other side of the mat. Maybe, Finley thought, maybe this wouldn't be such a mismatch after all.

"En garde!" cried the instructor, and the two of them assumed stiff, unintentionally comic poses that they'd obviously gotten from old B-grade swashbuckler films, their left hands raised self-consciously behind them. Finley felt like a statue in a water fountain. "Alley!" the instructor called again, or whatever it was (it was *"Allez!"* she learned months later), and she and Spencer set to.

Perhaps in some sort of misguided masculine overcompensation for his earlier clumsiness, Spencer attacked Finley with a ferocious barrage of Zorrolike flourishes. Her pulse racing, Finley fought back, barely effectively, managing only to ward off each attempted blow. The metal of their swords clanked just as it did in the movies; *swish* and *swish* went the air between them. Neither of them, of course, had the slightest idea what they were doing. Finally, endeavoring to administer a final *coup de grace,* Spencer drew back his sword arm and then thrust it, *hard,* at Finley's shoulder. Instinctively and without conscious thought, she shut her eyes, ducked, and lunged herself. As Spencer's blade soared masterfully into and through the thin air where Finley's shoulder had been, her own blade reached forward precisely, like an anatomist's forefinger, and tapped him, ever so lightly, at dead center of his groin.

Spencer's head tilted down, apparently looking at the trembling length of steel whose rubber tip seemed so finally to have punctuated their first encounter. But the mask of course still hid his face; was he grinning or embarrassed or what?

"Er," Finley at last brought out, *"touché."*

He laughed out loud at that, and removed his mask. Finley's sharp intake of breath stopped her own laughter. He wasn't gorgeous, really, with that long Roman nose cleaving the air before him like a locomotive's cowcatcher. But he wasn't bad, either, with a sensitive mouth that promised both easy laughter and ready passion, and in those laughing green eyes Finley saw a definite spark, even as they swung to one side a bit, away from Finley, and locked with the eyes of a redheaded fellow student standing behind her.

Looking back on it now, Finley could see that that first fencing match had told her many things about the course of their relationship.

Clumsiness first. She continued to marvel at how his grace when standing still was so dramatically and unequivocally refuted when once he began to move. Beer spilled, doors opened into his face and then shut upon his fingers, sidewalk cracks leapt up and grabbed him by the ankles. Even as a lover he was seemingly awkward and ill-balanced, as though not quite sure of himself at first; but in this case he made up for it with patience, persistence, and—well, courtliness.

"I didn't hurt you, did I?" he'd ask as Finley lay, gulping air, on her back in the bed, tears and sweat running together from her face down her temples and into her pounding ears, pooling there in itchy dampness about the ear molds of her hearing aids. Hurt me? she'd think. *Hurt* me?

Months after they'd completed the class, for his birthday, Finley had had a custom sweatshirt made up. "SPENCER THE FENCER," it said, and his gratitude (like nearly everything else about him) was stumbling and maladroit. "Uh, gee, well, I mean *thanks,*" he'd said. He'd obediently tried it on for a token few minutes, then taken it off, and that was the last Finley had seen of it.

Professionally, Spencer's life was spent half in the glare of publicity and half in the flickering light-and-dark of movies. Sometime a few years before Finley had met him, must be six or seven by now, with twin master's degrees from Princeton tucked in his back pocket (business administration and fine arts), he'd come up with an idea that many people had written off as cockamamie and badly timed. The economy the way it was, sheesh, what was he? Crazy or something?

Except that he'd not only come up with the idea, but pulled it off.

He proposed, he said, to establish a chain of movie theaters across New Jersey to show exclusively foreign and other "art" films. No more than one theater in each city, he said, and only in cities that met certain minimum requirements: there had to be a successful college located in the city or very close nearby; the city had to be committed to renewing its downtown, or already be thriving there; and there had to be existing building facilities of a certain type and age—he would not build new, but renovate.

Princeton and New Brunswick had been the first beneficiaries of his brainstorm, each local government lending him the down payment for its own Cinema Europa, as he called them. Each was housed on the first floor of what had been adjoining town houses within close walking distance of the downtown area. Two shows a night, special family matinee showings of old classics and animated features, seating for no more than two hundred patrons per location, and the money—ever so slowly—started to roll in. In the year before Finley met him, he'd even received some grant money from the state arts commission, enabling him to expand the chain with additional Cinema Europas in Trenton and Montclair.

"Nonprofit enterprise" it was in fact as well as in name. It would never be a business in which Spencer would make a fortune, but neither would it ever be a business that he'd have to justify to anyone. Never dogged by scandal nor tainted by greed; never featured in any section of the newspapers other than business and entertainment.

And his favorite part of the whole enterprise, as Finley quickly learned: previewing films.

In his condominium in New Brunswick, on the second and third floors of the first Cinema Europa to be completed, he'd made a point of installing a "screening room," outfitted not only with projector and screen but even with a short, five-seat section of cushioned theater seating. It was a haven to escape to, to remind himself, he said, what the real point of his career was—not hobnobbing with state and local arts communities; not arranging charity screenings; not, God knows, reviewing the monthly receipts and popcorn budget. And until Finley, so he said, he'd never escaped there with anyone else.

In its magic and mystery and even its slapstick comic touches, each preview was like a turn-of-the-century illusionist's show. He would set up the first reel of film, usually managing at least once to trip over a power cord or to drop a film can onto the tiled floor of the projection booth with a clang and clatter, and then be seated, one hand draped over the arm of the seat and touching Finley's knee. Using a set of switches mounted in the opposite arm of his seat, he'd simultaneously dim the lights and start the projector. The lush music would come up, and the titles and credits with their unfamiliar juxtapositions of familiar portions of the Roman alphabet would coalesce out of the darkness and onto the screen, and Finley gasped with sheer excited pleasure the first time she experienced it.

Why had she never before been attracted to foreign films? she wondered. With subtitles, especially, they were perfect for her: no need to worry if the sound system was blurry or an actor's voice distractingly accented.

But it wasn't just the films themselves, nor the watching of them, that had her so mesmerized. There was something about Spencer himself, something magical about being able to peek out of the corner of her eye and see his own eyes glistening, rapt by the flutter of images on the screen, or being able to look down and see the hairs throwing shadows on the back of his hand like a forest seen from a great height, or the charming way, when a reel was suddenly over, that it always took him a few seconds to collect himself, his heart thumping, to turn the lights back up and swap the exhausted reel for a fresh. There in the dark, swept up in visions and words of distant lands that Finley had never seen, she felt that distance itself had been abolished as a concept—as though she and Spencer had themselves merged and were spectators, participants even, in a grand drama of unity.

Maybe he felt the distance shrinking, too, and felt not liberated but confined, and that was why he'd evidently decided (perhaps unconsciously) to do something about it.

He'd gotten a new receptionist at his office last spring. "Europa Enterprises," this Alberta person would say in a crisp, confident, competent voice when Finley called to speak to Spencer. "No, Mr. Mann is not here at the moment. May I ask who's calling, please?" Finley did not imagine that someone with such a voice ever wore jeans and sneakers to work; such a person would certainly have normal hearing.

"Alberta?" Spencer would say. *"Alberta?* She's just my receptionist, for crying out loud." But then came a time when he was suddenly referring to her not as Alberta but "Bert"—"Hey, come on, Finley, she *asked* me to call her that, I didn't just nickname her myself!"—and before very much longer his conversations with Finley had less and less to do with extended runs and first showings and even with cinematography and acting, but simply Bert this and Bert that and Bert the other thing.

"Spencer," Finley said to him at last on the phone one night, "do you want to, to—are you interested in Bert instead of me?"

All awkwardness; even Finley could almost hear a gulp. "Uh, well, *sure,* she's nice and she's attractive, she *really* knows the business, I mean I could still see you sometimes, too, couldn't I, talk on the phone—"

She hung up on him. "Touché yourself, asshole," she muttered. At the rate he was going he'd soon confess that he hoped to remember her face every now and then.

For a good long while after that Finley would not answer the phone without first monitoring the answering machine—for as long as it took him to realize that she would neither talk to him nor return his calls, and he finally stopped trying altogether. That had been two, no, three months ago, and Finley had retreated almost desperately into the warmth, the unselfconsciousness, and above all the distant light of her on-line friendships. She couldn't imagine that she'd ever venture back out of it, and into darkness, again.

And she knew one thing for sure: she'd never fence again.

Today, back here in the real world of bytes and electrons, Finley spent her lunch break at the computer, checking her regular boards for mail. On STACKS, Jon Little-Olden was complaining, yet again, about his library's conversion from the Dewey to the Library of Congress classification schemes, a process that seemed to have taken years already:

> To: All
> From: Jon Little-Olden
> Re: Dewey to L of C - AAARGH!
> Message: Yes, friends, it is STILL going on! Why the hell
> didn't the Library of Congress consider the needs of
> LIBRARIANS when they put the damned thing together.
> God. This is like Chinese water torture, no it's worse than
> that, it's like trying to figure out my girlfriend's method of
> filing new names in her phone book, she's got the
> veterinarian's name not under the first letter of his name or
> even under "V" for veterinarian. It's under "D" for dog.
> Maybe she chaired the L of C committee that dreamed the
> thing up.

Finley really didn't know sometimes why Jon's girlfriend put up with him, assuming he acted like this around her as well as on-line; that she stayed with him at all, rather than her phone number-filing system, seemed to Finley to be the woman's defining lunacy.

But she didn't reply to Jon; she was looking for a message from Tracy, still harboring a glimmer of hope. But there was, unfortunately, nothing at all from Tracy, addressed either to Finley or to anyone else.

Nor was there any Earwiggery on ABLE to help leaven the growing worry, just a brief note from Jane:

To: Finley
From: <jane>
Re: Where are you?
Message: Hello, Finley dear. I hope you're having a good day at work. It just struck me that I have no idea where you live. I know it's not important but it's SUCH a nice way to help form a picture of other people here, especially my favorites. Still, I understand how you feel about your privacy; I feel that way myself, many a time! Share if you want. Love you, dear. <jane>

Finley smiled; Jane was a dear herself, and Finley said so in her reply:

> . . . Jane, aren't you sweet to be so concerned about my privacy? Not for you to worry about that! I'm in central New Jersey, I live in an apartment overlooking the Raritan River just a little outside New Brunswick. It's nowhere near as smoggy or traffic-bound and polluted here as everyone thinks it is. . . .

She supplied some further details, little descriptive sentences about local shopping and her neighbors and about McGarrity's, Falco's coffee shop, the bus ride to work. Then she signed off, "Love you, too, Jane. Take care," and sent it on its way.

Finally, on to FORENSIC. Nothing from Flokati; there was nothing unusual about that, since he was nearly always very busy and frequently didn't get to check or post his mail for days. But Finley had a message to post to him:

> . . . Hi, Flokati! I have a question for you: What can you tell me about knife cuts? If you see a cut, can you tell if it was made with a knife or a razor blade? Can you tell the difference between cuts made by different kinds of knives?
>
> I can't really talk about this now, not in detail. I just wanted to know the answers to these questions. Can you help?

She proofread the message very carefully before sending it off; even after years of exposure, Flokati was still grappling with nuances of the English language and she wanted to make sure that this would be unambiguous. And she also tried to read it through Morris's eyes; she didn't *think* it violated his gag order, and she hoped he'd think that way, too. "*If* he knew," she added mentally, and sent it.

"Finley!" brayed a sudden familiar voice from the doorway, startling her nearly backward and out of the chair. Oh, God, she thought, her heart pounding as she cleared the screen and Bill Lord ambled in, coffee in hand. Back to normal. She should have known it wouldn't last.

In the Shadows
1

*"I believe in my Self above all, free both
to will and not to be willed."*

The Pelagian Creed, Article I

"Finley," he began and then completed the message and sent it on its way. He sat back in his chair then, rubbed his hands over his face, and sighed. It was a long, deep sigh, deep with the contentment that springs from the commission of a purely spiritual act.

He stood and stretched, arms and fingertips reaching out, a-tingle with satisfaction. The veins and musculature along the length of his bare arms flickered like pale-green tributaries of the computer screen's green-glowing pool of light; the glow was picked up and reflected around the room—across the rippling chrome surfaces of the weight machines in one corner, across the lacquered high-gloss surfaces of the chests and cabinetry, across the gleaming steel of the blades mounted on the wall.

From a certain angle the glow was reflected, too, in the glass which covered a framed document on the wall. Not long ago, there was no document on the wall. There was a blank spot there and in his heart, waiting to be filled by the words there now. If you asked him, back then, he would have said he was a seeker after wisdom; but he probably would not have added that he was a *lost* seeker, a seeker of a sort of wisdom which he could not name and, he feared, would not recognize if he found it.

Not that he had failed to search far and wide for it, oh no; indeed, he had searched the world. Of the lands above the equator, he had gone first to the East: through steaming jungles to the feet of great stone gods; to the peaks of mountains whose very heights seemed to bespeak their holiness; to the serenity of paths lined with perfect round pebbles and flanked with carefully random gardens of green and flowering plants. But the mind of the East, he determined, was too thin and insubstantial to contain his truth.

He had gone to the West then: to forests dense with trees and the overgrowth of folklore; to cathedrals whose vaulted ceilings arched high above their incensed chambers, swooping up in the direction of an imagined afterlife; to ornate prayer and meditation chambers, their walls carved fantastically in rare woods, their floors thick with the weight of elaborately woven carpets. But the West was too heavy and coarse.

So he had journeyed to the South, then, to the dark lands below the equator—lands with a deceptive complexity to their truths, a complexity dense with much material but apparent little weight, like the wood of the balsa tree, or like a wafer. And like a wafer, when he blew against these apparently substantial truths they slid away from him and across the floor, leaving dry, rattling echoes in his mind.

He was discouraged when at last he returned from his travels. He returned of course to the city, his last hope, he feared, the city where there was something—so the folk wisdom said—for everyone. But it took him a long time, many months till he'd found his Master.

His Master's sanctum would be thoroughly banal to the unseeing eye: a walk up a dusty staircase behind an anonymous, street-level door; a gray anteroom and a gray office, with an adjoining meeting room full of gray folding chairs. Gray filing cabinets and gray steel shelves lined the walls. In the filing cabinets and along the shelves were arrayed the truths he had sought for years, and now found.

Motive is a fraud, the truths whispered to him. There is no

Reason in reasons, they said, no excuse for excuses. Man acts, and assigns motive later.

" 'Responsibility' is a tool of societal control, and a convenience employed by decadent minds to mask their absence of will," he heard his Master say. "It is not an inherent property of the human soul." Some actions cause us to feel pleasure, some pain, his Master said; some actions "help" others, some "harm" them. The goodness and badness of the acts can and will be assessed later, using subjective devices and yardsticks of the assessor's choosing, his Master admitted; but in the absence of motivation and intention, no act is good or bad in itself.

"In the context of a belief in the purity of your will, you must *do*, simply *do*," his Master insisted. "Do not ask yourself, 'Is it right that I do this?' or 'Why should I do this?' If the will moves you thus, thus shall you act."

Other students of his Master besides him had decided upon courses of action which they declared to be without motivation, actions which they, childlike, held up for the Master to examine and, they hoped, to approve. "Master," one would say excitedly, "I've decided that this afternoon I will steal an orange from a fruit stand, an orange that I can easily afford to buy. I don't have any reason to steal it!" And the Master would frown. Another would say, "I plan to walk backward through a museum tomorrow!" And the Master would waggle his head, cover his eyes with the palms of his hands, and laugh aloud in scorn.

Only he, he knew, had truly absorbed the Master's lessons. The Master sensed it also, and smiled at him, the Master's gray eyes glinting in satisfaction and pride. Only he sat in each session in silence, not deigning to offer up a catalogue of deeds performed as an act of obeisance, as an expression of the Master's will. The point was to establish a wholly *willed* life, not a kaleidoscopically impulsive one, nor one bounded even by his Master's approval. Only he acted on his *own* will, for no reason other than that he willed it then and in that place. He alone, of his Master's students, had experienced the warmth and glow of union with his will, a warmth and a glow of passion and power, a warmth and a glow which literally suffused his soul whenever he first bent to kiss the forehead and then drew one of these gleaming blades slowly, lovingly, across the throat of a limp and unconscious but still-warm victim: still warm with life, yes, with the life of flesh and blood and final breath; but still warm, more importantly, with the flash and frenzy of electrons, the life of wires and warm silicon, the life of her link—warm, intense, and finally ever so intimate—to *him*.

Chapter Seven

Constricted white light of the overcast morning sky filled her windows and spilled over into the apartment itself the next day, saturating it and everything in it with pale claustrophobia. A jittery breakfast, its tone established by the weird, frenetic, paranoid rhythms, on the oldies station, of Del Shannon and "Runaway." Stupid twittering nervously in his cage; milk pouring sloppily and sloshing over the side of her teacup; the kettle on the portable burner shrieking irritably, through all of which noise Finley heard the phone ringing. Who, at this hour . . . ?

It was Warren, calling to badger her about her Thanksgiving plans, for God's sake. She didn't know yet what she wanted to do for Thanksgiving, she told him. It was still weeks away; did he need to know today, right this minute? Sheesh. Yes, she'd let him and Nancy know as soon as she'd made up her mind.

She'd no sooner hung up from talking with Warren than the phone rang again. She jumped a few inches, startled. Wrong number this time. This was nuts; she was scaring herself.

She logged in to FORENSIC. Nothing yet from Flokati; given the time zone difference, he may not even have picked up her message yet. And on STACKS, ever more sadly, nothing from Tracy. A note from Uri said:

> Message: Hi, Finley. We had a request yesterday from a professor in the history department. She's looking for a BBS for academics with a special interest in turn-of-the-century Eastern Europe. If she can't find one, she's thinking of setting one up herself. I haven't been able to find anything like that. You have any ideas? Thanks for your help, as usual.

By the way, where do you GET all this information, anyhow? You work for the government, right? Is this some kind
of information service or something?

After checking the on-line directory on her PC, which matched
the one she had at work, Finley replied:

Message: Uri, you show a touching faith in my powers
<grin>. No, nothing specifically on the place and time
period she's interested in. I found one she might want to
try, though, called "Bismarck." It's for turn-of-the-century
GERMAN historians, but she might find what she wants
there. (Oh, and if she decides to set up one of her own,
could you forward to me the name and phone number
and so on, so I can add it to my directory? Thanks.)
And yes, I work for the government. Nothing you've
probably ever heard of, though. A criminal-investigation
agency, sort of an offshoot of the FBI, called CIAC. So
watch your step! <grin>

She tacked on to the message the log-in parameters for "Bismarck," and posted it to Uri.

As for ABLE, there was no mail for Finley from any of her
regular correspondents except Jane:

Message: Hello, Finley. What a delight to find out you're
in New Jersey! Why, I'm within an hour or so, in New York.
We should really get together sometime. It would be rather
fun, don't you think? Especially for the waiters taking care of
us, given your ears and my voice! Seriously, though, would
you be able to fit something like that into your calendar? (I
don't think I know, by the way—are you "seeing" anyone,
as the expression goes?) Let me know! Love you, dear.
<jane>

But Jane's maternal ebullience felt a little cloying this morning.
Finley would wait to answer it till she felt a little more upbeat.
Lunchtime, maybe.

Yesterday afternoon, having left Lord to his own office, she'd sat down with Helen Walker in Helen's cube and laid out what she could of the armed-robbery/weather project. Helen had recently moved to on-line from paper, and still viewed both the process and the products of electronic information retrieval almost religiously, with mixed terror and awe. "You got all *this*," she kept repeating, "on-*line*?"

Finley pointed out a few remaining loopholes and said she'd forward to Helen any late replies from outstanding queries. Then she went on to describe to Helen how to tie up the whole package into something like a conclusion, before actually handing it off to the requesting agent.

Throughout, Helen nervously tapped her fingers against the papers before her, as though confirming their reality; she now and then dabbed with a tissue at a sweating upper lip. The handoff went rather smoothly, once you'd made allowances for Helen's anxious befuddlement. But it left Finley with a feeling as though she were putting her affairs in order before embarking on some horrible ordeal.

That was truly what it would be, she thought: an ordeal. This whole on-line world was built, yes, of solid objects, of semiconductors and wire and circuit boards. But it was a world held together not only by artfully applied solder and precision-manufactured connectors, but also by the good old-fashioned mortar of trust; it was the last neighborhood still mostly untainted by suspicion. She didn't want to think about the possibility, however remote, that there was really a BBS connection in these killings; if not only the victims but the killer himself turned out to be a BBS user, then the whole precious essence of the neighborhood was threatened.

She tried to explain some of this to Gus when they went down to the cafeteria for tea and coffee. He nodded sympathetically but absentmindedly, not really paying particularly close attention. His eyes kept wandering to the glass-block wall, distracted by the motions of a single bird, transformed by the wall's weird optics into an entire precision-flying flock. He brushed a smear of cigarette ashes from the lapel of the same brown suit he'd worn yesterday. Of course, Finley reminded herself, he couldn't really understand. Not yet.

"Can we go check on the hardware-store question now?" he asked finally.

Finley smiled and nodded; maybe he'd understand pretty soon, after all. "Sure. And see? That's what I mean. There's just a natural tendency to believe what people tell you, and so you look forward to hearing from them."

Back at Lord's desk, Finley logged in to NJBBS. It said she had eight messages waiting to be read. Five of them, it turned out, had specific suggestions ranging from large national or regional hardware chains to independent local stores, local to wherever the sender lived or was otherwise familiar with. Two messages said it depended on what kind of hardware you were interested in, for example power tools vs. hand tools; of these two, one also suggested that Finley check a BBS called WOODWORK, giving the phone number and other necessary information. Someone else had chimed in with a reply to this last message:

> Message: Wait a minute. I thought WOODWORK was just
> supposed to be for manufacturers of woodworking tools,
> not for the general public?

"Huh?" said Gus. "How'd that guy read the message addressed to us?"

"That's another neat thing about BBSs, Gus: everybody can see and reply to messages from everybody else, unless they're sent in what we call 'private mode.' It's like a big barbecue or convention or something, with everybody milling around and butting into each other's conversations."

As for the eighth message, it didn't answer the question at all, just said:

> Message: Depends on where you live. Whereabouts are
> you?

Gus said, "You're not going to answer that, are you?"

"No—*you* are." She slid the keyboard over to him.

"Er, what do I type? Tell you the truth, I don't feel real comfortable telling this guy what hotel I'm staying at."

"Just reply that you're in the New Brunswick area, that's all."

He did so, and sent the message off as Finley instructed him.

He looked thoughtful for a few moments afterward, then said something to Finley. She missed it.

"Gus, I'm sorry," she said, "you're going to have to speak up. I really do have a hard time hearing your voice."

"*I'm* sorry, Finley. I just asked, this kind of thing happen often? Where you trade addresses with these people?"

"Well—not necessarily addresses; general areas of the country, the state, usually, unless you need to get more specific for something like this. Sometimes you want to mail something to somebody, a magazine article or birthday card or something, so you need to get at least their work address. And then there are special cases, people you get especially friendly with. I've met a couple of on-line friends before. Like my friend Jane, who lives in New York; we'll probably get to meet each other soon, and of course if that goes okay we may end up visiting each other at home."

"I see," he said, nodding in thought.

Finley waited, but he said nothing further. "Anyway, here's what I thought we could do," she said, finally.

She planned, she said, to start out by checking the floppy disks that she'd asked Gus to obtain. Many people used floppy disks to make backup copies of data on their hard disks, in case the hard disks accidentally failed. The victims' backup floppies, if any, might contain important information like letters to friends and business contacts, financial records, and so on; and if it turned out they'd used any BBSs, the backups might indicate which boards they'd contacted regularly, maybe even with whom they'd regularly "chatted."

If there were no backup floppies or no data on them, Finley could contact the sysops of all the boards in her directory, in the off-chance that something would turn up that way. But there were literally thousands of BBSs in her directory, though, some of whose sysops monitored their users less carefully than others, so this would be the more difficult and hence less preferable alternative.

"Sounds good to me," Gus said. "It's a start, anyhow. What can *I* do?"

"Been thinking about that. First, any word on the victims' backup floppies?"

"Oh, yeah, sorry, I meant to tell you. Each of the young ladies did have a bunch of floppies in her apartment. I asked the police in New York and Atlanta to send them via overnight express, to you here—the ones from the Bristol and Taylor cases in New York will arrive this afternoon, I guess, Atlanta by tomorrow morning. Can I do something with them when they get here?"

"Sure! Just check to see if they really do have backups on—" Finley halted when she saw the look of terror which Gus had built out of his nervous eyes and twitching mustache. Like Helen Walker, Finley thought: Aunt Helen. "Of course, Gus, I *meant* take them to one of our tech-support people, explain what we're looking for and let that person do it." Relief flooded his features. "For now, though, why don't you bring me up to speed on some of the details of the killings?"

He nodded eagerly; briefings were familiar ground for him, not like all this whiz-bang technoid baloney. He pulled from his briefcase four manila folders—one for each of the three cases, and a fourth for general notes and the Evsee reports.

The three cases, Gus said, shared the following characteristics: the victims were single women; they lived in apartments; they were killed in the same manner; they were killed within a short distance of their computers; the computers were on, but devoid of data or software. Oh, and there was one other thing: no traditional motive had as yet been established. None of the three had been sexually assaulted, and none of their apartments or purses seemed to have been burglarized. Aggie Bristol and Tracy were white, and Dorothy Taylor was black, so if indeed the cases were connected, there wasn't likely to be a racial motive. Aside from those features, as well as some trivial ones—each of the victims, for example, had American Express and Visa cards—nothing seemed to link all three.

"How about phone calls?" Finley asked.

"You mean, like correlating their phone bills to see if they ever called each other?"

"Umm, well, yes, that, too. But I was thinking more along the lines of seeing if they called any boards, even maybe the same ones, and—hey! Not a bad idea, I can correlate their phone bills with my BBS directory—good way to cut down on the work!" She explained that having a record of the victims' phone calls would obviate the need to contact every one of the hundreds of sysops in her directory; she'd just have to contact the sysops of the BBSs (if any) that the victims had used.

Gus nodded and seemed to perk up; looking into telephone records also put him in familiar territory. He made a note to himself in a small looseleaf pad.

"Okay, Gus—what else is there? Any other little details?"

"Well, the local cops didn't find any fingerprints at the scenes. None they could use, anyhow. Looks like he was wearing gloves —they did get some glove prints. And he may have black hair. Each apartment has turned up strands of the same kind of straight black hair. Caucasian. Of course, the hair itself doesn't point to anybody specific, and it's possible that it's not the hair of the guy himself but just somebody they all knew in common—"

"In which case you'd still like to talk to that person," Finley completed for him. "Sure, that makes sense. Nothing else about possible suspects, though—no eyewitness accounts of anybody seen visiting the victims?"

There were no such accounts, Gus said, not yet anyhow. As he'd said the day before, the first victim was reported missing by her employer, and found by the police; the second was found by a neighbor.

"And Tr—Ms. Williams, what about her?"

"Apparently, she car-pooled with a guy she knew from work." (One of *several* guys she knew from work, Finley amended to herself.) "He had a key to her apartment, and he found her that morning when he got there to pick her up. Lying at the foot of her desk. Her friend didn't have black hair, though."

But Finley wasn't listening. She was thinking back to two mornings ago. While the horrible scene with Tracy and her car-pool "friend" from work was being played out down in Atlanta, Finley herself was feeding Stupid, breakfasting, reading Tracy's last message. Singing along with Motown. Getting on the bus, sitting next to Bill Lord—hey, *Lord* had black hair. . . .

But nah, that was ridiculous even to think about. *Lord*? She didn't seriously believe there might be a connection between him and the killings; still, as a motive . . .

"Is it possible," she said, "that as a motive, the guy might be attacking them just because they were computer users? Y'know, like say he himself can't use a computer, maybe his job is threatened by automation and he overgeneralizes, like he's threatened by all computer users?"

"You mean—like, like *me*?" Gus said, his face reddening and his eyes narrowing a little.

Finley couldn't suppress a laugh. "Ha ha! No, Gus, no, I'm sorry, I didn't mean like you. Field agents aren't threatened by computers, they don't care *where* the data comes from. Besides, your hair's not black." She smiled teasingly.

He seemed relieved by her answer, and smiled back. "No, it's not black—not originally, and not now, even what's left of it. But on the general question, sure, I guess that's a possible motive." He made another note to himself. "On the other hand, doubt if he's really threatened by computers, though—seems to know his way around them okay."

"Yeah, that's true. How about the Evsee reports, Gus? What factors are significant so far?"

Although the Evsee fluctuated up or down with similarities between crimes, the various similarities did not all drive it up or down to the same degree. The Evsee reports indicated all factors above a certain minimum threshold of significance. For example, the first victim, Aggie Bristol, may have correlated just by chance to any number of others in CIAC's database, based on such things as location, profession, and so on. The blank screen and fully erased hard disk might have been noted as just a curiosity. But Dorothy Taylor's killing—although it shared few other characteristics with the first—would drive up the possible importance not only of the means of killing, but also of the victims' computers. When Tracy Williams died, those two factors raised the likelihood of a connection to near-certainty. At the same time, the specific locale went down in its likely significance.

"So what kind of killer are you starting to see, Gus? Anything yet?"

He thought for a moment. "Hmm . . . I guess, first, like I was just saying it's somebody who knows something about computers. Enough to erase their hard disks, anyhow, get rid of anything that might connect the victims to him. Or maybe, like you suggested, he's not erasing evidence of himself but just sort of erasing everything their computers were used for and stood for. At any rate, he knows *how* to erase everything. He knows how to use a very sharp blade of some sort—did I mention the pathologist's report said the cuts were apparently made from behind, by a left-hander? And he's also strong enough to knock his victims out long enough that he can cut their throats before they come to. Guy probably doesn't need money, he didn't take any from his victims and also he can afford a certain amount of travel. Or at least, his employer can. And he may have black hair. That's about all I can guess for now."

Finley nodded in agreement. She thought for a moment and added, "I suppose we don't really know that there's just one killer, do we? Could it be two or more, just acting together somehow out of the same motive, some kind of a club or cult or something?"

"Ah, no, you're right, should have thought of that myself. We can't assume it's the same guy, although there's obviously a connection of some kind."

The phone rang; Finley turned up the speakerphone volume. "FINLEY, MS. FINLEY?" a too-loud voice asked. "FRONT DESK HERE, EXPRESS PACKAGES FOR YOU." The miracle of overnight delivery. "Gus," Finley said as she rose from Lord's desk, "why don't you get started on obtaining the phone records? I'll check the floppies out myself."

He hurried off, and Finley retrieved the packages from the front desk. Not only the New York, but also the Atlanta shipments were here; amazing!

Back in Lord's office, she carefully slit the cartons. She inserted the floppies into Lord's PC, one by one, and scanned the contents. Neither Aggie Bristol nor Dorothy Taylor had done any backups, it turned out; it always amazed Finley how careless people could be—every hard disk eventually failed. Maybe people in New York were so inured to everyday disasters, human and technological, that they'd stopped wasting their time on precautions altogether. But she smiled to find, in the large plastic storage bin filled with Tracy's disks, over twenty floppies labeled, in a small, neat, cursive handwriting that Finley had never had a chance to see before, "BACKUP." Each label included a serial number and a date the backup had been made. But when she checked them further, she learned that every one was blank and unreadable: the killer had evidently gotten there first.

She imagined him sitting in Tracy's chair, his gloved fingers keying in the commands to erase the floppies, one by one. She imagined Tracy's silent form lying on the floor at his feet, staining the carpet. She imagined him then, just before wiping the hard disk, perhaps reading the mail which Tracy and she had exchanged, and a shudder ran through her as she imagined him smiling, evilly. She looked at the computer there on Bill Lord's desk, thought of the telephone wire trailing from it to the network, and she thought for a silly moment that she saw an intense, malevolent face, framed by black hair, looking out of the screen and into her heart. She closed her eyes, and when she opened them again the face was no longer there. Nonetheless, she reached over and shut the monitor off. Just, she told herself, to let it cool off for a while.

Chapter Eight

That Saturday, Finley's twin alarms went off at their usual times, six o'clock and six-thirty. As always on Saturday morning, the oldies station today awakened her with "Breakfast with the Beatles." Peering into Stupid's cage at him, sitting there with his head cocked quizzically to one side, she sang of seeing a face in an unforgettable time and place. "Chirp?" the parakeet asked.

Finley wasn't going to work today, oh no. She was going *away from* work. The last couple days hadn't turned up anything of particular significance, and she wanted not to think about it at all.

She'd started out a couple days ago, reading through the project folders more carefully, concentrating especially on information about the three victims' computer setups. Didn't seem to be anything significant there; they had different makes and models of nearly everything. They all had modems, of course, as Morris had said. The software lists were not especially revealing, either: different word processors, different spreadsheets. . . . They had all used BoardWalk, although because it was such a popular package she couldn't really make anything of that.

All three of them, as was the norm for nearly all computer users, had also apparently played a handful of games on their PCs. The only game that they all owned was one called "MindRace," some sort of arcade-style thing which (Finley vaguely remembered) featured squawking aliens in tennis shoes. Wondering if that might prove to be a connection, she logged into a games BBS, and spent an ultimately fruitless two hours reading hundreds of messages about dodging Neuron Blasters and Psychotropic Beams. None of these messages had originated from or been sent to any of the three victims, and none gave Finley any idea what MindRace might have to do with a serial killer. All these MindRace freaks seemed to spend too much time in front of their computer screens to think about killing anyone for real.

Finally, with neither enthusiasm nor conclusion, she wondered about the possibility of a BBS link among the three women. Until she could see their phone bills, she'd have no way of checking this further. Maybe she could at least start by checking Tracy's correspondence on STACKS, she thought; the sysop there, a guy named Frank, surely knew both Tracy and Finley herself well enough. She'd left a private message to him. But he had politely and firmly declined to provide any information about Tracy's on-line conversations with anyone else—"At least," he added, "not without a subpoena." Nuts; he meant a court order, of course, but that was still an angle she hadn't figured on.

It was true that she had finally heard, a little later, from Flokati:

> . . . Is possible, yes, to tell knife cut instead of saw for ex-ample. One kind of knife instead of other kind of knife, not so easy. Razor blade make very thin, clean cut. Japanese seppuku knife very sharp like razor, used in ritual of cutting own bowels rather than face dishonor. Is called hara kiri in USA I think. You know hara kiri?

She knew hara kiri, sure. But the message didn't really tell her anything she didn't already know—she wasn't even sure any longer why she'd even bothered asking. It was the local police's business, not CIAC's, after all.

But something gnawed at Finley that was CIAC's business, indeed virtually its reason for being: the killer's motive.

You were trained when you came to CIAC, and not just in information-retrieval techniques and formal criminal-investigation procedures. You attended classes in criminal and abnormal psychology; you learned to pick apart terms like "motive" and "paranoia" until they throbbed before you, oozing connotation, like organs on a vivisectionist's table. There were workshops in visualization techniques, conducted in a large seminar room with well-cushioned chairs and dimmed lights. In this room, the instructor's voice murmuring sonorously to you from the sound system, your eyes closed lightly, you learned to imagine a world refracted through the eyes of a criminal. It was a world in which a loaf of bread or a syringe of cloudy fluid might weigh as heavily on your mind as a pillowcase full of twenty-dollar bills, a world in which secrecy, despair, and suspicion, lies and innuendo, were not amorphous concepts but fundamental building blocks of the physical universe. Elements.

You learned to look at the facts swarming like a cloud of gnats about disparate cases, with your mind open and unfocused, using mental tricks which confirmed the absence of affiliation among most of the facts and most of the cases but which nonetheless often produced a near-audible *click* as one fact shifted into alignment with another, like a marble on a Chinese checkerboard. It was in fact called that, "The Click." "You get The Click yet?" you might ask a peer working on a particularly thorny project. That was the point of the daily event list, for example, scrolling past at least once every day on the screen of every computer and terminal in the building, dumping its seemingly random slurry of information into the subconscious sluices of all of CIAC's employees. You never knew when The Click would come, or what would trigger it, or in whose head. Key project-breaking facts had Clicked in the heads of nearly every level of personnel, from secretaries on up through managers as well as on-line searchers, and even the paper searchers were required—well, supposedly—to scan the event list every day.

This was one of her brother Warren's biggest (and simultaneously most feeble) gripes about the whole CIAC concept. "New Age cop talk," he labeled it, a drumbeat of disregard pounding with every monosyllable. "Criminalistics my foot," he'd said on another occasion, "how about criminal*mystics,* hey, how about *that*?"

But New Age hocus-pocus or not, in this case it seemed possible that there would never be a Click. Nothing truly connected the three women ("Not *yet,*" Finley forced herself to remember). Even Gus, with his two decades' lead on her, hadn't gotten The Click yet, *any* Click. It just didn't make sense—the computers, the blank screens; what kind of motive could they point to? It was no better than the dry mockery of a false Click.

So no: not a hint of a motive yet. Still, the killer had demonstrated great deliberateness so far; even in the absence of a motive, these homicides were all undertaken by someone with a *mind.* The guy *could* be a psychopath, Gus had said to her once—someone whose motive was unclouded by reason as we usually understood it. Gus had crushed out his cigarette then, and grimaced. He looked across the table at Finley and said, "Nuts maybe, but he's not stupid."

And that was right: perhaps crazy, certainly not stupid. But there was yet this damnable blank spot at the center, the one labeled, "WHY?" Finley was so puzzled by it that she'd again risked breaking Morris's order, and left another note for Flokati:

> . . . Thanks for the note about the knives, Flokati. Now I
> have a psychological question for you: why would someone
> kill people for no reason? Why would he pick complete
> strangers out of thin air, cut their throats, for no motive? I
> know there are sick people out there, psychopaths, but are
> there any sane "reasons" for doing such a thing, in your
> experience? Thanks again. Take care.
> Finley

Morris would have reason to kill *her,* she mused, especially if he saw that reference to throat-cutting.

But all that had been at work the last couple of days. Today, Saturday, she felt like she simply had to get away from killing and blood and, yes, even computers and BBSs. So she'd tucked all that into the back of her mind, dropped a beeper into her purse just in case, and after a brief train ride to Princeton and a brisk walk to Nassau Street, the autumn wind swirling her hair about and into her face, here she was at a gallery exhibit called "In Their Time: Three Centuries of Philadelphia and New Jersey Artists."

She'd been in this gallery before—but when . . . ? Of course, sometime in the spring was it? Yes. With Spencer. Another windy day, a different exhibit. It was a weekday, and they'd both taken the day off; nonetheless Spencer seemed—and, she was certain (especially in hindsight), *was*—awfully preoccupied by his work. He felt guilty being "out," he said, on a day when even his new receptionist was working. Finley tried distracting him in various ways, finally snaking a mischievous hand into one of his pants pockets as he stood before an Impressionist nude. But he'd not really been looking at the painting, and far from seeming to enjoy the massage, even repaying her in kind with one of his own large hands shoved into one of her jeans pockets, as he once might have, he had seemed positively annoyed by it. He had grabbed her wrist and yanked her hand from the pocket, twisting his hips violently away from her. "Finley," he'd whispered, "come on, we're in *public!*"

But now it was a different exhibit and everything else was different, too; with the departure of the previous exhibit, all its rounded soft-focus Bohemian floppy-hatted human figures and pastel landscapes, her very frame of mind seemed to have altered, irretrievably. Except for the memory of that prior visit, she might have been in a different gallery altogether. Most of the portraits in the present exhibit were stiff, formal poses. For residents of a country so caught up in Revolutionary fervor, she thought, these people all looked amazingly conventional and amazingly alike. Men and women both: ruffles, powdered hair, and rouged cheeks. The brushwork pinpoint-sharp. *Edged.* A room of folk-art, "primitive" paintings from about the same era, too: landscapes and cityscapes in plain unshadowed planes of color, populated by tiny stick figures.

There was in fact little in this exhibit that she hadn't seen already, in some place, in some form, and she was beginning to think of ducking out soon for a beer and a big hearty sandwich in a nearby tavern. But before her now was a large oil by one Horace Pippin. Finley had never heard of the guy. The painting depicted, and was titled, "John Brown Goes to His Hanging."

The sky was a deep blue in the painting, but it was confined to just the upper-left corner. Across the bulk of the canvas marched an array of figures in drab grays and browns and stark blacks and whites, standing out against the whitewashed building in the background like ugly handprints. But even the central figure in the composition—the demonic, obsessive abolitionist himself, riding to his execution in a cart, bound with rope and seated on his own casket—even he did not hold Finley's gaze. She was drawn, instead, to the face of a bystander at the bottom right.

The largest face in the painting, it was that of a white man in a rumpled grayish hat. His mouth was open, apparently in strong emotion, perhaps a fury and perhaps tinged with hatred. The skin of his face was a pale gray, as if he'd been long dead, and he was clean-shaven except for a droopy black mustache. His eyes were sharp, glittering pinpoints of vengeance.

What drew her attention to this face was not simply the depiction of the face itself, but the splashes of color on the people nearby, virtually the only color in the scene: a bright-red scarf to the right, slashing diagonally down and to the left, and a bright-red shirt to the left of the face. The face seemed caught there, as though pinned between a thumb and forefinger sticky with blood. She peered intently at the face, tried to see behind those white-hot points of hate, to imagine how and why someone would hate so profoundly. . . .

Her beeper went off, scaring the bejeezus out of her and a half-dozen other patrons. An elderly man with thick wire-rimmed glasses seemed to shrink in terror against a wall, his hands clenched apparently in prayer; a young mother ferried her child's stroller briskly into another gallery; a woman in a security guard's uniform moved in Finley's direction as though to arrest her for triggering an alarm.

Finley couldn't find the damned thing, let alone shut it off. She knelt, dumped the contents of her purse noisily on the marble floor, at last grabbed the beeper and silenced its shrieking. (Stupid would have had a field day with this thing.)

In the display panel on its face was Morris's home number. Scooping her belongings back into the purse, Finley asked the guard for a telephone. "You will have to go outside to the kiosk on Nassau Street," the guard said with an imperious Ivy-League sniff, and Finley turned to leave, glimpsing, for one last moment, the angry face dominating the corner of the John Brown painting; it now seemed to be jeering at her.

Morris's voice was tinny and ridiculous in the receiver of this old pay phone, almost swallowed up into inaudibility by the traffic noise here.

The same killer, apparently, had struck again, Morris said—this time in Philadelphia. With luck, Finley could catch a train from Princeton to Philly and get to the crime scene while the police were still there. Gus was already on his way, Morris said, and would probably arrive just about when she did, in about an hour.

"Some differences this time, Finley," he added. "A couple things you might want to know before you get there. The victim this time was a man, got that? M-A-N, *man*, I know it screws up the Evsee but there it is." Morris hesitated and cleared his throat. "And Finley? Take along a barf bag, there's a real mess there."

There truly was a real mess there; Morris had not exaggerated.

It was a large, tastefully furnished apartment on the second floor of an old brick building in a pre-Revolutionary section of Philadelphia; the streets here were cobblestoned, which played hell with a car's undercarriage but did nothing to diminish the gossipy enthusiasm of the crowd outside, milling about just on the correct side of the police barricades. Inside, the living room was neat, and appeared to be largely undisturbed (except for the splotch of red-gone-brown on the inside of the door, by the door-knob).

One detective was leaning back, ashen-faced, against a wall, his hands shoved deep into his armpits as though he were freezing, his eyes watery and body trembling. Finley steeled herself before looking into the victim's bedroom. But probably nothing could prepare her for the carnage there, on the other side of the cordon preventing entry to that room.

The pathologist's team had already been through once, literally picking up the pieces. The victim had not been eviscerated, exactly, but in some kind of unimaginably gruesome struggle with his assailant had lost whole swatches of flesh and chunks of muscle. Numbered chalk polygons around the floor and wall showed that there had been one, two, three . . . six such patches scattered about. One polygon on the wall ended in a yard-long streak of deep red, apparently left when the meat slid down the wall.

"Don't touch nothin'," admonished a detective sergeant, "we're not sure we got it all yet."

Touch anything? Finley thought. Fat chance of that, it was hard enough just to *look* at it. Geysers of blood had sprayed across the carpet, walls, drapes, and windows. Worst of all was the bed itself. The ivory bedspread had been soaked, in the center, with an enormous deep-red blotch, already blotted up by the mattress from edges to center. It looked like a perverse parody of a Rorschach ink blot, rust-colored appendages groping out from the rust-colored core toward the edges of the bed—as though toward, perhaps, an imagined escape.

"What the hell *happened?*" Finley asked the detective.

"Don't know for sure, yet," he said. "Near as we can tell so far, the guy with the knife or razor or whatever the hell it was surprised the guy who lived here. Surprised, ha, yeah, to put it mildly. He must have put up some fight," gesturing here at the weight-training equipment along one wall, stainless-steel surfaces splattered with red, "but I guess the guy who broke in was too much for him."

Finley waved a hand toward the bed. "The body was there?"

"Yeah. Looked like it'd been chopped pretty good, too. Guy with the knife must have been pretty pissed off or somethin'. Ran out the other door there to the back room, then out the apartment door and down the stairs. Set off the alarm at the fire exit, that's what got us here in the first place."

Finley thought for a moment. So much of this event seemed so different from the three previous ones; why did Morris think it was the same killer? "Look," she said, "I'm really a computer specialist, not a detective. The other homicides I've been looking into all had something to do with PCs, you know, computers. Is there a computer in the apartment somewhere? I don't see one here."

"Oh, yeah, come on this way." He led her down the hallway, around a corner; they passed the other door to the bedroom, from which paraded a line of red blotchy shoe prints—the left foot only —to a room at the back of the apartment. The detective gestured at the bloody trail in the carpet. "We think he ran into the back room here, then saw the footprints and took the shoe off. No prints goin' back the other way, see?"

The computer was indeed there in the back room, through the door and to the left, positioned off to one side on the top surface of a varnished door lying flat and astraddle two brightly painted sawhorses. There was a desk in this room, too, and a large steel file cabinet; one drawer in the file cabinet was open, and the files were in slight disarray. As for the computer itself, its keyboard was smeared with dried blood. The PC was turned on, and its screen was glowing. But as Finley confirmed when she approached, the screen was not blank. Starting at the top, along the left side, were a series of commands which someone had typed into the computer. Each command line alternated with a line showing the date and time when it was typed; the date was to-day's, and the times began a little before 3:15 that morning and ended a couple minutes later. The commands and corresponding responses from the computer said:

```
C:\> format c:
Bad command or file name

C:\> cd bdwalk

C:\BDWALK\> erase*.*
Are you sure? (Y/N)y

C:\BDWALK\> cd\

C:\> rmdir bdwalk

C:\> cld
Bad command or file name

C:\>
```

The killer, Finley saw with the tiniest of thrilling Clicks, had tried to erase the entire hard disk, failed, then erased some very spe-cific files and finally tried to clear the screen, but mistyped the last command. She pointed out the series of commands to the detec-tive.

"Yeah," he said, "I saw that. It mean somethin' to you?"

"Well, for starters, that first date and time there at the top is probably a pretty good indication of when all this occurred. The killer probably came into the back room here, turned on the PC, and after it got warmed up it displayed the current date and time there."

"Yeah, okay, that's right—that's a little before the fire alarm went off. What about the rest of it? Looks Greek to me."

Finley smiled. "No, not Greek. It says that the tracks on the floor aren't the only ones our friend was in too big a hurry to cover."

She closed her eyes for a moment and could almost see him, this time: his black hair shoved every which way in the struggle with his victim, perhaps a smear of blood across his forehead like the mark of Cain; the frantic trip to the room here, sitting at this very chair, striking the keys in a frenzy, his eyes darting nervously about; mistyping the last command but then suddenly distracted by the sight, out of the corner of his eye, of the bloody trail leading to his left foot; jumping up in haste, grabbing the shoe off his foot, rushing to the file cabinet (for what, though?), and dashing—shoe in one gloved hand, blade perhaps in the other or perhaps sheathed—down the stairwell and out to the street, into the night and the darkness of anonymity.

She reached out to touch the keyboard, but the detective yelled at her, "Wo, waitaminnit! I said not to touch nothin', didn't I?"

"Er, yes, sorry, I wasn't thinking. Any idea when I can sit here and browse around this computer for a while?"

The detective looked at her. Computer freaks, he thought. Christ, middle of a fuckin' slaughterhouse, they wanna play fuckin' Space Invaders. "I'd say—well, really not that much left in this room that we need to get at. We already dusted the thing, the chair and desk, too, I guess, checked for hairs and fabric samples, took blood samples off the keyboard and carpet . . . maybe no more than an hour, that all right?"

Finley nodded. "Okay. If possible, could you make sure nobody fools with the computer or takes anything away from this room? I mean, without letting me know?"

"Yeah, yeah, yeah," he said, and Finley thought, ludicrously, of "Breakfast with the Beatles." "Don't worry about that, we run a professional shop here."

As they entered the hallway again, Finley peeked in through the bedroom's back door. Gus was standing in the hallway at the other bedroom door, leaning over the cordon and craning his neck about, shaking his head, notepad and pencil jiggling nervously against his brown trouser legs, exchanging mutters with another detective. He looked over at the door where Finley stood then, rolled his eyes, and motioned with his head in the direction of the hallway.

"Let's get out of here for a while," he said when she met him in the hall, "and let the boys finish tidying up."

Chapter Nine

A banging jangle of Country-Western music from the jukebox belied the name and the shamrock painted in the window of O'McMurphy's Triple Irish Tavern, which Finley and Gus had entered after a short walk from the scene of the bloodbath at the apartment of Victim Number 4. Each of them was now sipping at a draught beer and waiting for a sandwich.

"You sure you can hear okay in here?" Gus said loudly.

Finley leaned forward, away from the thrumming back of her wooden chair, and smiled. "Yes, Gus, no problem. As long as you talk loud enough I'll be able to hear okay. And as long as I keep my back away from the chair."

"Your back?" He looked dubious.

"Trust me. Anyway," she said, "you were saying, you still think it's the same guy?"

"Well, don't know for sure, of course." He pointed down at Finley's napkin, on which she had scribbled an approximation of what she'd seen on the computer's screen. "But yeah, I think it is. Based on what I think you just said, especially. You said before that this 'BoardWalk' thing is one kind of program that dials up BBSs, lets you send and receive messages and so on. If that's just one kind, how'd he know that was the one on this guy's computer?"

"Easy. BoardWalk is the best seller, probably three-fourths of all the BBS users in the world use one version of BoardWalk or another, instead of something else. So it was a lucky guess for him, but not all *that* lucky."

"Thanks," Gus said to the bartender, who had just stepped out from behind the bar to deliver their lunches. "Another round, Finley?" She nodded. "Yeah, two more. . . . Anyway," he continued after the bartender left, "so let's say he gets lucky like you said, goes right to the BoardWalk area, directory, place, whatever-the-hell, and erases it all. So BoardWalk's gone now. Why didn't he check to see if the guy he killed had any other of these, these BBS programs? Could he have missed one, or some?"

Finley's eyes widened. She finished her mouthful of sandwich, then said, "Y'know, Gus, if you keep this up I'm not going to believe you anymore when you say you 'don't get all this computer crap'!" He blushed a little and smiled, obviously pleased. "That's a *great* idea, that's one of the first things I should check for when I go to look at the PC." She took a small notepad out of her handbag and scribbled a few words to herself. "And I guess the reason he didn't check for any other ones was, he was in a hurry, like I was thinking. Probably forgot to check for backups for the same reason."

She picked up her sandwich again. But just before biting into it, she looked across the table at Gus, lowered the sandwich again, and said, "I'm serious. You really are picking this stuff up pretty fast. You sure you never took any computer courses or anything? No computer at home? Maybe your desk back at your own office?"

"Nah," he said, popping the last little chunk of his own wolfed-down sandwich into his mouth. "No computer. Pure as the driven snow."

Like Warren, she thought, though maybe in his case purity wasn't exactly the first thing she thought of. "So then how'd you get into CIAC in the first place? Were you a police detective before this?"

He nodded, and took a swallow of beer. "Yeah, well, actually a sheriff's deputy. Pretty mundane stuff most of the time, chasing down deadbeat husbands skipping on alimony payments, that sort of thing."

" 'Most of the time'? What about the other times?"

He looked out the window at nothing in particular, at passing cars and parked ones, at people hurrying past, oblivious. He didn't like to remember all the other times, especially not all the later ones. "Well, I guess I was—*am*—a pretty good investigator. So after a while I got a chance. A pretty good assignment, got to work on a so-called 'drug strike force.' The kind of stuff you read about in the papers all the time, you know, stakeouts, raids, photos of bags of white powder stuffed in some guy's trunk, all that. Guns 'n' glamour."

Another sip, another cigarette. He played idly with his book of matches, holding it in the same hand as the cigarette, turning it, tapping it on the table.

"So anyhow," he went on, "I was in on a raid once. They started shooting at us and I got a little jumpy and shot one o' *them.* Trouble was, he wasn't really one o' them, he was one of *us,* inside guy, undercover. Oh, he *lived,* yeah, thank God for that; he lived. But it was touch and go for a few weeks there and he was never able to testify. Couldn't talk, couldn't even write. Everybody said don't worry, not your fault, so on; but I'll tell you, Finley, when they had to let all those guys go because the key witness couldn't testify, I wanted to crawl into a hole. Made me sick."

Finley nodded; she understood but yet didn't understand. This world of drugs and undercover police and the roar of gunfire was as far away as she could imagine from her gray little cubicle with the Garfield cartoons on the walls, the hushed ricky-ticky of a computer keyboard. It made her feel inexperienced, naive, as though she were still in high school. But Gus was still talking, albeit more quietly, and even the jukebox, silent now, seemed to be listening. Finley leaned forward, she hoped unobtrusively, and turned up the volume of one of her hearing aids just a notch.

". . . I could just imagine," he was saying, "how it must seem, you betcha, 'Gus lost his nerve.' And I was even jumpier from then on. Too bad, 'cause a couple months later there's another raid, even more shooting this time even though we were only up against one guy in an apartment. I had the cleanest shot at him but I *missed* him, goddamnit, and then the next shot he got off missed *me* and killed a local cop in on the raid with us—guy had a wife and five kids. And my shot . . ." He paused. His eyes were blinking a little too fast and they might have been just a little wet, or maybe it was just an effect of the strong city sunlight pouring down like a waterfall between the silent attentive office towers across the street and in through the window.

"My shot," he repeated, "the one that missed, went up through the ceiling. Damn, I *still* can't think what the hell I was doing aiming that high. Went up through the *ceiling*. There was a kid, a little six-year-old black kid, in the apartment upstairs, watching TV. 'Sesame Street,' damn it. Nicked him square in the eye. Didn't kill him, no, in fact when he got over the pain and the surgery and all, when they gave him the patch he thought it was kind of *cool*. That's what he said, 'Way cool!' and then he laughed. A pirate. But I couldn't help thinking of that kid growing up, all the jobs he couldn't ever have 'cause he just had one eye. . . ." He stopped for a second, his gaze flicking over to Finley and then back out the window again. "I know, I know, nuts, right? But I said to myself, pardon my French, 'Fuck *this*.' It could've happened to anybody but it happened to *me* and I knew I'd think about that kid or that cop every time I put my finger on the trigger from then on. Hesitate in *that* line of work, might as well keep the undertaker on retainer, right?"

He looked back at Finley, smiled ruefully, took a swallow of beer, and lit up another cigarette. "When I first heard about this CIAC thing it sounded—well, kind of dorky. Bunch o' little ferrets, y'know, runnin' around with encyclopedias and Reader's Guide to Periodicals tucked under their arm." He chuckled at the memory. "But then I started to recognize some of the names signing on as field agents. These guys, yeah, some women, too, they weren't patsies but the real thing. Sounded like all the ferrets were gonna be back in the back office, no offense.

"The best thing about it: no guns. I heard that and I jumped, you bet, and hallelujah, they took me. And that," he concluded, "is the complete professional life of August Merrill, crack CIAC field agent."

Finley smiled. She glanced down at his left hand, hovering with its cigarette by the ashtray. The plain gold band on his finger gleamed, dully, in the light which splashed across the tabletop. "Gus, I do understand, a little, how much all that with the two raids must have upset you, but *boy* it sure sounds a heck of a lot more exciting than any job *I* ever had. What did your wife think about all this?"

He grinned. "She said, 'Fuck *this*' even before I did. Stayed right there, I mean, but she helped me see the light. Why make yourself nuts?"

The bartender returned to their table and gestured at the empty mugs. "Another round?" he said to Gus as he picked up their plates. "Or coffee?"

Gus looked across the table at Finley. Finley answered for both of them, "Nope. Nothing else, just the check."

As they counted out their respective halves of the tab, Finley said, "I'm going to run back upstairs to that guy's apartment and check out the PC. You want to come?"

"Nah. Got to get back on the road."

"On the road?"

"Yeah. I was on the turnpike on my way out to Pittsburgh when the beeper went off; this is 'Parents' Weekend' at my kid's college. He'll understand that I had to miss the game today; I hope his mother will. I was supposed to meet her at the airport—hope she waited for me to catch up." He grinned. "Again."

They were at the door now, and Finley said, just before they shook hands and parted ways, "Okay, Gus. I'll give you a holler if anything comes up this weekend. Oh, and one other thing." She paused. "I just wanted to say I'm proud to be working on this project with somebody like you, Gus."

He reddened, mumbled thanks, and shuffled off down the sidewalk, a rumpled man in a rumpled brown suit, with a head full of rumpled memories. Uncle Gus.

She was sitting a short time later before the keyboard in the latest victim's apartment. John Redman, she'd been told by the young uniformed officer on guard by the front door: that was the victim's name. Redman. Ha; almost a sick joke, Red Man. Fortunately, she'd thought, not a name she recognized from any of her own BBSs—then mentally kicked herself; it wasn't any better for a stranger to die like this than a friend.

First, she followed up on Gus's idea: were there any other BBS access packages on Redman's hard disk? She did find one that she'd never heard of, called "CROSSOVER." It was clearly meant to be such a package, she could see after a few minutes of looking at some of the files in its directory; maybe a special-purpose one for accessing just one particular board and no others. But the program and the files with it didn't work at all; she'd take a copy of it home with her to fool around with. As for BoardWalk—maybe Redman had backups somewhere. . . . She walked back out to the front door.

"Officer, is it okay for me to look around in Redman's closets and so on? I'm looking for some floppy disks, spare computer things, you know?"

The cop looked her over. A kid still, practically a baby; must be no more than nineteen or twenty, tops. Bad case of acne ravaging his forehead. "Well, lemme see," full of authority now, "let's just make a note of your name again, badge number. . . . Okay, well, yeah, Sergeant said you could monkey with the computer. But he also said stay outta the bedroom. So yeah, okay, just no bedroom, all right?" He grinned and nearly winked, and looked her up and down again.

"Got it," she said, keeping her voice level. "No bedroom."

As it happened, she didn't need anything from the bedroom anyway; that was a good thing, because the detective team had already ripped up the carpet, cut out portions of the walls, removed the drapes and furniture, and trucked it all to the lab for analysis. Redman's backups were in a stack of diskette boxes on the floor of the closet in the back room. The most recent ones were dated over a month ago, but they'd still give her some idea what BBSs Redman might have frequented. She copied the backed-up files back onto the hard disk, but they didn't work, either, any more than the CROSSOVER ones had. Maybe a problem with the phone line—? The phone line, of course. Redman's phone service was probably shut off already. So she'd take along the BoardWalk backups, too. And finally, she herself backed up onto some spare floppies the more recent data from both the CROSSOVER and the BoardWalk directories—completing the backup cycle that Redman himself would now never get around to.

As long as she was there, she thought, she might as well check out the rest of the hard disk. The usual clutter of miscellany meaningless to anyone other than the PC's owner: old stray little bits of files that hadn't been touched in five years; files with garbage names, obviously mistakes, like "3{6AB?XX"; files that went with a different word-processing package than the one he had now. . . .

A couple of games; no "MindRace," though, so no connection to that game then. There was a spreadsheet package, too, but the only data stored with it were just row after row and column after column of numbers. Who knew what *that* was?

She checked out the files that went with his current word processor. Looks like he was a photographer: lots of letters to photo supply houses for film and darkroom chemicals, a list called "MODELS" with names, phone numbers, and so on. . . . She printed it all out; the sergeant, Sergeant Whatzisname, might be able to use it.

On the way out, she handed the sheaf of printout paper to the young cop. "Here's a present for your sergeant," she said. "Tell him it's information I found on the computer, might be useful." He gave her the once-over again, and made a note on his clipboard. "And also tell him I took some of Redman's floppy disks with me."

"Weeelll," he drawled, "I don't know about *that*. Sergeant didn't say—"

Finley thrust another several sheets of paper at him. "I already thought of that. Here's a list of everything I'm taking with me. Just give it to him. My name and so on is also there, if he has any questions."

He looked the pages over, visibly without comprehension and also with much less relish than he'd shown while examining *her*. "Hmm—hey, wait a minute," he said, "you didn't put down your home address and phone number." His eyes were lightly lidded, masked you might say, and he seemed on the brink of laughing out loud.

Some people . . . ! "Listen, Junior. Just give it to him, here's my *boss's* home number, see? If he wants to reach me at home he can reach me through my boss."

"Umm. Well, I guess that'll just have to do him, won't it?" Now he was grinning openly. "And, uh, no bedroom, right?"

"No bedroom. *Right*. Pleasant dreams, officer," she concluded, adding to herself, Don't forget your Teddy Bear!

She left Redman's apartment then and walked back out to the street, pausing only once, briefly, by the emergency stairway, to turn up her collar against a sudden chill breeze.

In the Shadows
2

He lay on the floor on a dense rubber pad the width of his shoulders, once, twice, a hundred times raising, then lowering, slowly, the gleaming dumbbells. The still-fresh wound on his left forearm throbbed relentlessly in counterpoint. One hundred *one*; one hundred *two*. . . .

It had not gone well, this last time; not gone well at all. It seemed all right at first; when he first arrived at Joanna's apartment last night, he slipped in as easily and soundlessly as on the last three occasions with the three other . . . friends. But when he discovered that Joanna was not there, right then he should have turned around and left, should have sensed this would not be an auspicious night.

But no. (One hundred *ten*. . . .) He'd riffled through the files, confirmed that she was, indeed, a photographer. That was *wonderful*. So wonderful that he had decided to hide behind the bedroom door, waiting. Not merely decided but willed it, in fact, he reminded himself. He'd been a little surprised by the weight-training equipment—she'd never mentioned it on-line—but not at all worried since he himself was superbly conditioned. Must have been two-and-a-half, three hours he'd waited. Had he known it would be that long, he might have looked around a little, and learned a lot, and spared himself the near-disaster.

One hundred *twenty*. He lay, panting, arms extended fully to either side, his eyes closed. Remembering the moment of awful revelation.

A little before three in the morning, standing there behind the door, rigid and alert, he had at last heard the creak of the front door's opening and the click of its closing; then a delayed, lighter echo from a closet door in the living room. A tune being whistled, the first few notes of an old tune which he recognized as "I'm a Yankee Doodle Dandy," and then a voice, clearly a *man's* voice, singing, ". . . A real live nephew of my *Un-*cle *Sam* . . . !"

A man? he asked himself. Joanna had brought a man home with her? But she'd said in her message . . . The man's form swept past in the hallway, visible through the crack between door and jamb, still singing, "I've *got* a Yankee Doodle *sweet*heart," and then the man was in the kitchen, and the words he sang next reverberated off the tile and walls and cabinets and appliances, reverberated still, horrible, in memory: "*He's* my Yankee pride and joy!"

"He's"? *Jesus*: "Joanna" was a *man,* a, a *homosexual man.* For a moment or two, there behind the bedroom door, all his training threatened to drain out the soles of his feet, taking his composure with it: *he wasn't prepared for this.* But then he collected himself. This would not merely test his training, but validate it. He focused his mind to a point, poured his will into the blade in his left hand, stilled the beating of his heart, and concentrated his vision on the view of the hallway through the crack behind the door.

The singing had stopped. Silence.

Suddenly, a voice behind him said, "Can I help you?" What the —? He looked, startled, over his shoulder. There, in the bedroom's other doorway, was "Joanna," staring right at him. . . . "Joanna" was wearing tight gray pants and a sleeveless T-shirt, one that showed him everything he wished he did not now need to know: that "Joanna" *used* all those weights along the wall, apparently several times a day, and that "Joanna" had every reason to be wearing as well a half smile of amusement and confidence as he advanced around the bed, his fists lightly clenched, and repeated, "I said, can I help you?"

Focus. Bring the mind to a point; *become* the steel in your left hand. This is not a muscular, two hundred-pound man advancing lithely on you, not even a "Joanna." This is a, a mere *It,* a thing to be wadded up and discarded after helping to fulfill your will. . . .

He flung the door away from him then, useless any longer as concealment. He brought forth the blade, crossed his arms right over left, and bowed to It. It stopped for a moment, Its eyes catching the gleam from the blade. Its smile evaporated, but only for a second; then It, too, crossed Its arms and bowed to him, and when Its head came back up It was smiling again. "Well, well," It said, "what've we got here? Little meat cleaver, have we?" It continued to advance around the foot of the bed, then stopped, hands raised slightly before It. Unafraid. Ready.

Precious little room to maneuver here—no way behind, not with the door closed, and no way to open the door again without becoming vulnerable. No way to go but forward. Forward, then, blade and yourself as one. . . .

"You better hope you're slicker with that thing," It said, still smiling, "than I am with these." It waggled Its hands and looked down at them for a split second—*now* feint with the right hand, strike with the left—but It expected that, had *drawn* the attack, and parried it neatly, receiving only a small nick on the upper-left arm.

"Not bad," It said, backing off just an inch, poised on the balls of Its feet. "Don't think anybody's ever cut me before. What *is* that thing, anyway, some kind of Japanese steak knife? Hey, yeah, that's right, sure, don't I know you from Benihana's?" Ignore It: ignore Its mocking voice, Its eyes, Its smile. Focus on Its weapons, Its hands, and the dangerous emptiness between you and It. Within distance now, and— Its right foot flew suddenly up, catching him for an instant by surprise, but his right arm reflexively came down and then he *slashed* with the left. . . .

It crossed Its arms again, again bowed, smiling. "That's two I owe you, friend," It said, and the smile disappeared. A thin line of blood, trickling through a gap sliced in the trouser leg on Its right calf, neatly balanced the trickle on Its left arm. Yes, balance; yes, harmony; *focus.* . . .

He and It traded no more than a dozen blows apiece. His, of course, were more telling. A neighbor in the downstairs apartment began to bang on the ceiling; "Keep it down up there," the neighbor yelled. "For Christ's sake, don't you ever *sleep*?" They ignored the neighbor. Once, It landed a blow to his collarbone that knocked him backward and into a wooden valet. Tangled in the valet, he'd somehow managed to turn the blade inward and, rising, had gashed the inside of his own left arm. Clumsy and unfocused; not to happen again. He advanced on It, blade extended fully up and to the left, right hand clenched before him as though defensively. . . . Just when It expected the strike from the left, *now,* the blade was suddenly in his *right* hand and slashing up and across, slitting It thigh to shoulder and now *jump,* while It is still surprised and before It can call out or scream, blade back in left hand and *strike* there at the throat, silencing It. . . . It staggered back, fell onto the bed, clutching Its neck, gurgling. No smile now. He leaned over It, knelt astraddle Its waist, slash and slash and *slash* and *slash.* . . .

Hours later, it seemed, though really only minutes, he was still kneeling there and slashing. His sweatpants and his own T-shirt were soaked with blood; blood ran down the walls and saturated the bed. The thing on the bed now truly *was* an It, barely recognizable from the waist up as human, no longer even twitching. He stood by the bedside, crossed his arms, and bowed to It one last time. Then he wiped the blade on the bedcovers and slipped it into the sheath in the fanny pack—

The banging on the floor resumed. "I've had enough of this, you son of a bitch! I called the super on you this time!"

The computer—where? Not in the living room, nor here in the bedroom; perhaps through the other bedroom door. . . . A short hurried walk to the back room, yes, there was the PC there on the left.

Must hurry—turn on the computer, warming up; format the disk—What's this? Oh, Jesus, the format command's been disabled on this computer, no time to erase everything now, just go directly to where the BBS and comm files are likely to be, erase what's here, and clear—oh no, *shit,* footprints, they'll trace the *footprints* . . . off with the shoe then, and then get out, no wait, back to the file cabinet, grab a handful and *go,* damn it, down the stairs and out the fire exit, all holy hell's bells breaking loose but don't worry, stay focused, get the hell away from here as fast as possible. . . .

He ran directly to the garage at his hotel, stripped, threw his sopping garments into the trunk of his rental car, and jumped in. Parked it on the street outside his apartment after a scary but *very* careful ninety-minute drive here. He'd sat in the car then, waiting till the street was empty, then run in his underwear up the stairs to his room. Cleaned himself off. A few bruises, he saw in the bathroom mirror, one eye blackened, he'd have to wear sunglasses for a few days to cover that up; "Not bad," It had said, but It hadn't been bad, Itself, all things considered. . . . Dressed, went out to the car, drove all the way downtown and threw his clothes from the night before into a dumpster. Came home again, grabbed some sleep. Drove back to Philadelphia this afternoon and checked out of the hotel like nothing unusual, dropped the rental car back at the airport and flew to Newark. . . .

So no, he reminded himself: the evening had not gone well, but there was no cause for panic. Relax, stay focused; close your eyes. Breathe deeply in, then out; in, then out. . . . His fingers curled loosely around the dumbbells' shanks, focused, still cruciform, he dozed. He dreamt of an omnipresent, impenetrable blackness in which floated, erratically, a single soundless point of light— soundless, that is, but for a faint and somehow ominous clicking sound.

Chapter Ten

Finley had found a little good news when she got to work on Monday, and a little bad news—and they were both the *same* news: her keyboard had been replaced, and she consequently had to leave Bill Lord's office. She trundled her logbook, her floppies, her manuals, and her file folders full of the new project's information, on a rolling chair from Lord's office, all back across the hall; back to Old Familiar. Maybe she'd come back in the next life as a hermit crab, toting a cubicle around on her back so she'd never have to get used to a new place.

She would not, of course, miss the virtual requirement to make at least rudimentary conversation with Lord at least once each day. And to be sitting at her own desk, before her own computer, with all her own supplies and reference materials handy, was indeed welcome. (She chuckled at Monday's wakeup message:

"Books are made not like children but like pyramids . . . and they're just as useless!—Flaubert."

Those guys who created the wakeups down in the operations room—tweaking the paper searchers again, obviously.) But she would miss working in a *room,* not worrying about whether someone might overhear a conversation, being able to use a speakerphone. . . . She sighed. Life.

Yesterday afternoon, at home, she had routinely checked her personal boards, but with a slight internal buzzing of suspense now that she was certain of the killer's interest in BBS users.

On ABLE, there was an exchange between one of the Earwigs, Bob, and an ABLE newcomer:

To: All
From: Visitor
Re: Ear disease?
Message: A friend of mine has been complaing of ringg sound in his ears he alsogets dizzy sometime and he waks up at night dizzy. He says he cant hear as well also. Is a disease? Tahnk you.

To: Visitor
From: Bob Melendez
Re: Ear disease?
Message: I am NOT a doctor but the things you say are bothering your friend sound a lot like a condition called Meniere's disease. Sometimes the dizziness gets real extreme, you wake up in the middle of your sleep it's so bad. It can cause vomiting too. Lots of famous people had it, I think Martin Luther for one. Your friend should definitely go to see a doctor about this even if it's not Meniere's disease. Good luck!

Finley smiled. She loved the way people offered information on-line without commenting on the form of the requestor's message. Elsewhere on ABLE, there was nothing from Jane, which was unusual—but not, Finley reminded herself, cause for alarm.

Flokati must have the weekend off; he'd already answered her question on FORENSIC about motiveless killing:

. . . One thing I am thinking is always assume motive. If no rational motive, seek nonrational one. Possible religious motive, human sacrifice, you see? Idea to check philosophy or religion BBS, I do not know myself so check BBS yes. One listing in my directory.

"BELIEFS," he said it was called, and he provided the phone number and other essential information. Good idea, Flokati, she thought, and logged in at once to BELIEFS (pretentious name, but maybe that went with the territory). The message she dropped there, addressed to ALL, said:

> . . . I'm seeking information about religions or cults that are known to practice ritual homicide or human sacrifice—contemporary groups, probably with some presence in the US. Do any of you know of any such organizations, or of any references where I could check further? Thanks for your help.

Then she checked over on STACKS. There was one message waiting for her, it said when she logged in, and for a moment her heart leapt up. But it was merely a status message automatically generated by the STACKS computer; it said:

> Your message To: Tracy Re: Knock, knock, knock! was not delivered and has been deleted from STACKS. Reason for nondelivery: Addressee has not read; deleted to free disk space.

Finley's spirit sagged again, then, and relinquished its last hopeful grip on Tracy's memory. Her Tracy was certainly, now, *the* Tracy.

She turned the burner on without rising from her chair at the computer. She needed another cup of tea. . . . One of these days, she meant to ask Flokati about the ritual of the Japanese tea ceremony. She'd only read about it before as an aside in one book or another, never really studied it, its purpose or practice; but her own observation was that sipping a cup of tea did wonders for the mind. As the tiny brown particles moved out, suspended, into the hot water, as she bent over her brown-stained mug and inhaled the slightly acidic vapors rising and bathing her face, she could sense clouds being pushed aside in her mind, not evaporating but merely, for the time being, made irrelevant. . . .

The phone rang.

It was her brother Warren, and as usual he began with an accusation: "God, don't you ever get off the *phone?* I've been trying to reach you for an hour. How come the line's always busy?"

Finley sighed; so much for peace of mind. He'd probably tried only once or twice, getting busy signals during the brief intervals while she was logged in. "Sorry, Warren," she said, "but really, I was only on the phone a couple times. Just logged in to a couple of boards. How's Nancy?"

" 'Boards'? Don't you ever talk to normal people instead of computers?" he said. Finley declined to point out that she was currently talking to *him*. "And Nancy's fine, just fine, she says to say hello and to ask you again, well, we *both* want to know, of course, you going to be joining us for Thanksgiving again this year?"

Cripes. If the word "querulous" hadn't been invented. . . . "Well, you know, it's funny you should ask, Warren—I was thinking, how about if *I* host Thanksgiving this year?"

"You? You mean at your place? Where would we sleep? I mean, there's the three of us, Nancy and I could take the fold-out sofa but what about Terri? I guess we could bring the cot, though, couldn't we? Of course Nancy's not due for another six months but—just let me ask her, hang on, okay?" He put the phone down to talk to his wife—or, more likely, was still clutching it, neurotically, to his belly. Muffled yammering and remote voicelike sounds issued from the receiver by Finley's hearing aid, whether from Warren's larynx or peristalsis, she couldn't tell. The teakettle sounded and she poured the boiling water into her cup, stirring it gently.

Then he was back. "You still there? Nancy said yeah, she thinks it's a great idea, we'll bring the cot like I said, all right? She said she'll give you a call in a week or so, straighten out the details, we'll spring for wine and you'll let us know if there's anything else we can bring, won't you?"

"Yes, Warr—"

"Hang on just a minute, Terri wants to talk to you, okay?"

A few seconds later, there was her four-year-old niece's voice on the phone. "Aunt Finley?" she whispered conspiratorially. *"Are we really coming to your apartment for Thanksgiving?"*

Finley attempted to copy the smile from her face into her voice. "That's right, Terri, in just a couple of weeks! You want to play some computer games while you're here?"

"Yeah! And Aunt Finley, can I talk to . . . *Stupid* again?" Terri giggled; she loved the bird's name. Daddy forbade her to call anybody stupid, but Aunt Finley positively encouraged it.

"Sure you can talk to Stupid, honey. You know what? You can

say, 'Hello, Stupid!' and he'll peep right back at you, and you can say, 'You're Stupid, aren't you?' and he'll peep at that, too."

There was a bonk at the other end of the line, then Warren's voice again. "What the heck did you say to her?" he asked. "She's rolling on the floor, for crying out loud, *laughing,* what's the matter with her?"

"Oh, we were just talking about my parakeet."

"Your parakeet? I swear, I don't know—Terri, get up off the floor. What's so hysterical about a stupid parakeet? Oh no, there she goes *again?*" He didn't wait for a reply. "Anyhow, listen, we'll give you a call, Nancy will give you a call about Thanksgiving details, that be all right?"

"All r—"

"Okay, and how's everything else? All right, I hope? Catch any spies lately?" He snickered; this was about the most inventive his humor ever became.

"No, Warren, no spies. The project, the case I'm working on now is—"

"Don't tell me, let me guess, an ax murderer, am I right? Or a notorious but mysterious underworld figure? Guess you never have to deal with small fry like burglaries and muggings up there in the Feds, leave all that to the locals, right? Eh, how's that, am I right or what?"

Finley sighed. "Yes, something like that, Warren. How about everything with you guys, everyth—"

"Fine, fine, fine, what could *we* have to complain about . . . ?"

It had gone on like that, endlessly it felt, for another half hour yesterday afternoon. By the time Warren had actually said, "Bye, okay?" Finley was exhausted. She couldn't bear the thought of answering another question. . . . Off went the computer, and out the door went Finley, determined to capture something of a real day off after her interrupted Saturday. As excited as she was by having made the BBS connection, she would tackle all the questions inherent in Redman's floppies at work tomorrow, Monday, *today.*

So here she was, settled at last back at her own desk, sipping at her second cup of tea from the cafeteria. Bill Lord she'd already brushed aside once today; he wouldn't be back at her, if her calculations were correct, till a little before noon—hoping for a shared lunch. Gus she expected at some point this morning, assuming he'd survived Parents' Weekend. As for the other man claiming her attention today, John Redman, he was starting to emerge as a real person from the floppy disks which Finley had retrieved from his apartment.

She'd already copied the CROSSOVER program and files to her PC here. Once she figured out how the commands on this BBS, whatever its purpose, apparently worked, she could see from the files that Redman had been skilled enough to modify them for his own use. His own ID and password were built right into these so-called login "scripts," for example, so he didn't have to type them while logging in. His CROSSOVER ID was "Pouch," for some reason.

There was also a file that seemed to be a list of all the IDs on the board; it contained two columns of data. In the first column, on the left, every line had an entry; many of the matching entries in the right-hand column were blank, and the ones that weren't blank contained names. Finley guessed that on this board every-one used aliases, which Redman had recorded in the first column of this file, the second column being for the corresponding "real" names that he'd come to know. One line in the file contained "Pouch" and "J. Redman," and that confirmed the theory.

But she hadn't been able actually to log in to CROSSOVER yet: the line was always busy. Boy, Warren would give them a real piece of his mind if he were here. . . .

Getting Redman's BoardWalk files to work, on the other hand, should be a snap. She had her own copy of the BoardWalk pro-gram itself, of course; all she needed of Redman's were the login scripts. Before actually running any of them, though, Finley ex-amined their contents.

She confirmed almost to certainty that he'd been a photogra-pher. One script was for accessing a BBS called FOTOBOARD, and it seemed that he'd had quite a bit of activity on it: among the backups were several huge files containing copies of old FOTOBOARD messages, both to and from Redman.

Huh. It looked like he'd been married, too, which surprised Finley because she'd neither seen nor heard any reports which mentioned a wife. But there it was in all the FOTOBOARD messages from his computer: *"John/Joanna Redman."* Of course, it wasn't unusual for married couples to share IDs, but it *was* unusual that she hadn't already heard about this "Joanna" yet. A sister, maybe? She made a note to check further on that, and went on to examine Redman's other scripts.

There were a couple of scripts for accessing boards for information about computer hardware and software. No surprise there; most BBS users accessed such boards—Finley herself did, although she subscribed to different ones than Redman had. No message files from these technical BBSs, though; either he'd never used the BBSs or just never saved any messages. She'd check with their sysops anyway.

Redman's wife or sister, "Joanna," also participated actively in a gourmet cooking BBS called "Eat&Drink." The message files here—ye gods, they seemed almost as big as FOTOBOARD's. . . . What a flirt this Joanna was! It seemed like she managed to come on to every guy on the board at least once apiece; there was almost as much *in* the lines as *between* them; and she gave her address to one, two, half a dozen of them at least—all Redman's own address, Finley saw, which made it unlikely that she was his sister. But if she really was his wife, his marriage must have been in big trouble. Finley checked the dates on the messages; maybe all this had been years ago—but no, Joanna had been sending and saving messages right into last week. So Finley wrote again in her notepad: "JOANNA?"

Nearly noon, she saw during a break. Where was Gus?

A knock came on the metal frame of her cubicle wall, and she looked up. Peeking around the edges of the cubicle doorway, only their grinning heads visible, were Monica and Ray.

"Helloooo, mysterious stranger!" Ray said.

"Ve haff come to kidnop you for ze lunch, no?" Monica added, and they moved fully into the entryway so Finley could see they already had their coats on. Finley laughed out loud. She'd told them once that they reminded her of Chip and Dale, the mischievous Disney chipmunks, and sometimes they seemed actively to work at it.

"You vill tell us all your secrets, ve vill make you talk, Yankee board-freak svine!" said Monica, tugging Finley to her feet.

"All right, all right!" Finley said, feigning annoyance. She put on her own coat, wrote a note for Gus and taped it to the cubicle wall, by the entryway. "I'll be back around one o'clock," it said. "Hold the fort!" She added a P.S.: "Was Redman MARRIED?" but then crossed it out; Morris would flip if he saw that.

"C'mon, c'mon, quit stalling!" Ray said, and he and Monica each grabbed an arm, pulling her from the cube. Giggling noisily, the three of them threaded their way out of the building and out into the fall sunshine.

Closer to two o'clock than one o'clock, the three of them, giggling even more hysterically and staggering just a little, trooped their way back up the same corridors in the other direction.

Finley had a monster case of hiccups, with which she had some- how infected Monica. Walking on either side of Ray, they were like two little pistons, firing alternately and in sequence— "Whoop!" "Hic!"—and propelling the trio up the hall. But Finley's hiccups went away the moment she saw the note on her chair: "Finley—Gus is with me in my office. Come on in. Morris."

She whipped off her coat, dragged her fingers through her hair, and scooped up her notes from the desktop. When she entered Morris's office, he and Gus were speaking quietly and earnestly. "Finley!" Morris said, brightening a little (whew, he must not be too mad), "Come in, take a seat."

"Hi, Morris. Gus," she said. "Looks like you made it through Parents' Weekend all right."

He grinned. "Yeah, well a little touch and go when I first got to the airport, you can imagine. But I got out alive." He plucked at the crease of his brown trousers. "Even had time to get the travel- ing suit dry-cleaned."

"Gus can fill you in on some stuff he learned this morning in Philadelphia," Morris said to her. "But first, why don't you bring us up to speed on whatever you've come up with since all the excitement on Saturday? You confirmed a BBS connection after all, that right?"

She nodded. So that was where Gus was this morning; he'd stopped in Philly on the way back. . . . She outlined for them what she'd learned about Redman from his BBS access files, con- cluding with the mystery about his apparently promiscuous wife/ sister Joanna.

A quizzical but unexplained look passed back and forth at this news, from Morris to Gus and back again. "Holy moly," Morris said, "this guy's life gets screwier every minute."

Gus turned a little in his seat, more directly facing Finley. "Here's what I got from the Philly police this morning, Finley. A few pieces of news, not sure which is more important so you pick if you want. First, Redman was gay, we think."

"*Gay?*" Morris was right: screwier and screwier. "How'd they find that out?"

"Autopsy. He had, well—he had semen in his stomach. Traces between his teeth, too." Finley's face reassembled its features into a twisted look of disgust. "Yeah, sorry, gross I know but that's what autopsies are for. Doesn't prove he was gay, of course, but it's a pretty good sign."

"So what are they, what are the police going to do with this . . . information?"

"For now, they're going on the assumption that the killer is gay, too. I felt a little weird about it, you wanna know the truth, that detective sergeant was practically smackin' his lips at the chance to shake down the homosexual community down there."

"God," she said. "So he was gay, and his wife or sister hits on every other guy she knows, at least when she's on-line. . . . And you say there's even more?"

"Yeah, one little detail from the autopsy—most of the cuts that Redman took seemed to come from in front of him, again made by a left-hander. But there was one biggie, kind of hard to tell for sure the way he was chopped up, but it looked like one big cut went diagonally all the way from his left thigh to just above the right side of his collarbone—"

"Which means?"

"It means he's either ambidextrous, at least with a knife, or there was another killer with him. A right-handed one."

"Great. Another complication. Was there anything else?"

"Yeah, 'fraid so." He hesitated, looked at Morris, then picked up a folder off the edge of Morris's desk. "Did you notice in Redman's back room, where the computer was, the file cabinet with the open drawer?"

"Sure. Looked like he might've gone through them, dried blood on the front, by the drawer pull."

"Yeah, that's right, good observation. He did go through at least one of the drawers, too, we think. Glove prints. The stuff in that drawer was almost all photographs of models—"

"'Almost all'? What else was there?"

"A few business records, not much, most of that is probably at his studio. Here in the filing cabinet in his apartment there was just some personal banking information, canceled checks, so on. But the police did find this folder there, too."

He handed it to her. The label on the tab said, "PERSONAL PHOTOS." Finley browsed through it. "Looks like more photographs, snapshots," she said, and Gus and Morris both nodded. "Mostly guys, of course, I mean if he was gay that makes sense. . . ." She closed the folder. "Was there something there I was supposed to notice?"

Gus took another snapshot from another folder on Morris's desk. "This *was* in that folder," he said, and handed it to her.

Finley examined the color picture, a 3×5, taken from maybe ten or twelve feet away. The scene was a bar; a bunch of guys leaning forward with mugs or bottles of beer, smoke drifting and highlighted in the camera's electronic flash. The balding bartender was laughing, heartily, his head thrown back and mouth open. But the subject of the picture, clearly, was the woman in the center, looking right at the camera. Cute, too, real cute: short-cropped brown hair, big toothy smile, the sort of moon-face without an ounce of fat on it. She was sitting on a bar stool, short-skirted legs crossed, in an ostentatiously fake cheesecake pose, with one hand on a hip and the other behind her head.

Finley turned the picture over. On the back, in the top left corner, was a solid black rectangle, its edges ragged, apparently made with a broad felt-tip marker. In the center, printed in neat block letters with a finer felt-tip, was the name, "Mary Ellen."

Finley looked up; Morris and Gus both seemed to be waiting for a reaction of some kind. What was she supposed to say? "She's, uh, she's cute," she ventured, finally. Then a thought occurred to her. "Say—this *is* a 'she,' isn't it, not a guy dressed up like a woman?"

Gus smiled tightly. "Nope. It's a woman, all right. Did you see what was on the back?"

"Sure, 'Mary Ellen.' Is that, uh, is that supposed to mean something to me?" She looked nervously from Morris to Gus, then down at the picture.

"Not the name, Finley," Morris said. "The black blotch in the corner. Hold it up and look at it kind of sideways to the light. Edge-on."

She did so. She could see it now, now that she was looking for it, something else was written there under the black, something in ballpoint it looked like, little shiny grooves marking the surface. It said, hmm, can't quite make that out, is that a "T" . . . ?

What it said leapt suddenly out at Finley, the walls of Morris's office seeming to collapse in on her in fear and confusion, just as Gus confirmed, "It's a name, Finley, the name of the woman in the picture. Her name is, or was, Tracy Williams."

When she came to a minute or so later, she saw blue to both sides, faded blue, and white in front of, or was it above her . . . ? She was still sitting in the chair, she realized, Morris holding her head down between the knees of her jeans, her sneakers down there, or up there, by her head. "I'm okay, I'm all right," she slurred, pushing Morris's hand away and sitting up. Gus, his face anxious, was standing by her with a paper cup of water from Morris's cooler. "Must've been the beer I had at lunch," she said, and drank some of the water.

Now Morris was kneeling by her chair. "You sure you're all right? Jesus, I'm sorry, Finley, we should've worked up to it, not just dumped it on you. I, I thought maybe you knew what she looked like."

She shook her head. *Trrraaaacy,* a voice, Finley's own, wailed in her mind. "Can I see the picture again?" She handed the paper cup to Gus, and got the picture in return.

This was *Tracy.* It was almost exactly how she'd imagined her friend, now that she thought about it—not the face or the hair but the context: the Budweiser and Miller Lite neon logos in the background, football game on the bar TV, guys, lots of guys, and something perky and upbeat on the jukebox. . . . Something, in fact, like "I've Just Seen a Face," she suddenly thought, and then remembered Stupid's cocking his head and replying "Chirp?" and something about that memory just made the tears well up and overflow and she was sobbing and apologetic and embarrassed all at once, crying out of a deep well of grief for Tracy first but also for everybody else she'd sort of known, on-line or off-, but never *really* known. . . .

"It's okay, Finley," said Gus, crouching down by her chair. She sobbed for another minute or two into his shoulder while he patted her, awkwardly, on the shoulder and the back of the head.

Behind her, Morris's voice was saying, "Okay, back to your offices, all of you—nothing to see here, she's all right." Wiping with a hand at her teary face, Finley saw out of the corner of her eyes, past Morris's bulk in the doorway, a small crowd in the corridor. "Okay, okay, I said back to work, everybody!" Morris repeated one last time, and closed the door.

When they'd all three resumed their seats and awkwardly apologized to one another, Finley, still sniveling a little, said to Gus, "But what does it mean, Gus? Why was Tracy's picture in that folder of Redman's with somebody else's name printed on it?"

He hesitated, then shook his head slowly in bafflement. "What does it *mean*? Well, we don't know yet, tell you the truth. But I can also tell you the police have been real busy today, not just in Philadelphia and Atlanta but New York, too. Thank God for the photofax machine!"

"Did they, did they catch the guy?"

"Nope. Afraid not. But they've got another connection, Finley. We might be close to a Click."

"W-what's the connection?"

"Pictures, Finley. Except for the first victim, Bristol, it turns out that each of them had a picture of one of the others, of the *previous* victim. Dorothy Taylor had a picture of Bristol; your friend Tracy had a picture of Taylor; and Redman of course had a picture of Tracy. Like you just saw, the names on the back were all doctored. Bogus."

Finley blew into a tissue, then folded it and wiped it across her nose. "So, so, so what now? Do we just warn people to watch out for pictures that look like Redman, with the name blotted out?"

He looked grim. "I wish it was that easy, and that's hard enough. We can't send Redman's face to every BBS user in the country, I mean. No, it's even worse than that—"

"Worse?"

"Yep. Remember the file cabinet? The open drawer, the files shoved out of the way? All the files left in the drawer were in alphabetical order, and they all had pictures in 'em. But the police mapped one of your printouts to what was there, and there were a bunch missing from the middle. We think he grabbed a handful of files before he split, folders like the ones he'd shoved out of the way to either side. Maybe, who knows, a dozen missing folders. All of 'em filled with pictures of Redman's models."

Chapter Eleven

"The poor girl," said the voice of Gus's wife, Mary, over the phone that night. "I hope you look out for her."

"Yeah, yeah," he replied. "Kinda hard to do when I don't even understand half of whatever the hell she's talking about. But I try. I talked to her boss after she left his office, asked if maybe we should think about moving her off the project, maybe she's a little too close to it. But he said Nah, she'll be okay in a day or so. What do I know?"

"For one thing, do you know if you'll have this wrapped up by Thanksgiving?"

"Hey, come on, Mary, gimme a break. I hope to have it wrapped up, sure, a lot can happen in a week and a half. But I doubt I'll be able to get home at all *this* week. Maybe this weekend coming up." He sighed, he hoped audibly. "I miss you, too, hon."

But Mary wasn't letting him off that easily. "Yes, I miss you, Gus, but you know that's not what I'm getting at. We're supposed to be at Mother's house in time for dinner the night before, remember."

They bickered good-naturedly back and forth for a little longer before saying good night. As Gus replaced the receiver in its cradle, he leaned against the pillows stacked behind his back on the hotel bed, and turned his attention to the six o'clock news. But a piece of his mind was thinking, Finley. Yeah, *I* worry about her, too. Damn, she takes this on-line stuff seriously. Hope she holds together. Hope she doesn't do anything screwy. Hope she's all right because God knows I sure couldn't pick up the pieces of this project on my own. . . .

As for Finley herself then, she was sitting at the kitchen table, munching distractedly at her dinner, which was, tonight, two re-heated slices of pizza and a can of diet Coke. From the other room boomed the sound, *loud,* of her stereo; the Temptations now, sing-ing about being on Cloud Nine and having no responsibility. (Ei-ther her neighbors were as hard of hearing as she herself was, or extremely tolerant—they'd never complained even once about her music.)

The evening paper which she'd picked up at Falco's and was now spread before her carried, of course, the story of Redman's murder—its provocative elements, anyhow: the blood, the homo-sexual connection, the blood, the knife or razor, the blood. . . . Not a word about the computer or BBS link, or about the missing Joanna yet—no surprise on that last item, Finley herself having just discovered it this morning. And, naturally, not even a whisper of CIAC's involvement in the case.

Newspapers tended to focus on local crime, missing all but the most flagrant connections to crimes in other cities. CIAC itself was still an institution too new, its functions too little understood, to be recognized as a connection, let alone a flagrant one, and no reporter on his or her own was likely to see in CIAC's presence a connection among four murders in three cities.

Finley sighed, folded the newspaper, and dropped it into the recycling basket. Over at the sink, rinsing the little bit of silver-ware and few dishes she'd left there in the last twenty-four hours, she mulled over the balance of her frustrating afternoon.

After the shock of Tracy's picture, there had been nothing much else to discuss with Morris and Gus. Gus hadn't gotten the phone records of the first three victims yet; he expected them by tomorrow, and promised to submit the request for Redman's records as soon as their three-way parley broke up. Morris of-fered Finley the rest of the afternoon off, but she thanked him and said no, she didn't really want to go home to sit by herself right now. To sit there in the apartment, accomplishing nothing.

So back to her desk she'd gone—and accomplished, thanks once again to the perverse whimsy of modern technology, a maddening nothing. No power blackout this time; this afternoon, the problem was the phone lines out of the building. You could call other offices there within the Center itself, but you couldn't get a line out of the building—so no BBS connections were possible.

She wanted to *do* something, damn it, wanted to close this guy out of her life and out of Tracy's death, too. She wanted to login to and learn all about CROSSOVER, to try out FOTOBOARD and leave a message for the sysop there, to— But it didn't make any difference what she wanted to do; she couldn't do any of it without a phone line.

She boxed up all the floppies she'd received from New York and Atlanta and placed them carefully and with precision, as though stocking a shrine, in a cabinet in her cubicle. No phone lines yet. She'd straightened up stacks of paper, not really bothering to organize them but simply aligning their edges. Still no outside lines. She cleaned the screen of her PC; no lines yet. She turned the PC off, opened up its chassis, dusted all its components by running a miniature vacuum cleaner over their surfaces, reassembled the PC, turned it back on, rereviewed the day's event list. The lines were still dead, and Tracy was still dead. Finley was sitting, hands folded on the desktop, staring in fury at the unresponsive screen, when Monica came in.

Even after three years, Finley wasn't sure exactly how she felt about Monica. Monica was undoubtedly her best friend at work, and could be—as at lunch today—one of the funniest people Finley had ever met. She had a rubber face and surrealistically expressive eyes which she used to full effect, when in a light mood, slithering mercurially from personality to personality. But it was also true that Monica could be one of the least charming people Finley could even imagine; when she got "serious," you were usually in for a scolding about "not being practical." But this afternoon, cut off herself from doing anything productive and worried about the scene, glimpsed from the corridor, in Morris's office, Monica said, softly, "Hey. Wanna go for a walk? Just down the cafeteria?"

No point sitting here on your hands, Finley grumbled to herself, and nodded. "Sure, Monica—but isn't the cafeteria closed for the day?"

"Uh-huh. Vending machines are still open, though." She smiled. "And so are the tables."

A few minutes later, they were seated over by the glass wall, scalding their mouths on paper cups full of tea and coffee. (How the hell, and why, did the vending-machine company contrive to *brew* this stuff so hot?) Monica began carefully, "Finley, I know you can't talk about whatever you're working on. But don't bottle it up inside you, either, it's not good for you"—threatening, a little, to fall over into the not-practical lecture.

But then her tone softened, and she offered to Finley to talk whenever Finley wanted, about *whatever* Finley wanted, and she offered to take Finley shopping with her, or to take Finley bowling the next time she and her husband Bob went. . . . (Bowling? Finley thought. Does anybody still bowl?) And she'd concluded, her voice warm and heartfelt, "Please count on me, kiddo. On both of us, both Bob and me."

But for the time being, Finley thought, coming back to the here and now as she dried the last piece of silverware and wiped off the tablecloth, for the time being she didn't want to count on *anyone*. Not after Mom and Dad, not after Warren, not after Spencer, and certainly not after Tracy. She didn't want to get close and then ripped apart, or for that matter have them fade away, either. She just wanted to keep, at arm's length, just whomever and whatever she already had. Flokati, a handful of on-line friends on STACKS, and of course the Earwigs. And Jane.

Jane. She knew it was silly, but still—it had been, what, something like four or five days since she'd last heard from Jane. . . .

On ABLE, there were no messages waiting, addressed specifically to her. Nothing from Jane. One stranger had left a general message, addressed to "ALL," asking about the best place in New York to buy hearing-aid batteries. That was something Finley knew about, all right, but not tonight: no strangers tonight. Just the Earwigs, briefly. And then Jane. To the Earwigs first, and keep it light:

> To: All Earwigs
> From: Finley
> Re: Earwig Roll Call
> Message: All right, Earwigs, which of you guys are going

to be around for Thanksgiving? Earwig Roll Call, count off
now . . . ! "Finley!" Who's next?

Her message to Jane, a bit more urgent, said:

. . . Jane, if you're out there somewhere please let me
know. I can't talk about this in detail, not right now, but
one of my on-line friends on another board recently died a
very sudden and very sad death and I guess I'm just getting
a little paranoid. Please just, ha ha, raise your hand or
something.
Finley

Flokati would be difficult to approach on that personal level,
even though she'd known him a lot longer. But she could still
touch base with him:

. . . Hi again, Flokati! I've been so caught up in my own
troubles lately that I haven't asked, how are YOU doing? Are
you keeping busy? You haven't asked me for technical help
with anything for a long time—you must be feeling pretty
confident with your computer now, huh? (ha, ha)
Finley

A pretty weak bit of teasing, and for that matter the whole message was pretty weak. But it would elicit a response, and that was
all she cared about.

She'd covered Stupid's cage, brushed her teeth, and was just
getting ready to turn in, when she thought: BELIEFS. She'd never
checked back on the philosophy/religion BBS where she left the
message last night. . . .

So it was back to the PC.

Ye gods, there were fifteen messages waiting for her! Long
suckers, too; these Ph.D. types wrote in complete sentences, oro-
tund paragraphs. . . . But they all, or nearly all, told her the
same things: voodoo, they said. Look at voodoo. Research Jones-
town and the People's Temple. Satanism. One woman gave her
the complete history, or so it seemed, of human sacrifice down

through the ages (including six paragraphs, God help her, on the Incas).

Nuts. None of this was anything she hadn't thought of, or couldn't have thought of, on her own. Not *news,* and she doubted she could use any of it.

But all the way down at the end was one fairly concise message, concise for this milieu anyhow; its author assumed, as had several of the others, that Finley was a "Dr.":

> . . . I've read most of the responses the others have given you, Dr. Finley, and concur with most of their recommendations. But after thinking on it, I'd like to suggest that you might take an alternative tack.
>
> To wit: consider the possibility that a belief system might not espouse homicide per se, but rather that the system might come to be associated with homicide as a logical consequence (or, perhaps, merely a reductio ad absurdum) of its teachings.
>
> Specifically, I'm thinking that you might want to look into the (admittedly eccentric) teachings of an Edward Pince. His ideas, I believe, are/were based on those of an early Christian monk named Morgan, the Latinized form of whose name was "Pelagius." (The Catholic Church later condemned Pelagianism as a heresy, I believe.) Put most simply, Pince's ideas boil down to the notion that the exercise of "free will" does not necessarily presuppose a "motivation," that in fact having a "motive" or "reason" for doing something makes the will no longer free, but, rather, subject to external requirements and conditions.
>
> I suppose if you took that to one possible conclusion, you might view with approval, for example, the notion of killing someone not for any particular reason but simply because you "willed" it. This would in effect make the question of homicide an intellectual proposition rather than a strictly moral one. It would posit, I guess, a sort of explicitly motiveless motive for homicide, as opposed to the passively motiveless crimes which I believe are the norm for psychopaths and serial killers. I'm not sure if that's of interest or not.
>
> Pince was very prolific, if somewhat muddled, and made

something of a minor splash in the late 1960s (what with all that "if it feels good, do it" pseudo-thinking that was in the air then), but I don't know whether he's still alive or active. You might check back issues of the Journal of Motivational Philosophy, for the period around, say, 1964–68. Good luck!

"Explicitly motiveless motive." The phrase veritably jumped off the screen at her. She couldn't wait to get to work tomorrow; at least now she really had something to pursue.

Chapter Twelve

Finley's first log-in at work the next day was to a commercial database of information about articles in academic and professional journals. Called, reasonably enough, the On-line Academic Index, this was the amiable old friend who had helped her out with the Old-English-vowels problem back in college. She still returned to it from time to time, more out of curiosity and a touch of nostalgia than real need, and by now she knew its tastes and crotchets pretty well.

It presented her with several search options: she could search by the author's name, or the subject or title of the article, the name of the publication in which it appeared, the date of publication, or several of these options, or all. The more conditions she put on the search, the fewer articles would be retrieved as the software sifted all the information through a successively finer mesh. Out of it would pop information about whatever articles matched her search conditions; she could then request printouts of any or all of them, to be delivered via conventional mail or fax. Gimme it all, she thought, and typed simply, "Author: Pince." But she was surprised by the message she received after a minute's wait:

Maximum retrievals exceeded. Please narrow your search.

"Maximum retrievals"? What was the maximum?

She checked her user's manual for this database. Ye gods, the maximum was five hundred—Pince had over five hundred articles in here?

Back to the search screen then, to fine-tune the search. She'd search by author still, but limit it to the years 1964 through 1968, as her contact on BELIEFS had suggested last night, and also limit it to just that one journal, what was it, the "Journal of Motivational Philosophy". . . . Yep, that did it. The message "Fifty-two references" flashed briefly on the screen; then it cleared, and the citations themselves took its place, a screenful at a time:

> Pince, E.D. Problem of "free will," The: JoMP xxvi Mar64
>   p12–16
> Pince, E.D. Inherent pleonasm of term "motivation" as used
>   in philosophy, The: JoMP xxvi Apr64 p6 (letter)
> Pince, E.D. New Pelagius, The: JoMP xxvi Jun64 p10–
>   15. . . .

and so on. Jesus, he had something in all but a handful of issues over that whole five-year period! Mainly articles; looked as though there were also a few letters which, judging from their mostly argumentative titles, were responses to other letters criticizing *him*. . . . Finley selected a few of the more general-sounding articles and requested that copies be faxed to her here at the Center. From past experience with this database she knew she could expect the faxes within the next couple of hours.

Another angle occurred to her. Suppose Pince was still alive: how could she locate him? She called over the wall of her cubicle, "Hey, Monica? Got a minute?"

"Let's say," Finley said after Monica had sat down in her cube across from her, "let's say there's a person, a philosopher or some kind of academic maybe, who published a whole *load* of articles in at least one academic journal twenty or thirty years ago—too many to retrieve all at once. So you know he made a name for himself in at least one field. Out of sheer volume if nothing else. How would you go about finding out if the rest of the world knew about him, and if he was still alive?"

Monica thought a few moments, then she pulled her chair around to Finley's side of the desk. Finley slid her keyboard and mouse over so Monica could reach it. "Oh, no you don't!" said Monica, grinning and pushing them right back at Finley. *"I'm* not even going to *touch* your keyboard on this super-hush-hush project! I'll tell *you* what to type! Let's see . . . okay, first, you know the guy's name, right?"

"Yeah. Pince, Edward Pince." (Forgive me, Morris, I'm not really talking about it. . . .)

"Okay, now go to your on-line directory, that's right—highlight the one called LIFENOTES. Try that one first."

LIFENOTES, she explained, contained capsule biographies of tens of thousands of public figures, both historical and contemporary; writers, scientists, politicians, entertainers, saints, academics, artists, labor leaders—they were all in LIFENOTES. For those subjects still living, it even included their last reported addresses.

But when Finley logged in and instituted the search, this board drew a blank on Pince. "Oh nuts," she said.

"Okay, don't panic. Try CLIPSDB next." That was another commercial database, a huge, cross-referenced index to articles printed within the last twenty-five years in nearly all general-circulation magazines and most big-city newspapers in the country. But there was nothing on the elusive Pince there, either.

"Looks like your guy hasn't exactly set the world on fire," Monica said. "You say you don't know if he's still alive?"

"No, I don't know. Is there any way to find out?"

"Yeah, hang on just a sec, let me get a script from my cube." When she returned to Finley's cubicle, she had a floppy disk with her. "Try this," she said. "It's just a BoardWalk script."

The script logged into a database Finley had never heard of; no surprise there—at the rate that new BBSs and databases were established, Finley felt lucky to know of as many as she already did. But although she'd never heard of this particular database, its name was certainly suggestive: OBITDB. "Is that what I think it is?" she asked.

"Yup. Everybody whose obituary has ever been published—"

"But, God, there must be a hundred million entries in it!"

Monica grinned. "Some day, maybe. But the database has only been active for a few months so far. First, it's United States only. They limited the years, too, started with 1950 and went forward from there. And, of course, they're not quite sure they've got all the newspapers yet—they keep finding little weeklies out in the middle of nowhere that stopped publishing in 1960 or whatever. But there's still a heck of a lot there."

And so there was. Finley found her own parents' obituaries there, and hurried on, and then found Monica's parents' . . . but not Pince's.

So that stumped both of them. They just looked at each other, Monica gnawing on the eraser of a wooden pencil, Finley with her chin in one hand and drumming on the desktop with the fingers of the other. The next step occurred to them simultaneously, and they broke into broad grins. Monica stood up and tiptoed to the back wall of Finley's cubicle, calling, in a sultry voice, "Oh *Raaaaaaa-aaaay* . . . !"

Ray didn't have much more experience at CIAC than Monica did. But he was both ingenious and pit-bull persistent, a combination of qualities which commonly brought other on-line searchers to him whenever they (like Finley and Monica now) ran up against some stubborn nonanswer. Some of his resources were merely obscure; Finley remembered one project he'd worked on, for which critical information had come from a BBS for collectors of rubber-and-wire cartoon character figurines (like Gumby and Pokey). And some of his resources were just the products of his mind, playing with a problem till it came up with a solution through sheer brute force. Presumably, a variety of these resources were on the floppies in his hand now.

The first was a script to access CIAC's own PHONENO database: all the phone numbers in the country, unlisted as well as listed. "Everybody's got a phone, right?" he said.

"Huh," Finley said, defensively, "big deal; *I* thought of that! But you have to say what area code to look for the person in, and we really don't know in this case— Hey, you aren't going to tell me to type in *every* area code in the country, one at a time, are you?"

His eyebrows bowed upward, his professionalism wounded. "Don't have to. The box on your desk will do it for you." And he pointed at the computer. He had, it turned out, written a login script which asked you at the start what name you wanted, then dialed PHONENO and issued the commands necessary to check for that name, area code by area code. The script was a program, really, which had to be smart enough to know not only everything that *you'd* type if it were you, but also everything PHONENO might say in response, so it could react accordingly. "Might take awhile, though," Ray conceded. "No point sitting here watching it. Coffee? Tea? Or me?"

Ah, Ray! Once Finley understood what his PHONENO script did, of course it was obvious, but who'd even think to bother? A script like that was so damned *tedious* to write! But Ray had a whole stockpile of such scripts; he'd add a line or two here and there over a period of weeks, till he had a complete script. Then he'd file it carefully away, held against the day when it might be needed. This PHONENO script, for example, he'd completed the other day, during and just after the blackout.

But as they found when they got back from the cafeteria, all that the script produced for the "EDWARD PINCE" search were several sheets of paper printed over and over with area codes and the words, "No match found."

"You said you've got another script?" Monica asked.

"Well," he said, "no promises about this one—never tried it myself. It's not a real fancy script, just gets into a database I had a theory about once."

Finley looked at the label on the floppy. " 'PRINDEX'?"

"No no no, not 'prin-dex.' It's 'pee-ahr-index.' "

"P-R, like Public Relations?"

"Uh-huh—only here, it's 'Press Release.' " A few years back, he explained, he'd been reading in some trend-spotting newsmagazine about something the magazine called the "Publicity Explosion." It coincided with the time when the use of personal computers, laser printers, and powerful word-processing software first started to become widespread. Everybody with a hot new idea or an odd specialty or a one-of-a-kind product to sell was suddenly printing up his or her own personal newsletter, stationery, business cards, and especially press releases, and mailing the latter to local newspapers. The papers welcomed the releases at first—it was an easy way to fill up all the little spaces between the advertising, while seeming to perform a more or less timely community service. But eventually it got out of hand. The papers were buried under an avalanche of press releases, and couldn't print even half of them.

"So this guy out in Chicago," Ray went on, "had this bright idea of setting up a database of info about press releases. Took a load off the newspapers—all the small fry's releases, as well as the big companies', are in PR Index now. Stuff, you know, like, 'Joseph Blow of 123 Main Street announced today that he would be available for consultation—' "

Goggle-eyed, Monica said, "It must be *huge!*"

"Nah. Big, yeah, but not *huge.* He only indexes the titles, keywords in the release, date, and where to contact for more information, like if you want the whole release itself. My theory was, well, you never know—I figured that people might show up in there even if the standard biographical references like LIFE-NOTES wouldn't toot their horns for them. Maybe this guy Pince, for example."

Finley logged in as Monica and Ray looked over her shoulder. It said:

Date, Title, Keyword(s), or Contact?

"Contact," Finley typed, and when the system asked for the contact name she typed, "Pince." The system paused a few seconds, then said:

No match found.

"Damn," said Finley. "I thought you were on to something here, Ray."

He was thinking, tapping an index finger against pursed lips. "Y'know," he said, "don't use Pince's name as the contact. Try using it as a keyword."

Finley did so, and sure enough:

Date: 8/19/86
Keywords: Motivation, Pelagius, Philosophy, Pince, Self-help
Title: E. Pince Establishes Pelagius Institute in New York City
Contact: Pelagius Institute

Both the institute's address and its phone number were given, as well.

"Ray, you are a *genius!*" Finley exclaimed, and leapt from her chair to hug him. He blushed fiercely. "I owe you a lunch for this one!" she added.

" 'Lunch'?" said a loud, penetratingly nasal voice from the doorway. "Did I hear somebody say lunch?"

In the afternoon, after lunch—after Monica and Ray had returned to their own cubicles, and Finley had successfully disengaged herself from Bill Lord's clammy presence—she found Gus in her cube, reading a newspaper. He'd brought the phone bills for the last three months, but only for the two New York victims.

"We couldn't get Tracy's?" she asked.

"Nope—I've got to go down to Atlanta myself, I don't know what the problem is. Some kind of procedural BS, probably. Flying out later this afternoon, and I should be back tomorrow night. But here's the New York bills anyhow. How 'bout you—anything turn up yet on Redman's bulletin boards?"

Finley blushed a little. The whole thing with Pince was probably no better than a diverting sideshow, but she had let herself be diverted by it nonetheless. "I, uh, I haven't gotten on either FOTOBOARD or CROSSOVER yet, Gus, I'm sorry. I spent this morning chasing down another angle I've been thinking of."

"Yeah? What's that?"

She explained to him her nagging curiosity about the apparent lack of motive. As they both knew, and as her correspondent last night had pointed out, many serial killers seemed to follow a "motiveless" pattern, at least at first. Such killers sought out strangers, killing not because of some quirk in the victim or in the victim's relationship with the killer, but because of something about the act of killing itself. But something about the motive would generally have Clicked by this point; a pattern would have emerged, probably unknown to the killer. "So I've been thinking —I wondered if in this case, the guy's not having a motive might be the whole point."

"The whole point? Afraid I don't follow you there, Finley."

"Remember the other day, when we were talking about the

guy's clearing the computers? And I said maybe he belongs to some cult that is just antitechnology or something? Well, I started to think about that. And I thought, we're assuming that the computer thing points to a motive—just because it's the only common thread. But doesn't it make better sense that he's just clearing the PCs to cover his tracks? That the PCs don't signify a common motive, but a common M.O.?"

Gus nodded. "Yeah, okay, but then that kills the only common thread that might point to a motive. So what's the motive then?"

"Well, it *could* be just a series of motiveless homicides. I mean, it probably *is* that, I know; we've seen or heard of enough of them between the two of us. But there's another possibility: the motive might be that he in fact doesn't *have* any motive. It's kind of hard to explain—"

"I noticed," he interrupted, grinning.

Smiling to acknowledge his kidding, she went on, "The other day, the day after Redman got killed, I started thinking again about someone who might kill people because of some crazy religious belief. So there wouldn't necessarily be any connection among the victims, but there'd still be a motive." She explained about her question on the BELIEFS board (carefully not mentioning, of course, that she'd corresponded with Flokati first), and summarized the set of replies she'd gotten. "They were all pretty obvious, I thought, except for one. It mentioned a man named Pince, Edward Pince, who apparently has this theory that you should do what you want to do even if you can't think of a reason for doing it. Something like that, anyhow."

Gus looked skeptical, cocking an eyebrow and pursing his lips a little in disbelief.

"Yeah, it sounds crazy to me, too. But it might explain things, you know? Anyhow, I also found out he's got this thing, this institute for promoting his ideas, apparently, in New York. And this afternoon I should be getting a stack of articles he wrote, to help me understand it all."

Gus smiled, approvingly, and muttered something. Finley shook her head and leaned forward across her desk. "Sorry, Finley," he said again, "I just said that I like the way you think. Like an agent." She smiled softly and looked away in embarrassment at having asked him, in effect, to repeat the compliment. "Keep after that angle," he went on. "But just don't forget the other stuff. Having Redman's files available could be a real breakthrough, you know—especially if, like you say, the killer is messing with people's computers to cover his tracks. Our guy might be in there somewhere," he concluded, pointing to the boxes of Redman's floppies.

"Or in there," she said, pointing to the stack of phone bills. "Or both."

After he left for the airport, Finley reluctantly put from her mind the whole complex of Pince-related issues. Gus had been too polite to say so directly, but he'd implied—correctly—that for the time being Pince was just a fascinating outside possibility. A ghost. And until the faxes came in, she reminded herself, she couldn't look into it any further anyway.

So it was on to CROSSOVER. Still busy the first few tries. The larger BBSs had lots of telephones and modems, so even if one were busy you'd automatically get switched to the first nonbusy one. But the smaller ones—and CROSSOVER, obviously, was one of these—only had one or two lines available, so busy signals were common.

She got through, finally, on her fifth attempt. But she didn't log in under Redman's ID, that weird "Pouch." Most boards had some sort of "registration" process for new users; this process told you something about the board itself, its purpose, and whom to contact if you had questions and so on, and then it asked for information about you, in exchange. So when she logged in as "Finley," she wasn't surprised when the system responded:

The name Finley is unknown to the CROSSOVER system. Are you a new user? (y/n)

Finley typed, "y," and got what at first seemed like a standard announcement for new users:

*****Welcome to CROSSOVER, Finley!*****

But then it went on:

```
**************NOTICE**************
```
Contents of the CROSSOVER bulletin board may be offensive
to some users. Parents should take extra precautions to ensure that their children are denied access to the CROSSOVER
bulletin board.
```
*********CAVEAT EMPTOR!*********
```
Do you still want to join CROSSOVER, Finley? (y/n)

With a little bit more trepidation this time, she nonetheless again
typed, "y."

Is Finley your real name? (y/n) Y
Are you a man or a woman, Finley? (m/w)

Huh? But she typed "w."

Do you prefer to be known as a man or a woman, Finley?
(m/w)

"Damn it, you just asked me—" she began to say to herself, but
then reread the previous question and noted the different wording
with its different connotation, and realized: CROSSOVER was a
bulletin board for gay users! Of course! She typed "w" here, too,
just to see where all these questions were leading. She was asked
her age, her height and weight, her interests, her address— This
was going too far. She broke the connection without completing
the registration process, and immediately logged back in using
Redman's own script.

Welcome back, Pouch!
You have 12 messages waiting.

Finley briefly scanned the contents of the twelve messages, then
printed them out. Most of them were pretty innocent, the kind of
things friends hurrying to different appointments might shout
across the street to one another. A handful of them, from various
users, discussed details of parties and dates, either in the plan-
ning stages or in retrospect. They'd probably be useful to the
Philadelphia police, especially the one sent to "Pouch" on Satur-

day morning; it thanked him for a "great time" on Friday night, and asked if they might "get together again. SOON." Shouldn't be too hard to track down the sender, whose ID was "Blake," as long as he was on Redman's list of IDs. . . . Hey, was it possible—?

Most BBSs operated pretty much the same way; they performed pretty much the same functions, differing if at all only in the specific commands you needed to enter in order to *get* those functions. For example, to create a message on one system you typed *"create,"* on another, *"write,"* and so on. One function that Finley now thought of was one that would tell her what Redman himself had entered during his first log-in—the one that would display his so-called "user profile." And that was the command, too, as it turned out; she experimented by typing, "profile," and the system responded:

Choose a number:
1   Change your profile
2   Display your profile
3   Exit profile function

She typed "2," and the system said:

ID: Pouch
Name: Joanna Redman

Huh? Joanna had used this board, too? But the profile display was continuing:

Sex: Man

Wait a minute; *"man"?* Had Joanna mistyped her response?

Prefers to be known as: Woman
Age: 30
Heigh—

Finley halted the display; she didn't want or need to know what Joanna's vital statistics were. For now, she had a puzzle to deal with.

Joanna *might* have mistakenly registered as a man. But then she would have realized her mistake at some point and gone back to change it—wouldn't she? Clearly the twelve messages addressed to "Pouch" were from *men,* writing to *another man;* would Joanna have been handling her husband's mail for him, for some reason . . . ?

It hit her suddenly with the force of a blow: *there was no Joanna Redman.* Joanna and John Redman were the same person, united in this "Pouch" persona. And what hit Finley the hardest about this was not surprise that John Redman might have been masquerading as a woman; Finley supposed that was fairly common among gays although she didn't really know, ha ha, first hand. No. What took her breath away was that a *BBS user* might pretend to be a sex other than what he or she really was. And he—or she—hadn't just done it here, on this aptly named CROSSOVER, but even over on FOTOBOARD and especially on Eat&Drink; Finley had *seen* all the messages from and to "Joanna": Redman had, on a general public BBS, pretended to be a *woman.*

Again, Finley wasn't totally naive about such things. She knew that you had to take with a grain of salt whatever someone said about themselves on-line. She knew that people used aliases on-line, like Redman's own "Pouch," which blurred their outlines still further. But she'd never imagined that someone might pretend to be the opposite sex. . . .

Morris seemed to think it was pretty funny, though, when she went in to report it to him. "Ha ha ha! Should have thought of that myself—ha ha!"

"But Morris, it's *dishonest,* it's *sneaky,* it's—it's *gross!*"

"Yeah, heh heh, Finley, I keep telling you not to trust everything that comes over the wire too much. Heh heh heh. . . ." Gradually, he recovered himself. "You, uh, you want me to call Philadelphia and let them know about it? Or do you want to?"

She sighed. "No, I'll do it."

And she did. The detective sergeant, like Morris, didn't seem particularly upset by the news; if anything, he seemed relieved. "Hey, great—one less thing we gotta track down. You got any other good news for us?" Bang. That was it; not even a second thought; next subject, please. Finley told him about the messages to "Pouch," and the detective asked her to fax copies down to him.

"Okay," he wound up, "keep the faith and keep in touch." And he hung up.

Finley couldn't wait till this project was over so she could talk to Monica and Ray about it. They probably wouldn't be surprised, either—but at least they'd register sympathy.

FOTOBOARD was a less complicated problem. Redman had saved all his (and "Joanna's") old mail on floppies, and Finley had already seen all that and turned it over to the Philadelphia police. But she wanted to check two things further: first, to see if Redman had received any new messages since his last login; and second, to check his FOTOBOARD user profile.

As it turned out, he had no messages waiting. So what was on the floppies would provide at least close to a complete start-to-finish snapshot of his FOTOBOARD usage. As for the user profile, she noted that there was a single profile for John/Joanna. FOTOBOARD, unsurprisingly, did not include gender and measurements in its profiles.

Nonetheless, it looked like she'd have something further to report to Gus about Redman's boards after all, she thought. She was thinking the word "Gus" and reaching across the desktop for her logbook just as her hand passed over the neat little stack of phone bills.

Aaaarrrgh. She had already forgotten about them, she realized —"forgotten," hell, she'd probably intentionally repressed all awareness of them, since matching them to her BBS directory was going to be incredibly tedious. The directory of course was on the computer, but she'd have to match it the hard way—by eye —against the phone bills, line by excruciating line.

Let's see . . . the directory was currently sorted by subject matter, since that was how she normally used it; but for this task, it would be a lot simpler if she sorted it by phone number itself. So *swish, swish,* a couple passes and clicks of the mouse and there it was, sorted as she needed it. And that was it, the last bit of anything even remotely resembling fun for the next ninety minutes. Line by line of every page of the six phone bills, matched against the directory; if it's in the directory, circle the phone number on the bill in red; if it's not, cross the line out lightly with pencil. Then go back through the stack a second time, just to be sure you got it right.

Boring, tedious work. When she was through, Finley's neck and shoulders ached grumpily, and her mind was feeling cramped and sore as well. She stood up and stretched, the heels of her hands curling up and away and brushing lightly against knick-knacks on the shelves in her cubicle. She blinked and looked down at the bills, at the numbers she'd circled in red and at the penciled list of BBSs, copied from her directory, that Aggie Bristol and Dorothy Taylor had used.

There were no matches. They hadn't known each other on-line. Scratch another possible connection, damn it.

Chapter Thirteen

"WALK," the sign said, and Finley walked—she, and what seemed like, gad, must have been five hundred other people at the same corner, swimming like a colony of jellyfish cells into the intersection and passing magically, osmotically, through an identical jellyfish from the opposite corner.

What was she doing here in New York? she asked herself. She had no right, no authorization, no *jurisdiction* as the term went. She'd even tacitly admitted this to herself by taking a day off to come here, on what was probably a wild-goose chase to the "headquarters" of the Pelagius Institute. But, she rationalized, who else would come? The only person on this project over whom she had anything remotely like influence was Gus, and he was in Atlanta, doing whatever it was that he had to do in order to get Tracy's phone bills. And he *had* told her to keep after the Pince angle, hadn't he? So, Jeez, she *had* to come in by herself, didn't she?

Last night, she'd read the faxed copies of Edward Pince's articles from the 1960s. He was a Class-A oddball, Finley thought, a spook, a twister of the language of morality and ethics in ways it was never meant to be twisted. "Do unto others," he said in one paper, like he was some kind of prophet, "and do not concern yourself with whether or not they would do so unto you." One of the pieces she'd read was an apparent response to a letter in a previous issue of the journal, in which the letter-writer had coined the term "Compulsivism" for Pince's cockeyed complex of beliefs. But far from taking offense, Pince had latched onto the term enthusiastically. Weird stuff.

And now here she was in Manhattan, on Eighth Avenue in the lower thirties, standing at the address of the Pelagius Institute; so this was it—the Mecca of Compulsivism. Certainly an unprepossessing front door; dirty glass and brushed steel, with a tiny foyer and a flight of stairs dimly visible through the glass. The address to the left was a storefront full of dusty kimonos and bamboo thingums, and painted on the large fly-specked window, AMER-ASIAN QUALITY IMPORTER. A small sign at the bottom of the window announced, cryptically, "No Retail—No Wholesale." To the right, on the corner, was a grimy restaurant with high-gloss, apparently varnished chickens turning slowly on spits in the window. Finley looked at the panel of buttons alongside the door and pressed the one labeled, with embossed plastic tape, PELAGIUS INST.

After a moment, the tiny speaker beneath the button crackled to life. "Whehh?" it said, metallic and completely unintelligible. Cheap intercom.

"Whehh"? Finley thought. She said, aloud, "I'm looking for the Pelagius Institute, I'm a researcher, is this it?"

"Whehh?"

"I said I'm a researcher, Pelagianism, Mister Pince's teachings and so on. Ideas of, of motivation." God, *please* let this be the right button. . . .

"Whehh whehh?"

"Uh, can I come up? Is Mister Pince in today?"

"Whehh?"

This was like arguing with Donald Duck. What more could she say? "Can I come up to talk to him, or you?" she repeated.

"Whehh! Whehh, whehh whehh *whehh!*" And then, miraculously, the buzzer sounded. Finley opened the door.

The first thing she noticed about the entryway and stairs, now that she was inside and on her way up, was the gray color. Oh, the upper portion of the walls had once been white or off-white, and they were now, yes, gray with dirt and dust; but the floor and stairs and a waist-high band at the bottom of the walls were all *really* gray, what was it? *battleship* gray, yes. The color had clearly been *chosen,* for some reason (or, ha ha, maybe for none). It made her feel as though she were wading across a muddy river—she wanted to lift her hands over her head to keep them clean.

The steel door to the left of the second-floor landing was

painted the same gray, beneath and around the frosted glass pane which was lettered with the single word, PELAGIUS. Finley was about to knock on the door, uncertain whether she should simply open it, when a shadowy gray form moved across the glass from the other side, extended a pseudopod to the doorknob, and opened it, out, toward the hall.

The gray form was a man, Finley could see now, a small man with thin gray hair and steel-rimmed glasses. A strip of some silvery material, duct tape maybe, lashed the eyeglasses together at one temple, by the hinge. (Looked like one of her landlord's repair jobs, Finley thought, and coughed softly to hide a giggle.) He was dressed in a white shirt, nondescript and slightly out-of-fashion tie, and gray suit.

"Yes?" he said.

"Mister Pince?"

"*Doctor* Pince, yes. Can I help you?"

"I'm a researcher, looking, you know, into Pelagianism, Compulsivism. Like that. Wanted to meet you, maybe ask you some questions. Interview you."

His voice constricted a little with suspicion. "What kind of questions? What kind of research are you doing?" He had still not admitted her through the door.

Think, Finley. What kind of researcher are you supposed to be? "I'm a—a graduate student. Columbia. Majoring in psychology. My, umm, my master's thesis is on motivation, how self-help groups, New Age therapies and so on, how they help motivate people. Not the big ones like est and Alcoholics Anonymous, you know, just the . . . lesser-known ones."

The man hesitated a moment longer, then smiled an icy smile and stood aside.

Finley could see now that this was not the office, just a reception room. Hat rack, small gray desk, a few chairs of gray molded plastic here and there around the walls. A door on the wall to the right, and, on the wall across from her, another door, this one wood-veneered and labeled with a fake-bronze plaque that said, E. PINCE.

"Please wait right here a moment," said the man (was it Pince, or wasn't it?), and disappeared through the labeled door. A minute or two later his voice called to her from the other room.

Now sitting at a large steel desk, gray of course, bent over the desk like a manuscript illuminator when Finley entered, he was writing something in a journal or ledger—pretending to write, more likely; pretending to be busy. At a gesture from him, Finley sat in a chair by the desk.

Five minutes passed before he finished recording whatever profound insight had suddenly occurred to him, giving Finley a chance to inspect the office from her seat. Gray everywhere: a bank of four-drawer file cabinets along the wall behind the desk; gray-enameled floor-to-ceiling steel bookshelves off to the left and down into an ell that obviously wrapped around the reception room; the gray door behind her and another in the wall to the right. Remarkably, he'd even come up with a cheerful-but-gray touch: a gray parakeet, chirping quietly to itself—even its voice was gray—on a wooden perch in a gray wire cage. Fluorescent lights buzzed overhead. No computer anywhere in sight; was that significant?

At last Pince put down his fountain pen, read over what he had written, nodded in self-approbation and closed the journal. He looked up. He had gray eyes, naturally; and he smiled a polite, tight-lipped smile. "How do you do?" he said and stood, extending his hand for Finley to shake. He looked even smaller when standing; bullies in school must've loved this guy, Finley thought. "I am Edward Pince, Ph.D. And you are—?" His voice was buttery-soft but audible. Velvety.

"My name is Finley, Mister Pince, just Finley." Then she went on, gaining confidence in the lie as she spoke, "I'm a graduate student in psychology, Columbia, looking into motivation, criminal motivation particularly, the reasons why people commit crimes? A friend who'd read some of your work many years ago suggested I look you up. And so here I am."

He was still wearing that artificial smile. "*Doctor* Pince, Miss Finley, *Doctor*. Not Mister."

Finley reddened a little, almost but not quite reminding him that it was "just Finley, not *Miss* Finley." She said aloud merely, "Yes, that's right. *Doctor* Pince."

"Do you have a list of questions, Miss Finley? Something to help us move along? As you have seen, we are quite busy today."

Busy, ha. "Well no, *Doctor* Pince, no actual physical list of questions. The list is in my head. It's not a very long list—I've already got information about, you know, your background and so on. Just a couple of questions actually, theoretical questions? Questions it'd be impossible for me to ask of books and old magazines and newspapers."

"Ah, *theoretical* questions!" Pince clapped his hands and seemed almost gloating, as though Finley had yielded some significant philosophical point. He stood up and moved to the parakeet cage, poked his finger through the wires and made a parakeet owner's typical silly clucking noises. "Tick-tick! Theoretical questions are our favorite kind here, aren't they, tick-tick-tick! And what might be the first of these theoretical questions?"

"Well, for starters—can you explain the contradiction between your ideas of doing something for no purpose at all and, say, all the *gray* here? The floors and walls, your suit, desk, even the parakeet—surely that was all chosen for some *purpose?*"

Pince was chuckling to himself before she even finished. Then he was outright *laughing*. It was really a rapid-fire wheeze, but it literally had possession of his body; he had to leave the parakeet, sit down at the desk again, and remove his glasses in order to smear at his watering eyes with the heels of his hands. He gasped for breath and said, apparently to himself, "She wants to know about the *paint!*" "Chick!" exclaimed the parakeet, joining in the general merriment.

"I am sorry, Miss Finley," Pince said at last, recovering his composure and what passed for his dignity. "It is merely that the paint is a little inside joke with us here. But I will let you in on something, on the *joke,* Miss Finley, and then I will answer your question. Please," he said, rising from his desk and moving this time to the side door, on Finley's right, "step over here for just a minute."

Finley got up, and he opened the door. He didn't swing it open fully, so she sensed she was not to enter the room beyond. But she could see it, clearly enough.

It was obviously a lecture hall or meeting room of some kind. At the front wall was a projection screen, a little threadbare, patched here and there with adhesive tape, it seemed. There was a lectern, too, with a small wooden box on the floor behind it, standing on which (Finley thought) a short person might make himself seem taller. Folding chairs, a dozen or so, were scattered in ragged formation in front of and around the lectern. But what she was almost certainly meant to notice was the decor. The folding chairs, yes, were gray; otherwise, the room looked like a paint factory after a bombing.

Splotches and sprays of blue, off-white, orange and yellow; streaks and smears of green and red; decorator varieties like Heather Green and Autumn Sand—paint factory *nothing*, it looked like the inside of Jackson Pollock's stomach after a Chinese-Italian dinner, she thought, and at first had to close her eyes in order not to be sickened. When she opened them a moment later, it seemed merely ugly. Then she noticed the shades and drapes on the large windows along the back wall: jet-black.

Finley turned, her face quizzical, to Pince. He said nothing at first, waiting until they had resumed their seats. But even then he didn't speak, merely cocked both eyebrows in an unspoken, "Well?" And he was still chortling.

"Well," she said, "that was certainly . . . *different*. Would you mind explaining it all now?"

"Not at all, Miss Finley, not at all. To begin with, you make the same mistake that others have made, others who like you are not perhaps of a particularly philosophical nature. You confuse absence of purpose with absence of pattern. As a result of this confusion, when confronted with pattern or consistency of behavior, you decide that the pattern must have been *chosen* in advance, for some logically deducible or even discernible purpose."

He removed his glasses and placed them on the desk blotter, alongside the journal; he was speaking from habit now, Finley guessed, not particularly to her. "This conclusion of yours is nonsense, of course. Consider the shapes of the stars and planets, for example; spheres they are, or nearly spheres. Perfect form, you see. Pattern. But they acquire that form as the result of physical forces, gravitation, the properties of gases and so on, not to satisfy some *purpose*, Miss Finley." He closed his eyes, and pinched the bridge of his nose between thumb and forefinger.

"So," he went on, "in the case of the walls and furnishings here in the office and downstairs, you assume that if I were rigorous in my beliefs, in practicing what I preach so to speak—at least as you understand what I preach—I would have arranged to have them painted in odd, chaotic patterns or rather *non*patterns. Antipatterns. But you have also, I am afraid, confused *motivation* and *will*. In purely Pelagian terms, Miss Finley, having *willed* out of no particular motivation that the bottom step shall be gray it is perfectly acceptable to *will* for no reason at all that the second shall also be gray, and the third, and so on. Each step a new decision, you see."

He stood again, and again walked to the parakeet's cage while continuing to talk. There was something a little intellectually slippery going on here, something that Finley couldn't quite grab hold of with her mind. But Pince wasn't waiting for her to catch up, nor was he tick-tick-ticking at the bird; he was just in playback mode now.

"The meeting room next door, Miss Finley, the decor there was, yes, more in keeping with your rudimentary concept of 'purposelessness,' was it not?" The question was rhetorical; he continued without pausing. "Rather we would say, here at the Institute, that the colors in that room represent the chaotic web of 'decisions,' of so-called 'purposes,' that are carried around in the minds of people of everyday ilk.

"And the curtains, the drapes on the windows? We might say that they represent geometric and chromatic purity, pure forms anchored within but not partaking of the chaos around them." He turned and looked straight into Finley's eyes. "Pure forms, Miss Finley. That is what the participants in my workshops aspire to become. Imagine a creature of pure perfect unmotivated will, *in* but not *of* the everyday world of so-called 'decisions.' Solid. One or two of my students have in fact attained such a plane of existence. Can you see such a creature, Miss Finley?"

Without really intending to do so, Finley shut her eyes. She did indeed see such a "creature": it was a man, looking rather like the figure in the painting in the Princeton art gallery. She could see him as clearly as if he were seated before her now: dressed like the windows all in black, smiling dreamily, even beatifically, and absolutely motionless. All that was needed to complete the picture was a ray of sunlight streaming in through the window and striking him on the forehead. Finley might have guessed he was in a trance.

"Look at him, Miss Finley. Purity, you see? As close to a perfect *will* as you are likely ever to encounter."

Eh? At the moment, in suspended animation as it were, the creature in her mind's eye seemed to represent a perfect *absence* of will. A mute; a dummy. She opened her eyes. Pince having paused long enough to return to his seat and put his glasses back on, Finley said, "But if you've decorated the room next door to *represent* some ideas like you just said, for that matter if you've created this hypothetical creature of pure will here at your Institute, then haven't you done it for some *purpose,* Mister, Doctor Pince? Aren't you just playing games with semantics?"

He peered at her frostily. Smug bastard. Then he suddenly waved his arms, vaguely indicating the file cabinets arrayed like palace sentries along the walls. "You see all this, Miss Finley, all this paper? My life's work is here, my legacy so to speak. Oh, I grant you I have not written all this myself. Most of the books on the shelves there were written by others, and serve as supporting references for what I *have* written. But my writings are all here, going back to the time when I was a mere boy. They represent quite possibly three-fourths of all the paper in this room. My Bible, you see? My point, Miss Finley, is in plain English that I know what I am talking about. Do you seriously think that after more than forty years I would not have obliterated all trace of contradiction in my thinking? I have defended myself against, and subsequently successfully counterattacked, far more rigorous minds than your own, you know. It is *you,* Miss Finley, not I, who is caught up in petty semantics."

Jesus, Finley thought, he wrote all this stuff? Of course, no idea if the filing cabinets all have anything in them but even so, only a nut would ever read a Bible this big. Let alone believe it. Let alone *write* it. She said, carefully modulating her voice to betray no sarcasm, "Umm, well, yes, I see what you mean. I really ought to defer to your longevity and experience. . . ." Must have succeeded; he was nodding in agreement. "But to get back to my thesis, Doctor Pince. Criminal motivation. Does it sound reasonable to you, say a particular criminal commits a crime that makes no sense at all, a murder say, a victim he doesn't even know. Or barely knows them, anyhow. He doesn't rob them or anything, just kills them and walks away. Would that be a good example of what you call 'pure will'? Would that be a, umm, a Pelagian act?"

"Yes, certainly that is possible. In an infinite universe anything is possible, Miss Finley. Of course I would have to talk to the person involved, the one you referred to as the 'criminal,' to determine unequivocally if that were the case." He leaned back in the desk chair and folded his hands across his vest. "Alternatively, he might, for example, be a mere psychopath. As a student of psychology, Miss Finley, you surely know that even psychopaths have their reasons, merely imagined or nonsensical reasons perhaps, but they are reasons nonetheless. If so, of course, his behavior would be anti-Pelagian.

"But you know," he said, his tone perking up a little, "you really might want to consider attending one of our sessions. I can see your sincerity, and I do believe that a meeting or two might help you understand better. They might even," wheeze, "they might even help you to understand the paint. Here, I shall see that you get our standard materials on the way out." The interview was apparently at an end, and he led her from the office.

"Well, Miss Finley, perhaps we will see you again soon. Every other Tuesday. It is all in the brochure."

"Thank you, Doctor Pince, I feel like I should—"

"No no no!" he interrupted. " 'Should' is not a word in our vocabulary here!" The wheeze again.

Here in the reception room, he extracted from the desk a single sheet of paper—gray—folded twice into a small brochure; the "standard materials," obviously. It asked the reader, in large letters on the front flap, "WHOSE Will Be Done?"

"Here you are!" Pince said. "Maybe we shall see you again soon, then?"

Carefully matching his tone of voice, Finley said brightly, "Yeah, maybe you will!" But she thought, as she let herself out the door and down the stairs, carefully holding her hands above the dirty gray, waist-high tide, pushing her way past a man in a black shirt turning a key and opening the door at the foot of the stairs— one of Pince's pure disciples no doubt—"See you soon? Fat chance, you little gnome, ha! Over my dead body."

Chapter Fourteen

"You went *where* yesterday? And did *what?*" Morris exclaimed the next morning, his face florid and openmouthed with disbelief.

"Just, just into New York, that's all. To, to interview this Pince guy."

Morris stood up and walked from his desk to his office window. One arm rested on the ledge formed where his abdomen met his chest; the elbow of the other arm rested on this one, and its hand was clamped over his mouth. He stood like a statue, staring in silence out onto the grassy courtyard and bare November trees. When he turned back to face Finley, he was obviously fighting to maintain control of his temper.

"Finley, I just—I just don't know what to say. What you did was *wrong,* that's all. At best, you wasted a day's worth of your real work on your real investigation, maybe giving a dangerous killer the extra day he needs to kill someone else. At worst, you may have compromised the *police's* investigation, if it turns out that Pince really is inv—"

"But—"

"No buts. Effective immediately, Finley, I want you to drop all further investigation of this Pince angle. Write up whatever you've learned so far, write it up as objectively as possible—no speculation, got it?—and then turn it over to Gus. Make a copy for me, too. And then *wash your hands of Pince,* understand? If I hear one more word of another stunt like this one, I will take you off the project, and give it to Helen, yes, *Helen Walker,* Finley."

"Morr—"

"That's enough. I'm glad you told me about it, and I'm impressed by your initiative. But we have rules here, damn it, rules that put limits on individual initiative but with good reason. And you just violated a good half-dozen of them."

"I—"

"Go. Back to your desk. To *your* job, Finley—not Gus's, not a policeman's. *Yours. Go.*"

Finley went, all right. She had never seen Morris like this, not even remotely like this. She hoped she'd never see him like it again. But she hadn't really done anything, had she? She knuckled away a tiny wet spot at the corner of one eye, and sat down at her desk.

Nearly two hours later she had her "report" completed. One copy was in a manila envelope here in her cube, for Gus. Morris's copy she hand-delivered; but he was on the phone when she brought it in, which watered down the drama she'd hoped to arouse by completing it so fast. He merely waved absentmindedly and went back to his phone conversation, oblivious to the frosty set of Finley's mouth and to the sarcasm implicit in her salute when she turned to leave. Ha. Again with the Helen Walker routine. Just let him *try* to ask Helen Walker for one tiny point of stupid clarification. Let him try to ask stupid Finley herself, for that stupid matter. "Pince?" she'd say, all wide-eyed and innocent and stupid. "Pince who?"

As for the rest of the project, her "real work," as Morris had snidely put it, she knew just what she would do next. Tracy's picture gave her the idea: examine the messages that had gone back and forth between "Joanna" Redman and the fictitious "Mary Ellen."

Finley quickly narrowed down the search to the Eat&Drink BBS. There it was, the paper trail of an apparently innocent on-line friendship, rooted in what seemed to be a common interest:

> . . . Hi, Joanna! I've been following your conversations with everybody here and just wanted to say that you SURE seem knowledgeable about all this stuff. Lots of folks here seem to be just hobbyists but you seem to have it down cold. You MUST be a professional, right? How else could you have learned so much about food and wine?

Mary Ellen

. . . Why, thank you, dear Mary Ellen! What a lovely compliment! But no, I'm afraid I must disappoint you: just a
mere enthusiast like many of the others around here. A trifle
more obsessed with detail, perhaps, but other than that no
special qualifications. . . .
                                                    Joanna

They'd then proceeded through a series of mentor-protegé exchanges, with "Mary Ellen" professing a profound sense of mystery about such things as dairy substitutes and fermentation technology and "Joanna," on the other hand, pirouetting about in a
showoff dance of expertise. Redman really *had* known a lot, Finley
could see—not the least of which was how to keep his own secret
about "Joanna." Unfortunately for him. For soon the conversation
dipped down into private mode, down where not even the sysops
would look at it:

. . . Joanna, I've got to tell somebody this story before I
explode. I met this guy the other night at a party. We hit it
off pretty good, he was coming on pretty aggressively but
so was I (if you know what I mean). We came back to my
place afterwards and painted the boudoir red. Wow!
    But then four hours later he jumps up out of bed and
while he's pulling his pants and shirt on he mumbles something to me about he has to get back home or his wife will
get worried. His WIFE! I ask you, is this normal? How would
YOU handle a guy like that?
                                                    Mary Ellen

. . . Good heavens, Mary Ellen dear, I'm afraid I'm past the
point where such situations are even IMAGINED. I haven't
"dated," as I suppose the term still is, for some years now,
and the straits in which you youngsters place yourselves are
quite beyond the scope of my matronly understanding
<smile>.
                                                    Love, Joanna

. . . Come on now, Joanna—how old ARE you? Not that
old, I'll bet! I mean, the way you come on to the guys
around here? (And I'm a grand old lady of 24 myself!)
Mary Ellen

. . . You make me blush, dear child. I'm old enough, as
they say. 35 going on 50 is another way to put it. See? I'm
old enough to be your jaded older sister.
Love, Joanna

Knowing what she did, Finley got a morbid thrill out of reading
the two "women's" correspondence: watching "Mary Ellen" ever
so artfully draw forth details of "Joanna's" life, golden details
which "Joanna" agreeably spun out of the dross of "her" longing
and imagination. Fascinating.

And also, as Finley came to realize, a little creepy. Creepy, because the killer had stolen not only Tracy's picture for his own,
but also her very *persona*. The voice of "Mary Ellen" was Tracy's
voice, right down to that flippant "painted the boudoir red" line.
Indeed the whole rhythm and tone of "her" life, not just the expression of it, were Tracy's. Finley remembered her own first
exchanges with Tracy; they had evolved pretty much along these
same nearly organic lines, branching out from the solid roots of
fact into the fragile twigs and leaves of wishes and loves. It was
beyond creepy; ghoulish, it was, like watching someone you loved
having the blood sucked out of her neck.

"Yo!" came Monica's voice over the wall. "Finley! Lunch?"

She looked up. Monica appeared to be standing on a chair or
carton; her elbows rested along the top of the wall between their
cubes as though being eight feet tall were the most natural thing
in the world.

But Finley wasn't hungry. "No thanks, Monica. I'm going to
spend some time at lunch checking into some of my personal
boards."

Monica frowned comically and dropped out of sight without
looking down—maybe Ray had been holding her up there? Finley
spent no further time wondering about it; she really did want to
check on her on-line friends.

On STACKS, Jon Little-Olden and Uri were engaged in something like an argument:

To: Uri
From: Jon Little-Olden
Re: Say what?
Message: I pretty much stay out of your way, Uri, you seem to be an all right guy from what I can tell. But who the h*ll are you to be telling me that I don't know what I'm talking about in the L of C vs. Dewey battle? Maybe I don't have as much real-world bigshot academic experience as YOU do, but . . .

To: Jon Little-Olden
From: Uri
Re: Say what?
Message: I didn't say or imply any such thing, my hot-tempered friend. I said it didn't seem fair to turn a comment about the L of C vs. Dewey issue into one about your girl-friend, although by now I guess those of us who hang around here regularly should pretty much EXPECT it of you, right?

Whew! All right, Uri! Finley couldn't resist putting in her own two cents' worth, though she was careful to make it sound more or less neutral:

. . . Uh, guys, you want to try keeping the volume down here in the library? Can't you read the sign, "SHHHHHH!"? (But Jon, Uri does have a point—you really do have a tendency to shoot off your mouth more than most.) (There's a <grin> attached to that!)

And over on ABLE, what a relief: a message from Jane, finally, after what was it, almost a week now?

. . . Hello, Finley dear! I'm so sorry I haven't been able (ha ha) to reply to your mail over the last few days. It's been dreadfully busy here since last week; I even worked over the weekend. Surely you know how that is sometimes!

But you know, now that I think about it, it occurs to me that I don't know what sort of job you have. Isn't that funny, that we should have skipped such a basic piece of information! For the record, I myself am a secretary, although around here we call it an "administrative assistant."

And so sorry, dear, to hear about your friend who died. Was it a man friend, or a woman friend? Talk about it if you want; I'm always willing to listen. Love you, dear. <jane>

Jane was right; it was funny that they'd not discussed work yet (except in a general, world-weary-muttering way). Finley's reply said:

. . . Actually, Jane, my job is pretty interesting. I do on-line research for a government criminal agency, and the project I'm working on right now is pretty interesting, too. A serial killer. I can't talk too much about it, but one of his victims was a pretty good friend of mine named Tracy. So sad, you know? Tracy was a "she," yes, and she was kind of wild but also innocent. And I think she might have gotten too friendly with the guy who eventually killed her. But I'm in a unique position now—maybe I can actually help find the guy myself.

Right now I'm sort of upset about my boss. I got in trouble today because I was a little too eager and did something yesterday that I shouldn't have. I can't give you details, but I took off from work to play undercover cop. Lots of fun, but Against The Rules.

Ah, well. Back to the trenches. Take care of yourself, Jane.

Love, Finley

As for Flokati, there was waiting for her on FORENSIC one of his occasional, spontaneous, lyrical expositions of the wonders of forensic pathology, couched in his usual enigmatic syntax:

. . . Finley, I hope everything is fine. I attended autopsy last night. Is always a mystery to me, a mystery and a wonderful thing to be bystanding at autopsy! To see incision made just with craftfulness and so beautiful too organs inside the skin gray and red and shining in light have never seen, even fat beautiful then, you see? And examining pathologist physician whispers into Sony recording Walkman around neck whole time, is like great mysterious drama to me. I love bodies yes!

Finley giggled a little at that. Flokati was such an inadvertent charmer; his prose, like the organs he described, glistened in her Western mind in ways he couldn't possibly imagine. "I love bodies yes!" indeed!

But then she thought of Flokati in another light: could this unmistakable voice of his be the voice *not* of someone Japanese, someone at the University of Hokkaido? Could the on-line, irritable voice of Jon Little-Olden, for that matter, be masking the true voice of, say, an even-tempered saint? Could someone pretend so thoroughly to be someone else on-line that you couldn't tell the difference between that Other Self and the real thing? She was cheering or giggling no longer now, but shuddering: not at Uri, Jon, or Flokati, certainly, but at the wispy presence of that Other out there, unseen, the Other waiting, she thought absurdly (the thought, after all, based on absolutely nothing): waiting now for her.

Like Morris, Gus was surprised by Finley's excursion into New York. The rumpled appearance of his forehead as she told him the tale closely matched that of his brown "traveling suit," which clearly would soon need another dry cleaning.

When Finley reported what Morris had said about staying away from the Pince angle, Gus chuckled a bit. But he refrained from voicing anything like "I told you so"; instead, he merely picked up his copy of Finley's report and said he'd look it over at his first opportunity. "For now," he said, extracting from his briefcase one of his ever-present manila folders, "here are Tracy Williams's phone bills."

She sighed. Even if it was Tracy's stuff she was working on, she knew, bleech, that it would just be more of the same. More boredom. The way things were going, she would emphatically welcome even the arrival next week of Warren and his family. God knows, she could use some excitement.

In the Shadows
3

His Master had been pacing in agitation about the office when he arrived late yesterday morning. It was all the fault of the young woman who had just left, his Master had explained—she was intelligent but really quite naive.

"Who was she?" he had asked, and his Master had stopped pacing for a moment, a perplexed look on his face.

"A Miss Finley; I do not believe she ever gave me her first name. Graduate student. Lots of questions. Confused, like most people. Still, she seemed willing enough to be instructed. . . ."

Finley? he'd thought to himself. Could it be the same Finley? How many women could there be who went just by that name and no other?

"Now what the devil is the matter with you all of a sudden?" his Master had asked then. "Did you see her on your way up here? You are not daydreaming, I hope? Surely not fantasizing? She was attractive, yes, but allowing yourself to be distracted by superficial so-called beauty is not a healthy symptom, Smith, in fact it is a disease all to itself. Always remember that: consciousness and will in every act."

"Yes, you're right of course," he'd agreed. "It really is just a case of distraction. I'll try to be more careful about it."

Shaking his head, his Master had left for the day, then, journals as always tucked under one arm, leaving him to "straighten up" as they called it although the term was not precisely accurate. He'd moved about the premises of the Pelagian Institute, shoving chairs into random positions, emptying the contents of each trash can into another, raising or lowering the window shades according to the dictates of his will. But he was aware all the time of an insistent high-pitched voice piping annoyingly at the back of his mind, squeaking maniacally, over and over, like the voice of a small bird, "Finley! Finley!"

And now it appeared that the voice's urgency had been justified. Finley was a—what had she called it? a "researcher," whatever that was, for some criminal agency. And she left no doubt that she was onto something. But *what* was she onto? What did she suspect?

She certainly did not suspect his on-line self; she was still answering any question he thought to ask. Nor did he think she suspected his Master, judging from the tone of the questions she'd apparently asked. But she was getting close, and by whatever route she had gotten this far, he had to keep her from getting closer. . . .

An interesting experience, it had been, actually to *see* one of them. Beforehand, as it were, even just a glimpse at the foot of the stairs. Finley reminded him even—a little—of a girl he had loved once, years ago, before embarking on his search for wisdom.

That girl had been slightly deaf, even. She, too, had had sandy brown hair and brown eyes. But his Master had described Finley as uncertain and tentative, more bravado than bravery, as if groping her way along, walking in the dark on a steeply sloping surface; *that* girl, on the other hand, had been confident, assertive, almost frighteningly sure of herself. She had always known just what she wanted and always been unafraid of saying so, of doing whatever she needed to do in order to get it. "*That* car," she'd said, and bought it. "*That* job," she'd insisted, and gotten it. And, finally, "*Not* you," and slammed the door on him.

She'd tried to, at least. But she hadn't been able to dislodge him with the mere slam of a door. He'd badgered her with phone calls; when she stopped answering the phone and then finally acquired a new, unlisted number, he'd followed her everywhere, from a distance, from his car and on foot, confronting her unexpectedly in shopping malls and movie theaters, his persistent pale eager face glimpsed through crowds of strangers in fast-food restaurants and airport terminals.

And when, at last exasperated beyond all tolerance, she had confronted him in her kitchen, screamed at him, *"Get* away *from me!"* and slapped his face, he had . . . well, he had become someone other than himself at that moment, someone else for good, as though by the mere act of touching his face one more time, even in violence, she had transmuted him. Reflexively, he had hit her in return, surprising himself as much as her, and then hit her again, and kept hitting her, her voice rising first to a scream and then diminishing to a whimper until she was silent and still and all her life force had been, so he believed, transferred into his own soul. Her will into his. Utterly *with him,* at last.

Silence had followed, then, an awesome silence he had initially mistaken for awful. But he had stood in contemplation for a long time before a window in her house, looking out at the uncomprehending world.

The silence from the kitchen behind him had come to seem not a true silence, but merely a dull distant booming just beneath the threshold of hearing, the subaudible pulse of an eerie sort of life whose existence he had never even glimpsed before. He had looked down at the hands which had introduced him to this strange new sort of life. They were no longer the hands he had grown up with, the hands he had previously thought of, all his life, as timid and shoved deep in his pockets. They had become, with this simple act, the hands of a new self, a self he wanted to know more of. . . . Inspired, he then had oh so carefully disposed of her mortal remains, and gathering up into himself the last shards of her soul, had left on his search.

And now here, it seemed, she had returned to haunt him—returned to claim what she thought to be hers, perhaps: her soul, her life, a future, the promise that when she opened her death-dimmed eyes he would be *gone*; returned, seeking reparations, in the apparently innocent form of this Finley.

And that was a pity, really; he'd have to accelerate the schedule this time—and he did so hate to rush.

Chapter Fifteen

Nothing that happened the next day, Friday, did anything to dispel Finley's sense of just spinning her wheels. Oh, the electrical power remained on, all right; all the Center's phone lines were up and trouble-free. But Finley herself still seemed to be doing stuff without accomplishing anything.

Tracy's phone bills, for example: using the same primitive, dull, screen-to-bill comparison method that she'd used for the New York victims' bills, she learned that Tracy had used two other boards besides STACKS. The first was one of the common technical-support boards that everyone seemed to subscribe to; the other, a BBS for Atlanta singles called "The Party Zone."

But as with STACKS—indeed, as with the BBSs to which Aggie Bristol and Dorothy Taylor had subscribed—the sysops for these two boards refused to provide copies of Tracy's correspondence without first seeing a court order. Gus, with a weary shrug, had gone back down to Atlanta yet again; his purpose this time was to help the Atlanta police obtain such an order for each board, focusing especially on The Party Zone because it seemed a more likely place where Tracy might have met the killer. Once Finley had copies of all of Tracy's messages on The Party Zone, she knew that she'd have to zero in on messages to and from a "Liz," since this was the name the killer had inked onto the back of the photo of Dorothy Taylor that he'd sent to Tracy. Copies of all of it, Gus assured her, would be express-delivered to Finley as soon as it became available, not only from Atlanta but also from New York, where similar efforts were underway to obtain Aggie Bristol's and Dorothy Taylor's on-line messages from their board's sysops.

Finley dreaded the likelihood that, as usual, it would all arrive at about the same time, burying her under an enormous quantity of paper—all of it needing to be absorbed, digested, and sorted for significance as quickly as possible. She saw, in her mind's eye, massive twin rivers of rustling white, wending their circuitous ways from their sources on a dozen faraway BBSs, through the courts and the police departments of the two cities—both rivers sluggish and lazy for now but gathering momentum and about to converge in a gigantic onrushing tidal wave at a point here, yes *here,* at the center of her desk. She dreaded further the thought that the deluge would hit on Wednesday, the day before Thanksgiving, which would be a nice way for the police to give themselves a breather. Great for them, but what about her own plans? Sounded like something her brother would do, if you wanted to know the truth. And in the meantime, she just had to sit and wait. There was little to do—little to do, that is, but speculate.

"Gus," she'd asked him once, during one of his phone calls from Atlanta, "why are we assuming the killer is a man?"

He'd paused to consider the possibility, but only for an instant. "Well," he'd said, finally, "you're right, there's no evidence that says it's *got* to be a guy. But that *is* the usual pattern with serial murderers." Far easier, he said, to accept that the killer might be masquerading on-line as a woman, than to jettison what they knew to be true of serial killers in general.

But Finley was trying to keep an open mind about it, trying to demonstrate that she could, as Gus had put it a few days ago, "think like an agent"—even though in this case Gus himself, clearly an agent, did not think as she did. She wondered, for starters: if you stripped away the "From:" information in a message's header, were there any cues that the message was really in a woman's "voice," as opposed to a man's?

Over lunch at Burger King, Monica and Ray seemed almost to shrug at the question, as though it were no big deal.

"Sure, men imitate women on-line all the time," Monica said. "Not too often in the other direction, but that happens sometimes, too. Whichever way it goes, it's called cross-typing."

"But isn't it *weird*?"

Monica chuckled and inhaled a French fry. "Maybe so in real life, Finley. But on-line isn't real. You've only been doing this for a couple years now—wait till you're an old hand at it, right, Ray?"

"Oh *yeah,*" he agreed. "For a real kick, you ought to check into one of the BBSs sometime that are set up just for so-called 'serious conversations about human sexuality.' Stuff like that goes on all the time. Ahem, so I've been told." He bit off a huge chunk of a chicken sandwich.

But Finley still wasn't satisfied. "But how do you *know*? Is there something that gives it away? So you're just, you know, reading along in a message and all of a sudden you sit up and say, 'This isn't a real woman, this is a *guy!* '"

"Sure, uh-huh," Ray said, one cheek bulging as he continued to chew while speaking, his eyes glittering mischievously, "you read between the lines."

"Read between the lines? For what?"

He swallowed and said, "A salami. If there's something hidden between the lines that looks like a salami—"

"Oh, Ray, cut it out," Monica interrupted. She half turned to Finley, who was trying to suppress her giggling in the face of Monica's earnestness. "Seriously, Finley. It's probably not easy to tell from a single message. You need to see a whole series of them, over time. There'd be a pattern, like with the Evsee. You'd look for, let's say, somebody who seems almost exclusively concerned with being a *woman,* like they're trying too hard, you know? Flirts a lot with guys—"

"—and at the same time," Ray interrupted her, this time, "the guy would also be real heavy on the schmoozing with other women, trying to establish, y'know, his sisterhood credentials or something."

"That's right. And there's a contradiction there, Finley, you see it? The fake woman is trying to fit into two stereotypes at once: the total-woman-to-all-men, and the true-sister-to-all-women. When in fact, *real* women on-line are very seldom the first, let alone in combination with the second. Real honest-to-God flesh-and-blood women are more complex than that, and they're too cautious, after years of being leered and grabbed at by guys, to flirt openly with ones they don't even know. I mean really, Finley, think about it, how many times have *you* volunteered sexual fantasies to a guy on-line?"

"Oh, I don't know," Ray jumped in again. "Finley and I frequently share our innermost thoughts and desires over the wires, right, Finley? Remember the tapioca scenario?" He wolf-winked at her.

Finley blew him a raspberry in reply. "So basically what you're saying, *Monica,* is that if you were reading a series of messages where a 'woman' seemed to be trying too hard to be a woman, you'd get suspicious?"

Monica thought about it as she slurped the last strawful of soda. "Well, no."

"No? But you just said—"

"I know what I said. But that supposed I was *looking* for something, you see? In most cases, I pretty much just roll with whatever personality the other person, man or woman, wants to wear. Doesn't make any difference to me."

Well, all right; Finley could see that. It didn't usually make a difference to Finley herself, she thought as she sat in the back seat of Monica's car on the way back to the Center. Not in general. Who cared if someone was really a man or really a woman, or for that matter was Japanese or Russian, disabled or "normal"? Wasn't that a beauty of on-line communication, that it obscured or eliminated all that cultural and ethnic and gender baggage? But on this project it did indeed matter; it might make a crucial difference, the difference between finding a needle in a haystack and just finding more hay. If she could only set the perspective of her mind just *so* as she was sifting all the on-line printouts she expected to receive—just tune her sensibilities to catch the slightest false note in a flirtation or a feminist proclamation, she could break the project open. She would be watching, she told herself, and she would be ready when he slipped up. *If* he slipped up.

Chapter Sixteen

But Friday afternoon, after lunch, was laden with even more wheel-spinning, more thumb-twiddling, more do-nothing inaction. Finley did a full backup of her hard drive; she updated her BBS directory to include the new boards she'd learned about over the last couple weeks; and she spent a sluggish, mind-deadening hour with Helen Walker, who wanted to check *everything* with Finley—every last little BBS citation, every cross-reference, the X and Y coordinates of every single colored dot on every single graph—before submitting her final report on the armed robbery/weather project. Morris, who'd been virtually tiptoeing around Finley since their little run-in on Thursday, stuck his head into her cubicle once only. "How's everything going?" he asked. "No more news? Breakthroughs? Clicks?" Not at all, she assured him; things were just as boring as he wanted them to be.

That wasn't fair, she knew. Not fair, but true. There had been nothing of substance, nothing *interesting*. That translated to no *progress*. And so Finley rolled with gratitude into the weekend; at least, she'd be able to start solidifying her preparations for Thanksgiving.

She visited McGarrity's on Friday night, briefly; turned aside three obvious attempts to pick her up, and one ambiguous one; but mostly, spent entirely too much time brooding about Spencer, and the last time she'd seen him here. . . .

The last time she and Spencer had been together was a sultry evening late this past August. Waiting for the heat to break, New Brunswick hovered, sweaty and panting, on the brink of the start of the Rutgers academic year. The air was thick with humidity, with the exhaust of automobiles headed for the shore, with expectation and anxiety.

Spencer was preoccupied by work, no doubt about it. He had plans "in the pipeline," he said, for two new Cinema Europas, one in Hoboken and one in Morristown, but still hadn't received word on the grant applications. He didn't know if he'd have sufficient cash reserves without the grants to do more than simply purchase the buildings; no money for renovation. And his nervousness was beginning to show, made manifest in an irritability and grumbling that was starting to bug Finley and make her more than a bit prickly, as well.

Booker T and the MGs' "Time Is Tight" was pulsating insistently from McGarrity's jukebox when Spencer had suddenly pushed his barstool back from the bar. "Let's go."

She had glanced down at her mug, still containing a couple inches of Bass. "You mind if I finish my beer first?"

"Oh, yeah, sorry," his words had apologized, but his voice and posture were unrepentant, slouching with impatience. He signaled Colleen for the tab and lurched awkwardly forward to grab it off the bar—knocking Finley's mug onto the floor and spraying a waitress with beer. "Jeez, sorry," he repeated, not to Finley but to the waitress this time, jumping up to dab at the woman with a napkin. Then he'd returned to his position at Finley's left, not sitting on the barstool but merely standing there. "Sorry about the beer," he said.

Finley shrugged. "Guess I really didn't want it anyhow," she said.

He had a film to preview tonight and they sat as always in adjacent seats in his screening room, his mood as always lightening perceptibly the moment he sat down there. The lights went down, the sound and subtitles came up as always. Not uncommonly, the film was French, what Spencer called *"nouveau noir"*: smoky jazz on the soundtrack, jaded characters, languorous story line and cloudy ethical premise. But something was different. . . .

It was Spencer himself. His hand was draped not over the arm of the seat between them, but across the back of Finley's seat and down over her right shoulder, his fingers playing first with the ends of her hair and then with the neck and shoulders beneath it, tracing along the surface of her skin as though he were a connoisseur of fine china admiring a new piece's delicacy. Finley felt her head tilting forward, her eyes closing, the sense of the movie's plot slipping away from her as she warmed to his touch. Her own arm slipped off the armrest and draped as though casually across his thigh. He shifted in the seat slightly, and then his hand slipped around and inside her shirt, its buttoned front popping open as softly and surely as if she had willed it.

The armrest was becoming a problem as they twisted toward each other, and Spencer removed his right hand for a moment from whatever it was doing with the back of her head and, the hand dropping lightly to the armrest, *lifted* it out of the way, she had no idea that was even possible, not a feature of the screening room he'd ever demonstrated before but she wasn't really thinking about that right then, just turning further and then lying down across him, her shirt fully open now and Spencer leaning down over her and somehow she became oblivious to the knowledge that never before had he interrupted a preview for such activity— oblivious, now that his mouth was pressed so tightly against hers and his hands everywhere and drawing forth pulses of longing from every square inch of her, oblivious to the uncommonness of it all, even as they moved from the seats onto the carpeted floor and Spencer suddenly rolled onto his back and Finley, for once the clumsy one, had flopped over him and rammed her teeth against one of the steel legs of the seating section, oh Jesus that *hurt,* stars winking suddenly but then she wasn't aware even of the stars any longer but only of Spencer's form beneath and within her as she rose and descended over him, the light from the projector flashing across her face and then off, light and then dark, and then Spencer groaned and Finley herself was overcome and the oblivion washed over her. . . .

She didn't know how long she dozed. Spencer himself was still unconscious, breath being sucked noisily in through mouth and nose simultaneously. She'd chipped a tooth, damn it, but she couldn't be mad at Spencer, sweet innocent clumsy and asleep as he was. She reached for his face with a fingertip, traced the outline of the bridge of his nose and down along his chin. In the rear of the screening room the forgotten reel of film suddenly ran out and the room was cast in a harsh white glare, thwik-thwik-thwik went the film over and over in synch with Finley's own heartbeat, and she leaned forward to kiss Spencer on the cheek, into consciousness, and that was when she saw, on the carpet under the row of seats, gleaming in the white light like a needle of ice, the earring.

Not her taste at all. When Finley wore earrings at all, which was not often, she favored the small and discreet rather than large and exotic, tiny pearls for formal occasions or silver beads for casual, wanting to attract no more attention to her ears than necessary. But this one was too flashy, like a huge sliver of crystal dropped from a candelabra. Gaudy. Not hers.

She couldn't bring herself to see Spencer again after that. He seemed, not surprisingly, awkward and confused—had he hurt her?—but she couldn't even talk about it. Then there'd been just that one last phone call, and that was that. . . .

Now, this Friday night, she downed the last of her beer, said good night, and finally slouched her way out and back to the apartment. To bed, and a different and chillier sort of oblivion.

Saturday "Breakfast with the Beatles": waking up to the old-timey saga of one Rocky Raccoon, who had come to shoot off the legs of his rival. . . .

She called her sister-in-law Nancy, the soft-shoe ch-ch-*cha* of "Rocky Raccoon" still skipping through her head. Terri answered the phone; no, Aunt Finley certainly did *not* want to talk to Daddy, was Mommy home?

Warren, Nancy, and Terri (Finley and Nancy agreed) would arrive Wednesday night. Nancy would bring a dessert, Warren would pick up some wine, and Terri (Nancy reported) would come prepared with a surprise for Stupid. And "of course," Nancy had insisted over Finley's nearly-nagging objection about Nancy's four-month pregnancy, "I will of course give you a hand in the kitchen on Thursday itself." But Finley didn't really want to, ha ha, belabor the issue; in truth, she would welcome her sister-in-law's help. Among her other worries about this whole deal, Finley had never cooked a turkey before; while one or two neurons in her brain knew, feebly and without a lot of conviction, that there was a little knob or button or something implanted in the turkey, she could never remember if the turkey was nominally "done" when this little thingum went in, or out, or—gulp—was it first in and then out, too?

Not just turkey preparation but the whole ritual of Thanksgiving was a mystery to Flokati, as he'd confided in the message she received when she checked FORENSIC a little later in the morning:

> . . . Finley I do not understand American Thanksgiving, Christmas OK yes, I see, Japan has birthday of Emperor like that, big sale in store like USA yes. But Thanksgiving weird, is that word? Understand concept of gratefulness etc. but why so close to Christmas, must make whole time so crazy! How is possible to be in grateful mind then I do not understand, like fiction to me.

Well, yes. Thanksgiving did seem a little nuts, when he put it that way. (She wondered, in her reply, if he'd ever considered the similarities between carvery and an autopsy.) Why, just the *thought* of entertaining three family members for one or two nights already had her nervous system aflutter with potential complications, fears of food smoking or raw, of hot beverages spilled or gone lukewarm, of schedules and habits disrupted, and yes, almost certainly, of fights with Warren—and now here she was, of all things, at the bowling alley on Saturday night with Monica and her husband Bob, about to complicate her holiday plans even further.

"Finley," Monica had said on the phone that afternoon, "you have any plans for tonight?"

"Weeelll, nothing really specific, no. I thought maybe I'd read."

" 'Read,' you say. That's *it?* Okay, listen, Bob said to tell you we'll pick you up at about seven-thirty. You ever bowl before?"

"Uh, Monica, sure I've bowled before but—"

"Now, Finley," she said, and Finley could almost see Monica's features settling into Lecture Mode. This would be, let's see, Lecture Number Forty-Three: You Don't Enjoy Life Enough. Yep, that was it: "You think entirely too much about work, my dear," Monica said, "and spend entirely too much time by yourself. It's not healthy. You're human, and humans are made to spend time with other humans even when they're not at work. Bob and I agree on this"—as if that made it so—"and it's something we want to do for you. We'll be there at seven-thirty."

It was about as dishwater-dull an evening as Finley feared it would be. She went gamely along with it anyhow, pretending to absorb with interest their pointers about foot placement and speed of approach and how lofting the ball played havoc not merely with the wooden construction of the lane, but with the efficacy of the bowler's delivery as well. While Monica took her turn, Bob doodled for Finley on the back of the score sheet, in excruciating engineer's detail (including graphs, God help her, of slippery quantities like angular momentum and coefficients of friction), the effects on one's game of varying the angles and twists of one's body. Finley didn't know how much all this might affect one's game, but its effect on her mind was sheer *paralysis.*

And, ye gods, how embarrassing: she'd practically nodded off in the diner where they'd stopped for coffee and tea afterward. Monica and Bob were yet abuzz with excitement about their "performances" that night, congratulating each other effusively, lingering lovingly over such true-believers' moments of triumph as "that terrific seven-ten in the fourth frame of the second game" and so on, and so on, and so on. . . . But then Monica noticed Finley's drooping eyelids and slackened jaw, and reached across the table to touch Finley's wrist.

"I'm so sorry, Finley! Here we are chattering away like bowl-a-rama robots and you must be tired as hell—Bob, take care of the check why don't you, Finley and I are going out to the car."

Monica and Bob had good hearts. Waiting while Monica unlocked the car door, Finley suddenly asked, "What are you guys doing for Thanksgiving?"

"Um, don't know, we haven't talked about it. Probably just eating alone like usual, why? You want to come over?"

"Well, no," Finley said as she plopped into the back seat. "My brother and his wife and my niece are coming over to my place this year—you want to come over, too?"

"Hey, that's sweet of you—hey, Bob," she called to her husband, just now seat-belting himself into place behind the steering wheel, "Finley just asked us to come over her place on Thanksgiving, sure, Finley, we'd *love* to!"

So it was set. "Crazy!" Flokati had said; ha! He didn't know the half of it.

In the back seat of the car, once again drowsing, sitting beside the two bowling-ball totes jostling quietly up against each other like necking Martian sweethearts, Finley came abruptly back to life. It was Monica's sudden question that did it; she turned in the front seat and asked, "So what can we bring with us on Thursday? How about if I make some dessert?"

Fortunately, it was too dark in the car for her to see Finley straighten and shudder.

She was remembering a "bake-off" at the Center last Christmas, for which everyone on the floor, in rotation, had contributed a cake or a pie or cookies for a modest entry fee, which they'd collected and donated to a local charity. Monica's contribution was a "Mediterranean coffee cake," whatever that was. When Finley had finished rinsing her mouth out with lots of tea and water, stuffed two sticks of spearmint gum into her mouth, camouflaged the remainder of her piece of this concoction by cramming it into an empty floppy-disk box, and then finally unobtrusively slipped it into a wastebasket, she quizzed Monica, apparently out of innocent admiration, about its manufacture.

Monica rattled off a dozen or so ingredients, none of them sounding particularly lethal. "But I did make one substitution," she confided, and leaned forward, lowering her voice to a loud whisper in order to Impart The Secret. "It didn't really sound Mediterranean enough to me, even with all the dates and figs and almonds and so on. It sounded like a kid's fantasy of what the Mediterranean would taste like, you know? So I replaced the vegetable oil in the recipe with olive oil. You like it?"

"Oh *yeah*!" Finley had averred, gagging a little despite her best efforts.

Monica had not won the bake-off. And there was no way Finley would let someone with such culinary instincts grace her Thanksgiving table with a dessert. Somebody brings a dessert, everybody else is obligated to try it. So, "No, really," she insisted now, "everything's already accounted for."

"Wine—how about wine?"

"No, *honest,* Monica, it'll make my brother nuts if there are two of anything. He's probably already gone out and gotten the stuff they're bringing, and it's probably already in a gigantic paper bag in his fridge with a big sign on it saying, 'FOR FINLEY.' Really, don't worry about it. I'll just be glad to have you guys there, you and Bob. It's my first year ever to make Thanksgiving dinner for other people."

So at any rate she was fully awake when they dropped her off and she went inside. "Chirp!" exclaimed Stupid from beneath the Garfield cover when he recognized Finley's creak on the floorboards. "Chirp yourself!" she said, "Go back to sleep!" "Sleep?" he answered.

One more cup of tea before hitting the hay tonight, she thought. She turned on the burner and, while the water was heating, turned on the computer as well, and checked her mail. She didn't expect to find much, if anything—most people went out on Saturday nights, had plans with *real* people which hardly included logging into a BBS to drop mail. And she was right; only a couple of messages had come in tonight, both on ABLE. There was a message from the "A" Earwig, Andrea:

> . . . finley, i haven't checked the messages on the board for a few days now. do you recall whether charlotte was going to be around for thanksgiving? did she say, do you know? thanks! hope you're doin' okay!

Andrea, unlike the other Earwigs, was one hundred percent deaf; she accessed ABLE not via PC, but with a "Telecommunications Device for the Deaf" (TDD) terminal which lacked the ability to transmit capital letters. She and Charlotte lived near each other, in the Seattle area, and communicated almost exclusively via ABLE. But neither of them logged in as often as Finley, and they often did this sort of touching base through her. Her reply to Andrea said:

> . . . Hi, Andy! Nope, haven't heard a peep out of Charlotte since she left her last "punk hearing aid" message. If I see

her around here I'll tell her you were looking for her. Take care of yourself.

And there was also a message on ABLE from Jane:

. . . Hello, Finley dear! Your job sounds ever so much more interesting than my own humble dreary occupation. Typing, filing, scheduling meetings, it's a wonder I don't expire from sheer boredom. Your job, by contrast, sounds positively exciting—hunting killers down, capturing them. Don't tell me you use a gun, even? <smile>

And have you made your plans for Thanksgiving yet? I will be doing as I usually do, eating in with some other girls from the office. How about you? Spending it with family, I hope? Take care. Love you, dear. <jane>

Boy, have I ever made plans for Thanksgiving! Finley thought. And she laid it out in her reply to Jane, all of it, certain of Jane's sympathy: how her friends Monica and Bob would be coming over for the day; how company would be arriving Wednesday; she wasn't sure if they'd be staying Thursday night as well, but they'd definitely be gone by Friday afternoon. By then, she would definitely be alone, blissfully alone, thank God. And, no doubt, thoroughly exhausted. Last, she added a postscript:

P.S. Do I come across like someone who'd pack a gun, or even know how to use one? No, dear Jane, of course I don't use a gun!

She finished her tea then and went to bed. Jane, she thought as she drifted off. Jane. Maybe the upcoming holiday weekend would be a good time to meet Jane.

Chapter Seventeen

No doubt, it was just a coincidence—just the normal rotation, say, of the same one thousand oldies in a year—that on Monday, all the music that Finley heard while getting ready for work seemed a little *off,* like an unannounced special program on the theme, perhaps, of undanceability. All of them middle-grade, off-tempo songs: "Spinning Wheel," "Rocketman," "Signs." Like that.

But coincidence or not, it was a cycle of songs that fit Finley's out-of-kilter mood as she faced her onerous task at work this morning.

Gus had called her at home last night. "Just got in from Atlanta," he'd said. "I've got your goodies, Finley. Interesting stuff!"

"Umm, I'll bet. Anything from that 'Liz' person?"

"Oh, *yeah.* Wait till you see it! I'll bring it into your office tomorrow morning, you won't have to wait for the express-mail delivery. For now, though, I'm gonna take some time to acquaint myself with the wife again."

So there was, after all, something for her to do here this morning; the Atlanta people and Gus had managed to get it to her before Wednesday. But Finley's feelings about this task were still muddy with ambivalence.

She had always trusted what the other party, whoever it was, told her over this on-line channel. What was the point of her job otherwise? Oh, sure, you had to cross-check facts, corroborate them with other sources, you couldn't build a real investigation without doing that; but what, really, would be the point in someone's lying? That trust, of course, was already draining away, leaking out through the hole punched in her innocence by the killer's dialogue with Redman. Worse, she now had to confront a loss of trust in some of the assumptions underlying the whole medium, the very context in which on-line conversations took place: that when you and the other party agreed to keep something private, it would *stay* private; that if someone "listened in" to a dialogue between two others, that person would make his or her presence known; that on-line confidentiality was as real and substantial (and as invisible and easy to take for granted) as the air shared by two people sitting in the same room. Finley was beginning to appreciate just how tenuous and volatile that trust really was, ready to evaporate at the slightest spark of insincerity or meanness by either person—or, as in the present case, even at a hint of unseen intervention by a "friendly" outsider: she herself was party to its violation. This whole court-order procedure for obtaining BBS transcripts made her feel as though she were wiretapping a friend's phone; listening, with a glass tumbler, at a friend's hotel-room door; prying a friend's diary open with a wrecking bar. . . .

The transcripts of Tracy's on-line mail, which Gus dropped off on his way to New York (to "light a fire under our friends there," he said with a wink), made up a *huge* pile of paper. Must be at least three hundred pages here, nearly all of it, she was certain, irrelevant. But she had to read it and analyze it, every bit of it, nonetheless, still fishing for The Click. . . . She sighed, pushed aside everything but the heap of printouts and a notebook, and started to plow through the pile.

She placed each board's messages into a separate stack. The technical BBS had only a couple of pages, inconsequential stuff about monitors and cables. More significantly, no "Liz" was recorded there.

Tracy's STACKS messages were more voluminous, running to perhaps fifty pages. From her own experience on STACKS, Finley was pretty sure there were no users there named "Liz," but she checked anyway. There was a guy named "John Alden" who had exchanged a few messages with Tracy a while back, then dropped out—hmm, hadn't Finley herself corresponded with him . . . ? And of course there were Finley's own messages to and from Tracy reproduced here. Eerie, it was, to see their messages in this context; neither she nor Tracy, of course, had known what was

coming, and their idle banter now came across to Finley as exceedingly shallow, like someone telling elephant jokes at a wake.
. . . But no, there was no Liz on STACKS, so she moved on, with some misgivings about the quantity of messages, to The Party Zone.

It had far more messages from and to Tracy than the other two boards combined. (No surprise there; if Finley had to venture a guess, she might say that Tracy's whole life had been lived in a party zone.) The messages were organized chronologically, with Tracy's oldest correspondence (going back more than a year) on top and the most recent—her last—on the bottom. This was probably the easiest organization for a sysop who had to produce a printout, she knew—it was just the order in which the backups took place; but it was damnably hard to trace through. The complication was that Tracy had had lots of correspondents, her conversations with them weaving back and forth, in chronological order, overlapping one another in a crazy, incomprehensible warp-and-woof of subject matter and in-jokes. A message to one friend on a Thursday, for example, might not be answered until the following Monday, and dozens of messages to and from dozens of other friends on a dozen other topics might intervene within that four-day window of time. It was as if someone had shuffled together the pages of eight or ten or twelve or fifty different books, then went through and inserted random newspaper and magazine clippings as well. Impossible to follow in raw form, and Finley was stumped at first at how to straighten it all out.

Simplify, she thought to herself. *Simplify.* First, she was really looking for someone named "Liz"; while she couldn't altogether ignore the other messages, it was probably only Liz she needed to go after at first. She picked a yellow highlight marker out of the desk drawer.

Downward through the stack she shuffled, scanning for a "Liz" in the message headers. There it was, all right, a "Liz Enright," first cropping up about four months ago, in midsummer. Finley stuck an index card into the heap at this point, its edge protruding like a thumb tab. Then she fast-forwarded through the rest of the printout, highlighting in yellow all the message headers with Liz Enright's name in either the "To:" or the "From:" portions. Finally, she went back, opened up the stack to that first message, and began methodically to read, one at a time, only the messages with highlighted headers. And there it was, yes, the development of the on-line relationship between Tracy and Liz laid bare, like a complex connect-the-dots picture against a cross-hatched background.

Liz had at first stepped only tentatively into The Party Zone (which its users all referred to, in shorthand, as "TPZ"). She (if, Finley reminded herself, Liz *was* a "she") spoke of being new to Atlanta, so she didn't know about all the favorite hangouts familiar to all the other TPZ denizens. And she was almost standoffish, shy of meeting anyone or of giving out her phone number. All of this, Finley could see from her special perspective, functioned as a convenient cover; it covered for what would otherwise seem to be Liz's gaffes from not knowing the local "singles jargon," and at the same time insulated her from meeting anyone except on her own terms.

But although standoffish, Liz was not unsure of herself. She had a dry, *dry* sense of humor, wildly inventive but eschewing all exclamation points or other hints that she might find her own jokes as outrageous as someone else might. Tracy, always on the alert for a complement to her own extravagantly effervescent personality, had been attracted to Liz's deadpan almost at once:

> . . . Hey, Liz! Welcome to TPZ! Tell us about yourself! You working? Where at? You grow up here in the Chicago of the South? (Don't worry, we are STRICTLY FORBIDDEN to ask one another our astrological signs!) Welcome aboard again!
>
> Tracy

> . . . Hello yourself, Tracy, and thanks for the enthusiastic welcome. (You shook my hand so enthusiastically that I damn near dropped my plateful of canapes.)
>
> Moi? Not much interesting to tell, I'm afraid. Lived in NYC all my life up till now. Now I've come to Atlanta to become civilized. (It's true, you know. Think how much more civilized "King Kong," for example, would be if it took place here, with Confederate cavalrymen charging all around and

poking cutlasses at his hairy ankles instead of biplanes shooting him in the nose and eyes.)
Liz

. . . Ha ha ha! FUNNY message, Liz, we need all the laughs we can get around TPZ—keeps us from crying in our beer too much!
Tracy

and so on. Although Liz's deft irony had at first attracted admiring attention from both men and women, she'd not for some time really gotten "close" to anyone. She did not, after all (and understandably), volunteer much information about herself. Nonetheless, she treated the problems of others with apparent sympathy and seriousness. And finally, about six weeks after first "meeting" Liz on-line, Tracy had dropped down into private mode, disillusioned, as she occasionally was, by the vagaries of her private life:

. . . Liz, life just really SUCKS sometimes. I get so depressed, you know? I can't tell what's important or why I bother. I met a guy a few weeks ago, well, actually I met him at work about six months ago but we just went out a few weeks ago. Anyhow I thought things were looking pretty good. He's good-looking, tan surfer-type if you like that, and drives this great car, I think it's Italian. Last night we went to a dinner theater thing, you know, where you eat at a table and watch like a real Broadway show? And then we went back to my place afterward, painted the boudoir red, ha ha. And then he suddenly jumps out of bed like three hours later. Says he has to get home to his WIFE. His WIFE, can you believe it?!? So why do I even bother?

. . . You sound, Tracy, like you could use some cheering up. I've been scorched sometimes by guys, too—the wife thing, never, though, thank God for small miracles. I think there's an undiscovered perverseness gene in the Y chromosome. Dominant in the male, like everything else. Unfortunately, as hard as it already is to meet guys there never seems to be a shortage of guys with carrot cake where their brains should be.

Interesting. Finley remembered Tracy's crying on *her* shoulder about that married guy, though not in these same exact words; she was a little surprised (and faintly, oddly annoyed) that Tracy had apparently gone crying down the street about him to at least one other friend, as well. But what struck her harder now about this message was the extent to which it resembled "Mary Ellen's" message to "Joanna" Redman. The killer had gone beyond merely plundering Tracy's image and persona; he had lifted even her exact words. No wonder he was so eager to erase the trail of messages. And it made sense, too, in light of what Monica and Ray had said at lunch on Friday—rather than try (and probably fail) to invent a realistic woman's voice of his own, he just replicated the voices of *real* women.

The whole series of Liz-Tracy messages evolved like this, innocently enough if, like Tracy, you didn't know what was really going on. Before long—within, in fact, no more than a week—Liz knew where Tracy lived, what her hours at work were, and what her weekend schedule typically was. . . . *Her weekend schedule.* Finley retrieved Gus's file on Tracy to see what time the coroner had estimated she died. Between seven and eight at night, it said. Sunday night. If, as they assumed, the killer was not from Atlanta but merely visiting, how had he known that Tracy would be at home at seven on a particular Sunday night?

Back, then, to the yellow-highlighted paper trail. Should be somewhere down here, down close to the end of the stack. . . . Yes, here:

> . . . Say, Tracy, I've got some time to kill on my hands this weekend. You interested in getting together for a drink one night? (We've probably put off meeting long enough, don't you think?)

The audacity. He must have burst out laughing to himself at that "time to kill" line. Probably explained why the rest of the message was so uncharacteristically straightforward, so un-Lizlike—he probably thought it was already too funny. Tracy's reply said:

. . . Sure, that'd be great! I've got plans Friday and Saturday; how do you feel about having a drink Sunday night? (Some people are strange about that, you know!)

Finley wanted to shout, *No, Tracy, no!* But it had already gone too far, especially for belated warnings, and the next (and final) exchange between Liz and Tracy sealed Tracy's fate:

. . . Sunday's all right for me. I'm going to be busy in the afternoon, but later on, say, 8:00 or 8:30 should be fine. That be all right? (We can have a drink and eat some carrot cake.)

. . . "Eat some carrot cake"—ha ha! Sure, 8–8:30's fine. I'll be out most of Sunday myself, but I should be home by around 6. Take me an hour or so to get showered and changed, check my E-mail. You can swing by here and pick me up, okay? I'm looking forward to meeting you!

. . . Will do. I'll get there between 8:00 and 8:30. (Oh, and I'm looking forward to meeting you, too.)

That was it.

Finley felt nauseous; Tracy had literally invited her death in the front door. Because there was no sign of a struggle, he'd obviously simply used the time to pin her down to her apartment, then arrived early. But late enough, Finley saw when she detoured over to the last page of the STACKS printout, her heart lurching unpleasantly in her chest, late enough to give Tracy time to send out that dippy last message, time-stamped, wrenchingly, 7:18 P.M.:

Good night, everybody!!!

"Yo! Finley! Lunch?" Monica was standing in the doorway of Finley's cube, and evidently had been standing there for some time, trying to break through the younger woman's concentration. Lunchtime? Already?

"Er, gee no, Monica, I can't take a break right now—"

"Listen, young lady. What did I just tell you the other day on the phone?"

Finley grinned, recalling Lecture Number Forty-Three. "Well, yeah, I know, but some days it's just impossible—tell you what. I'll walk down to the cafeteria with you, but I'm bringing lunch back here, understand?"

Monica chattered like a happy teenager all the way there, insisting that she still hadn't come down from Saturday night. "So much *fun,* wasn't it, Finley? We'd love to see you more often," that sort of thing. But Finley was attending to her friend with only half a mind. With the other, more active half, she was still worrying at something from Tracy's STACKS messages, some little fact clamoring to be noticed. . . .

But not until she sat down at her desk again and took her first forkful of tuna salad did she realize what it was. She pushed aside The Party Zone's voluminous transcript, and once again opened up the one for STACKS. Where was it . . . ? Here:

> To: Tracy
> From: John Alden
> Re: First Hello
> Message: Hi, Tracy. My name is John Alden (obviously),
> and I'm new to the STACKS BBS. I'm not a librarian myself,
> but my job does require me to keep a lot of complicated
> documents and stacks of books in some kind of order. Can
> you recommend some software to help me with this?
> Thanks!   By the way, I'm located in NYC. Whereabouts are
> you? And isn't this a great medium of communication? (Do
> you belong to any other boards besides STACKS?)
> John

Tracy's reply, like all her first messages to newcomers, was friendly and straightforward, and answered all of Alden's questions. She and Alden had exchanged a few more messages of no consequence in succeeding days until Alden, finally, had simply failed to respond to a message from Tracy. Gone.

But what was it about that first message . . . ? There was nothing explicit in it to arouse one's suspicions—it was simply a typical request for information, followed by a handful of social banalities of the sort that people on-line often exchanged. Still, there was an undercurrent, Finley thought—the ostensible reason for the message, the question about software, was a little too hurriedly dispensed with, the social banalities a little too much dwelt upon. . . .

On an impulse. she flipped through the TPZ messages again, to the first one from "Liz Enright," and checked its date and time stamp. There it was, on paper and in her head, a Click: John Alden had dropped off STACKS the day before Liz Enright materialized on The Party Zone. Coincidence, maybe?

She turned to her PC and logged into STACKS. There were a couple messages waiting for her, but she'd ignore them for now—for now she was after something in particular:

profile john alden

The system paused for a moment—it was always sluggish now, when STACKS subscribers from all along the East Coast were on their lunch breaks—and then presented her with an enigma:

Name: John Alden
Address: {EMPTY}
Phone: {EMPTY}

and so on, through all the rest of the fields in the profile. "{EMPTY}"? How did he get around the requirement to enter all this stuff when he first logged in?

Then she laughed out loud in response to a second Click, and experimented with a change to her own user profile: she simply altered her real address to read, "{EMPTY}." He hadn't gotten around the requirement at all, simply keyed in a value that made it look that way!

She changed her address back to its true value, then logged out and immediately logged back in, this time to The Party Zone, for one last check. She'd never signed in here before, of course, so she had to go through the whole tedious registration procedure. And the commands here on this BBS were different from the ones she was used to—there didn't even seem to be a "help" command, which she'd thought was nearly universal—so it took her several tries to learn that the command to display a user's profile here was "userinfo." But she knew this mild nuisance was justified when she finally saw Liz Enright's profile:

```
Name:      Liz Enright
Address:   {EMPTY}
```

and so on. No doubt about it now: "John Alden," whoever he might be for real, was "Liz Enright."

"We having fun yet?" asked Gus, grinning, when he peeked into Finley's cube toward the end of the day.

"Gus!" Finley exclaimed, looking up, bleary-eyed, from the heap of disheveled, marked-up printouts on her desk. "I wasn't expecting you till tomorrow, at least!" She looked, nervously, for another stack of paper in his hands; but he bent over, placed some sort of package on the floor outside her cubicle, and walked in empty-handed. He sat down.

"Yeah, well, when I got there they were just tying the stuff up to ship it here. I told 'em I'd bring it over to you, high-priced courier, that's me. How about your day? You come across anything good?"

Wishing, anxiously, that she could peer with X-ray vision through her cubicle wall, Finley first explained what she'd learned of "Liz's" friendship with Tracy. Gus was most interested in the killer's having adopted Tracy's language for "Mary Ellen's" messages to Redman.

"So then," he said, "if we work backward from that—"

"Right. If he's consistent, we'll probably find that his 'Liz' characterization sounds like Dorothy Taylor, the second New York victim. Probably even picked up that carrot-cake line from her, same way that he used Tracy's 'painted the boudoir red.' And his voice when on-line to *her,* Taylor—what was the name on the back of the picture he sent her?"

Gus flipped back through his notepad. "Uh, Renee? Yeah, here it is, Renee Jackson."

"Uh-huh, his 'Renee' messages will have the same voice as Aggie Bristol, the first New York woman."

"What about his messages to her, then, the first one?"

"I was afraid you'd ask that. I don't know. His own voice, maybe,

but it will take a lot of reading between the lines. For a salami,"
she added, giggling.

"A salami?"

"Never mind, Gus, in-joke. But I've also got some *real*
news. . . ." She told him then about the nearly simultaneous dis-
appearance of "John Alden" from STACKS and the appearance of
"Liz Enright" on The Party Zone. After a little bit of confused
head-scratching, he finally understood the significance of the
"{EMPTY}" profiles. But he latched without hesitation, indeed almost with ferocity, onto her casual remark that Alden had corresponded with Finley herself.

"Jesus H. Christ, Finley—you think you *know* this guy? Or
worse, that he knows *you*?"

Well, yes, now that he put it that way it was a little alarming; she
hadn't really thought of it like that before, so caught up was she in
the pursuit. But she sought to reassure him; "Don't worry, Gus,
I'll be on the lookout for him," she said. "*Waiting* for him, in fact.
And for all we know he may have corresponded with dozens of
women here on STACKS alone—"

Gus sighed wearily. "Guess we gotta get transcripts of all this
Alden guy's messages on STACKS, then? Your sysop friend is
gonna throw a fit!"

Giggling in agreement—Frank would never forgive her—she
said, "Good point. Let's give him a day or two to recover from the
last court order. Let me check to see first if John Alden or somebody like him shows up in the New York City transcripts." She
cleared her throat ostentatiously and raised her eyebrows. "Hint,
hint."

"The—oh, yeah, thanks for reminding me, almost forgot—" He
stood up and walked to the doorway, bent over and with a grunt
picked up whatever he'd left on the floor out there. Finley's eyes
almost started from her head when she got a real look at what
turned out to be not one but two enormous bundles, wrapped in
brown paper; there must be, ye gods, there must be two thousand
pages of text there . . . !

He dropped the packages onto her desk, *bang* and *bang*. He
smiled as though apologetically and said, "The, uh, the New York
folks seem to have had a little more on-line activity than Miss
Williams did."

But there was no apology in his eyes, Finley noted. "You are a sadist," she said.

"I can't help it! You know how us guys are, carrot cake for brains!"

He escaped, barely, before Finley could brain him with the yellow highlight marker.

On his way out of the building, Gus stopped at Morris's office.

"She *knows* the guy?" Morris exclaimed.

"Well, not quite who he is yet, but don't worry, I don't think it will take her long, you got a sharp young lady working for you there, Morris."

Morris replied a little ruefully, thinking back to last week, "Oh, she's sharp all right. Sometimes a little too sharp maybe. But you say she's actually exchanged messages with him? Holy moly. . . ."

After Gus had shuffled out of the office, Morris turned to his PC. He flipped through the on-line CIAC internal phone directory for a minute before finding the number he wanted; he'd never had to use it before.

"Internal security?" he said into the receiver. "I've got an employee I'd like to have covered . . . no no, not really shadowed—more like protected. . . ."

Chapter Eighteen

"Alden," Finley was thinking as she walked out of the building after work, and it was "Alden" she was thinking as she stepped onto the bus. "Alden" was at the forefront of her mind as she plopped her head against the back of the bus seat, as she stood to leave the bus by her apartment, as she ducked across the street to Falco's coffee shop, as she unlocked the door to her apartment and stepped back outside, briefly, to check her mail. Alden. Who was Alden? And why *Alden,* of all possible aliases? Need there, indeed, *be* a reason . . . ?

"Here, Stupid; stupid bird, stupid bird," she chanted as she replaced the water in the parakeet's cage. "Eh?" he asked petulantly, in jealousy almost, as though he knew she wasn't really thinking of *him.* "Eh?"

John Alden. That name meant something to her, but she couldn't remember what it was, not until she was seated at McGarrity's an hour later, moodily digging with a thumbnail at the label on her bottle of Bass. Not too crowded tonight. Of course, it was still early in the evening. . . . Even the jukebox was subdued and moody and neurotic, muttering rhythmically and obsessively of too many teardrops. . . .

She called to the bartender, down at the other end of the bar. "Hey, Colleen! The name 'John Alden' mean anything to you?" Sticking her tongue meditatively into her cheek, Colleen shut her eyes in a grand show of thinking hard. But the elderly man sitting on Finley's left—a professor, maybe?—looked up from a book of crossword puzzles and answered first.

" 'The Courtship of Miles Standish,' " he said. "Henry Wadsworth Longfellow. 1858."

Shoot, Finley, you dummy, of course that's where you knew the name from. "Hey, thanks, you just saved me a sleepless night!" The man smiled shyly, blushed a little, and turned back to his puzzles.

A perfect alias. John Alden, the guy whom Miles Standish designated to stand in for him in dealing with a favored woman. So that was one part of the mystery solved; that was the original Alden. But who was the one she sought now, the John Alden of Tracy's STACKS transcript?

Outside, the air was light and dry, the air more of early September than of near-Thanksgiving. The breeze through her hair rattled in her hearing aids as she walked home the long way. Who was *this* John Alden? What would he be like, not on-line necessarily, but *really* . . . ?

He would be someone who—well, someone who had certainly had some sort of bad experience with women in the past. With, with *a* woman, maybe. Someone with an ax to grind. He attacked only women, after all, Redman obviously having been a surprise and a mistake for him. . . . Judging from the boards he was drawn to, he would know something of food, and something of wine. . . . And, of course, he knew something of each of his victims: where to find each one. Every day.

She passed beneath the Amtrak railroad tracks, walking aimlessly now, and a train roared by overhead. She thought of another November night, a November night of last year, then as now walking the long way around from McGarrity's to her apartment. Rain that night, a chilly rain. Spencer and Finley standing right here, in this underpass, under a screaming commuter train. "What?" Finley had yelled. "I can't hear you!" "I said I *love* you!" he had yelled back to her just as the train left the bridge, leaving his voice too loud and echoing, "*love* you *love* you!" She had laughed and, feigning annoyance, he'd stifled her laughter with a kiss, long, and hard, and deep, nearly having to stoop as always to reach her mouth with his, tilting her head back, as the late-night taxicabs and buses splashed past, his hands and fingers tracing her shoulder blades through the layers of clothing. . . .

The sidewalk here on the other side of the railroad station

climbed a short steep hill, taking Finley with it. She was panting a little when she reached the hilltop, but she walked on, past taverns and a record store and an ice cream parlor and a handful of neighborhood restaurants, past seemingly hundreds of Rutgers undergraduates taking advantage of the Indian summer night to celebrate the onset of their first real midsemester break, the Thanksgiving calm before December's storm of final exams. A raucous, crazy, loonlike laugh rippled through the air from somewhere on the other side of the street; a young couple stood at a corner, engaged in a quiet, earnest but nonetheless unmistakable argument, and Finley walked on, her head still full, damn it, of Spencer.

How could she not have seen through Spencer? And now, having seen through him, how could she not just flush him out of her mind? "Real" life, *ha*. Was it more predictable than on-line, less hurtful, its denizens saner, soberer, cleaner, kinder? No. In real life you could look deep into someone's eyes, you could feel the touch of his fingertips against your goosebumped flesh—that was true. But when a flesh-and-blood love leaves, in fact or effect, he takes all that away with him, and the hollowness left behind in its place was bitterer and more profound than any that you would ever experience on-line. And not know anyone on-line? *Ha,* again —as if you ever really got to know anyone *off-line,* for that matter . . . !

On the far side of the street along which she was now walking, set back a short distance from the sidewalk, the Rutgers library glowed, glowed as if with the heat and light of all the information shelved inside. A handful of dry leaves skittered across the street, brushing up against and then crushed beneath the tires of a tiny Honda whose driver was trying, over and over and over and without notable success, to parallel-park in a space too small for him. Back and forth. . . .

And then in the real world, too, that was where you could find people like her brother, people you could not ignore even if you wanted to, people capable of making you crazy with their too-persistent *presence.* It wasn't like on-line, where you could just ignore someone pestering you and they'd eventually go away; in the "real" world relationships carried not only pain, but obligation. On-line friends would tell you of family emergencies and you could simply murmur sympathy in messages posted at your own convenience; you didn't need actually to buy them a drink, offer them a shoulder and the time to cry on it, drive them to the hospital on demand, see the pain in their own eyes let alone respond to it. . . .

No. This wouldn't do, this woolgathering and self-absorption. Whatever else the real world might be, it was *the* world: the world where a niece laughed at your stupid parakeet as well as the world where a brother condescended to your every word; the world where trains screamed by overhead and rocked you gently to sleep; the very world, the very *context* in which the off-line world existed. You couldn't escape it, shut it on and off at whim, and so you had to come to terms with it.

And worse, while she plucked like a self-conscious teenager at these little philosophical dust-kittens, somewhere out there in the darkness was a person, a force, who lived at the very edge which separated the two worlds, one foot planted squarely in each life, in the on-line and the off-, someone who threatened the real lives of real people. Someone whom she, Finley, had the best and perhaps only chance of finding and rooting out. . . .

Who was "John Alden"?

Back inside her apartment now, she turned on the burner for tea, and then the computer. She didn't know of course if *any* of her present regular correspondents were "John Alden." He might not have singled her out, after all, not yet anyhow. . . .

But before checking her boards she wanted to check out the correspondence that she was certain she'd had with this guy, this Alden. Searching through her back-up files . . . *here.* A message dated about a little over three months ago, on one of her technical-resource BBSs:

> To: Finley
> From: John Alden
> Re: Comm software
> Message: Hi, Finley. I see you know your way around bulletin boards quite a bit, and I have a question for you. I use BoardWalk, like everybody else almost, but it's an older version (version 1.5). Do you think I should upgrade to a later one?

> We haven't exchanged messages before. I'm still pretty
> new at this BBS stuff. What other boards do you visit regu-
> larly besides this one? I'm still amazed you know at how
> many people use these things, and how many different
> places they come from. I live in Kansas. How about you?

Kansas? Well, that was a new touch. But probably just an attempt
to vary the messages so they weren't all identical. Nonetheless
the format was the same—"business" question asked and dispensed with; social question broached and lingered over. Almost
too casual. But what had she told him in reply?

She checked her answer to this message. She'd answered the
BoardWalk question for him (yes, she counseled: upgrade). She'd
told him about STACKS, FORENSIC, and ABLE. And then, finally:

> . . . and I live in New Jersey. Not as bad as you might
> think, though!

That was it. Alden and she had exchanged a handful of other
messages over the next couple days, none significant, and then
the conversation had simply come to a halt—at least, she reminded herself, the conversation with him *as* Alden. So once again
she had to confront the question: if one of her regular correspondents fit the killer's profile as she understood it, which would
it be . . . ?

Sipping at her tea, she logged in to ABLE. A message there
from Jane, left late last night, telling Finley that she wouldn't be
on-line much this week but not to worry about her. Finley smiled;
she really did love Jane. It certainly wasn't necessary, she told
Jane in the reply, that her friend account for *all* her movements.
She apologized for the paranoid tone of her messages last week
and, the message posted, logged out of ABLE and into FOREN-
SIC. Nothing for her there, either.

But on STACKS was something which at first amused her and
then froze her blood in place. Jon Little-Olden, abrasive as ever,
had taken to task a newcomer, a young woman, on a casual reference she'd made to wine-bottle corks, nothing at all to do with
libraries or information retrieval but leave it to Jon to get his back
up anyhow:

. . . Well, Miss, whoever you are, I don't know if the news has reached the frozen wastes up there in Wisconsin but even here in Kansas we know better than to insist that our wine be corked these days. Screw caps are the way to go. They hold a much better seal, for one thing, and don't lose so much ullage to evaporation. And screw caps never get moldy. You want to know the only real advantage of corks? Snob appeal.

Characteristically smug and condescending, and not the first time he'd upbraided someone about their Philistinism. "Ullage," indeed! And then of all the nerve—to accuse the *woman* of snobbery! But there was also another message from Jon, this one addressed to Finley herself. A *private* message:

. . . Finley, thanks for trying to calm me and Uri down the other day. I still don't think it was really my problem to start with but you're right about one thing, public messages are not a good place to yell at each other like that.
　I don't think we've ever really corresponded much. I know you're some kind of on-line researcher for the government, right? Where is this, anyway? I think you told somebody else New Jersey once, but where in NJ? I'd like to meet you sometime off-line I think. You're one of the nicest and most level-headed people on STACKS.

No. Could it be? *Alden;* Little-*Olden.* Kansas. A thing for wine. And another thing, a different kind of thing, for women. A *problem* with women.

And now he wanted to meet her. . . . Her pulse booming in her head, her eyes suddenly burning and face flushed, she placed her teacup back on the surface of her workstation, and the brief, rapid, oscillatory rattle of ceramic against wood brought Stupid, screaming and paranoid, from his sleep.

In the Shadows

4

Despite the unremitting sense of urgency which jabbed at his consciousness whenever he thought about Finley, he had still nonetheless been practical, patient, and careful this time, hadn't he? Yes, he had.

To begin with, it had not been a simple matter to find out where she lived. He couldn't risk asking her for her address; she might be on guard about so specific a question (even—and he smiled at the thought—from his on-line persona). Worse, he didn't even know if "Finley" was a first name or a last. It sounded to him like a surname, but he couldn't find a matching number or address in any of his on-line sources. Probably unlisted.

Oh, there were some Finleys. But none of them was *the* Finley, as he'd learned after renting a car last Friday and driving all around New Brunswick, street map and list of Finleys open on the seat beside him, checking every address to see if it matched the description she'd provided a couple of weeks ago. But no: one address didn't provide a view of the river; one lacked a coffee shop or supermarket or a tavern anywhere within a few blocks; several had no bus stop nearby; and so on.

Frustrated at first, he'd then been inspired by another idea, and pulled into a service station. He had accosted the sole attendant, whose hands were out of sight, rummaging about in the greasy underside of a car up on a lift. "Excuse me! I'm looking for the National Crime Bureau's computer center; can you tell me where I can find it?" He'd had to make up the name, of course. And the attendant, of course, had obligingly corrected him.

"'National Crime Bureau'?" the man had asked, wiping his hands on his overalls and reaching for a pack of cigarettes in the pocket. ". . . Don't know about that, no, but there *is* some kinda government computer center a few miles or so out of town. Don't remember the exact name but I don't think it's the National Crime Bureau—"

"Oh, that's all right," he'd interrupted. "I'm sure you're thinking of the right one. Can you tell me how to find it?"

"Sure," the mechanic had said, "easy. You just head up Route 27 here till you come to your third light," and so on. Even sketched out a little map for him on a piece of scrap cardboard, smudged with grimy fingerprints. And, indeed, as the mechanic had assured him, it had been easy.

When he'd found it—"National Crime Information and Analysis Center," the brick-and-aluminum sign announced—he had parked at the curb, a little ways back from the bus stop right by the computer center. A little before five o'clock, a woman whom he recognized as Finley, the same one he'd seen leaving his Master's Institute the other day, had ambled out the front door of the building, across the wide asphalt driveway, and stood at the bus stop sign. She had boarded the next bus that came along, never even looked back his way while she was standing there, biting at her lower lip, raising an index finger once to touch at her teeth. . . . ("Hope you're not working too hard, Finley, you seem so preoccupied!" he thought, smiling.)

He'd followed the bus for the trip back into the city of New Brunswick, until Finley had stepped off by an older apartment complex that, yes, did indeed overlook the Raritan River. Parked his car then, and watched her proceed up the steps of what was obviously a shared entryway for, hmm, it looked like four apartments maybe—but which one was hers? A second after he'd asked himself the question, Finley had reappeared, leaning out the doorway, and fished around in one of the mailboxes mounted on the exterior wall of the building. After she'd gone back indoors, he'd driven slowly by the apartment entrance and noted the number painted in large, sloppy letters on her mailbox. So it had been simple, after all!

He would have to wait still longer, of course. At that point, last Friday, he still hadn't known her Thanksgiving schedule yet, and now that he *did* know it he'd still have to wait. Furthermore, of course, he'd have to pay for his own car rental or train ticket this time, since his Master would have the credit card with him over Thanksgiving. But it would be all right; he could afford the expense, and he could afford to wait the extra few days.

Her mailbox, that was his favorite part. It had given him another idea, one that would lower her guard still further. He remembered cackling to himself, demonically, as he'd pulled the car back into the flow of traffic on the street outside her apartment. And he cackled to himself now, at the memory, as he shut off the computer and left his own apartment to arrange a car rental.

He caught a train out of Penn Station and into New Jersey early on Monday morning.

When the train emerged from the tunnel beneath the Hudson and began to cross over the marsh to the Newark station, the sun was just barely up over the horizon, its rays not only warming his right side through the window here but also, he knew, miles up ahead there in New Brunswick, pushing aside the curtain of night in the windows of Finley's apartment. Somewhere up there, Finley was just about to be brought out of bed by her two alarms. The clock radio would be playing, say, Motown this morning. And then she'd be at her PC a few minutes later, sipping tea, picking up among others his little late-night message—the one giving her some silly excuse why "he" would be off-line over the next couple of days.

He was probably overdoing it. But he couldn't risk Finley's making a connection between her confessional outburst of last week, and his sudden absence on-line. She seemed so smart on-line sometimes—he wished he knew really what sort of law-enforcement job she had, it wasn't by any means clear even now that he'd seen the building where she worked. But he wasn't at the point yet where he could ask outright, and now that he thought about it he didn't know if there'd be time to *get* to that point. . . .

This time—this time with Finley—was so different from the others. He couldn't shake his sense that he'd crossed over a line of some sort: he seemed to be doing it this time for a *reason*.

Furthermore, he was *enjoying* it; he thought he'd never enjoyed anything so much, and almost regretted that it had to end so soon. It was—well, "fun" didn't go far enough . . . "thrilling" was more like it. Part of the thrill, he sensed with a fleeting guilty twinge, was in breaking his Master's taboos, nearly every one: do not think, merely act; do not rationalize, merely describe. Certainly he'd followed the dicta at first, having selected certainly all the others but also Finley herself for no particular reason; now, however, he pursued her for one. And, as he was learning, the far greater portion of the thrill that he felt was in this pursuit itself, in the deliberate stalking that he'd planned over the weekend while (ha ha) in bed with the flu, the stalking that he intended to carry out over the next few days.

He wanted not just to read about Finley's life any longer, but to see it; not just to imagine her daily routine, but to watch her living it; not just to know about her, but to know *her*. The first time he'd gained a potential victim's confidence on-line, he'd experienced a jolt of exhilaration, a visceral charge, as though from a drug. But that excitement had been steadily waning; it was almost too easy, so it seemed—he could get Finley to tell him almost anything. It, well, it needed more *zip*.

So now here he was on the train. Stalking.

He thought he'd visit New Brunswick by train first, ask a few questions about bus routes in the train station, and board a bus a few stops ahead of Finley's own; ride with her to her office building in the suburbs; disembark a few stops later. He'd already seen much of it once, the other day, of course, but he'd have a couple more moments to see and to reassure himself about what sort of place this computer center was, this workplace for police-without-guns, and to check out some of Finley's apartment's surroundings.

More importantly, he'd get to see Finley herself: to see the way she shivered in the New Jersey November cold; the way she sat in the seat first thing in the morning *versus* the way she plunked down at the end of the day; the way she walked and, if in a hurry, maybe the way she ran, too: would she run like a real runner, with arms and hands raised and swinging easily at her sides, or more tentatively, like an amateur, stiff-legged, with her hands jammed in the cold up under her armpits? He would see the way she *moved:* the way she bent at the waist, the way she flexed an ankle, the way a pink blush came to her cheek then faded away after she'd rubbed it with the back of her hand. It hadn't been true with the others, but it was true with Finley: before the final act of merging and, well, consummation, he wanted to *absorb* her.

He laid his head back against the seat, and the slow, evenly paced and continuous clack-clack-clack of the train into New Brunswick lulled him into a shallow and pleasant doze.

Some fourteen hours later, on the train back into New York, he reflected that it had been, indeed, a deeply satisfying day in every respect.

Finley boarded the bus in the morning—the bus whose back seat he was occupying—as he'd fancied she would, with the hint, maybe, of a Motown-special smile playing at the corners of her mouth. (He could almost hear the words and music in her head, the lovesick words about not being too proud to beg, baby.) Dressed in jeans and sneakers, of course. She paid by flashing a commutation pass at the driver, and walked back a half-dozen rows to sit by a window, on the side of the bus facing the rising sun. She removed her mittens, leaned her head against the seat, and—he imagined, although he couldn't see her face—closed her eyes. Once, when the bus driver sounded his horn in anger at some other driver's real or imagined discourtesy, Finley reached up with her right hand to fiddle with the hearing aid on that side. Turning it down? She spoke to no one on the bus.

The bus ride to her building was almost a half-hour long, although it couldn't have been more than five miles distant—all the Rutgers campus stops slowed it considerably. A couple of minutes before arriving at her building's stop, Finley stood up in the aisle by her seat, clutching the overhead handle; she spent the time glancing around the bus at her fellow passengers—including once, for a heart-stopping instant, at him. He was glad he'd worn the sunglasses today. Then she glanced away, and absentmindedly reached up just before donning her mittens again reached up and touched with a fingertip at one of her teeth. Had she forgotten to brush this morning?

She got off the bus, and as it pulled away from the curb he

followed her with his eyes, turning to watch through the rear window. She was walking, alone, toward the huge brick edifice. Once she stopped suddenly and looked over her shoulder at the departing bus; he himself quickly turned back and sat down again facing forward. But then the bus was out of sight, and she had surely seen nothing.

Throughout the rest of the day, although it was cold he was strangely warmed by the thought of haunting Finley's footsteps while she pecked away at the keyboard or did whatever else she did a mere few miles away. He visited the coffee shop across the street from her apartment building; went for a brief walk along the bank of the Raritan, which allowed him to check out the rear of her apartment; stopped in at the Rutgers main library; and ate lunch at McGarrity's Pub.

There in McGarrity's, he gave his order—including hot tea—to a gaunt waitress, and she hurried off after a brief and ill-disguised glance of curiosity at the sunglasses he still wore.

The sunglasses. Of course, he didn't need them here in this dimly lit fake-Tudor cavern of a tavern, surrounded by high seat backs and booth walls of dark oak. He removed the sunglasses, rubbed his eyes with the backs of his hands, and stretched. The wound on his left forearm still throbbed in concert with the memory that he'd actually been sufficiently clumsy and unfocused to acquire it. "Joanna," ha. That must never happen again; he must never let himself be surprised or caught off-balance again. *Never. . . .*

In his mind's eye now he saw Finley approaching and then coming up the steps outside McGarrity's to the thick wooden door with the plastic, fake-yellow-frosted-glass window set into it. This imaginary Finley opened the door, entered, walked the few steps to the cash register, and waited (as the sign admonished) to be seated. He imagined her looking about the restaurant, her eyes becoming adjusted to the dim light, her amplified hearing starting to blur over the background noise, looking for a hostess or waitress to seat her or perhaps simply checking to see if there were anyone here whom she knew. He imagined her gaze falling, finally, upon him himself; one corner of her mouth, in his fancy, began slowly to curl up a bit in recognition.

Then the gaunt waitress delivered his order and—with one final glance of acknowledgement at the Finley of his imagination—he drove his steak knife down into and through his sandwich, lovingly but firmly and deliberately, all the way through to the plate.

A little later, in the afternoon, after walking about the city for a bit more, he caught a bus from New Brunswick to a shopping mall that she had once or twice written of visiting during lunch breaks.

How many times had she placed her foot right *here*? he wondered. How many times had she stepped over this crack in the pavement, set her hand upon this door handle, purchased a candy bar at this counter, stood in front of this window looking not at the goods arranged on the other side but at her own reflection? There was a kiosk at the mall whose sign proclaimed it to be the home of "Batteries PLUS," and he wondered if here was where she purchased batteries for her hearing aids; he even approached the salesgirl to ask if they sold hearing-aid batteries, and when she said, "Sure. What size you after?" he merely waved her off and replied, "Not for me, just asking for a friend" and went off, shaking his head and smiling faintly.

The bus that went back by Finley's building in the early evening began its route at the mall, so he got on board and was sitting in a seat toward the rear, still wearing sunglasses even though the sun had already dipped out of sight, when Finley herself got on. She looked very perplexed about something; perhaps this was her normal end-of-the-day look? As he'd imagined, she plunked down in the seat with an ambiguous sigh that came either from her or from the upholstery, put her head back against the seat again, and did not stir until approaching her stop. As before, she perused her fellow passengers again—skipping him this time—and then got off, proceeding directly, he noted, into the coffee shop. He rode a few blocks more, then disembarked, and walked back to the train station.

On the way, he walked past Finley's apartment complex. He noticed a paperboy delivering evening papers to the entryway of selected apartments, and thought: evening newspapers. . . . Preoccupied by the phrase "evening newspapers" as he crossed the street to the station, he did not notice the late-model sedan pulling into the parking lot outside her apartment. Its driver did not take note of him, either; he was, after all, just a passerby—probably some kind of nut, still wearing sunglasses after dark like that. Maybe even on some kind of drug.

Chapter Nineteen

Gus, Finley couldn't help noticing on Wednesday morning, was wearing a blue suit—a well-worn blue suit, with shiny patches at the sleeves and with the elbow and knee wrinkles characteristic of his brown suit. A former "traveling suit," maybe? But Gus's attire was the second item of curiosity, the first being that he and Morris together intercepted her on her ritual walk to the cafeteria for her first cup of tea.

"Nope, uh-uh!" said Morris, grasping Finley by the upper arm and steering her back to her cubicle. "No cafeteria this morning—this morning, we go out!"

"Out? What is this, anyway?"

The two men grinned like impish schoolboys. Gus said, "Morris and I figured you deserved to see some daylight for a change. So we're taking you out for a little pre-Thanksgiving breakfast."

"Breakfast? *Out?* But I ate breakfast at home!"

"We're happy for you," Morris said, "but what about us? Besides, this is going to be a working breakfast, young lady. You will tell us all about what you've found in that scrap heap so far," gesturing at the mound of paper on her desk, "or in that one," pointing at her head, "and we in turn will offer you penetrating commentary and sage advice out of the vast well of our combined half century of law-enforcement experience."

Finley chuckled, a little nervously, but obediently picked up her coat and logbook. Bill Lord stepped into her doorway just then, saw the crowd, said, "Whoops!" and backed out, running backward into the office mail carrier and once again sloshing tepid black coffee—not on Finley's keyboard this time but on himself. Trailing watery brown droplets from his hands and wrists, he scuttled like a gigantic insect, still backpedaling, across the hall and into his own office, and shut the door. Finley was already enjoying this little excursion.

Soon they were seated in a booth in the back of a nearby diner's main room, Gus and Morris squeezed into the seat across from her. She felt vaguely on the brink of a third-degree.

But they were right: she did need to see some daylight, especially on a morning like this. Through the window alongside this booth, she had a wonderful view of the sky and trees; the sky was a brilliant sapphire, almost artificially blue—the sort of blue sky that no one ever believed you could see in central New Jersey—and while by this late in the season the trees were bare of leaves, there was something at once both majestic and delicate about their gray-brown textures against such a sky.

Majesty and delicacy were two concepts far removed from her work of the last two days. Few activities held less charm for an on-line searcher than even an hour of painstaking reading and analysis, hunched over printouts instead of a screen and keyboard, and Finley had just spent the better part of two solid days that way; for that matter, the portion of time spent on-line hadn't been all that enjoyable, but nerve-racking. Sure, she'd felt a guilty little voyeuristic electric charge at reading a stranger's BBS messages, but even that had fizzled away very quickly. The first time that Aggie Bristol made a joke, say, about the New York City subway system, Finley did indeed smile; if ten or twenty such jokes had been spread out over days and weeks, as they'd been in real life, she might even have continued smiling. But compressed into a few hours? Yuck.

"So all right, so a lot of it was boring," Morris said. "So save the boring stuff and tell us about something *interesting* you found." The way he stressed the word "interesting" made her think that maybe he'd gotten over her visit to the Pelagius Institute, that he'd gone back to teasing her instead of either fuming at her or keeping out of her way altogether. She smiled, and, grandly, forgave him, as well.

Pushing aside her silverware and cup of tea, she consulted her logbook. "Well, let's see. . . . . Did Gus tell you about Tracy Williams's messages back and forth to this 'Liz Enright' person? He did? Okay. So that gave me a theory to go on, that maybe I could trace the, y'know, tone of voice backward. I could find out 'who' he was to the second victim; after all, I already had his 'Renee' photograph to go on, so I knew the name he'd be using with her." She scribbled on her placemat for a few minutes, then turned it so Morris and Gus could read it:

Victim:	Bristol	Taylor	Tracy	Redman
Alias:	???	Renee	Liz	Mary Ellen
BBS:	???	Cooking	TPZ	Eat&Drink

"See? I wanted to fill in the spots where there were question marks. Monica told me—" Morris's eyes started to darken at Monica's name and Finley quickly changed the direction of the sentence. "Monica told me once, oh Jeez, *long ago,* must have been at least a year, that you can tell if a guy is imitating a woman on-line because the voice is all wrong. He tries too hard. I figured that this guy, if it is a guy, probably realized that himself, and that's why he was stealing his *victim's* voices. But for his first victim, Aggie Bristol, either he'd still be new at it, so he'd be kind of clumsy and forced, right? Or he'd be using his *own* voice, not even trying to disguise himself as a woman."

At that point, when their breakfasts were delivered, business conversation had to cease as Finley closed up her logbook to make room. That was fine with her. What came next was the most dramatic part of the tale for her, and she wanted to go through it once, beginning to end, without serious interruption. Except, of course, for the ones that she herself would devise.

Morris and Gus lapsed while they ate into the usual guys' small-talk about sports teams and personalities she'd never heard of. Munching on her order of toast, Finley tuned into their conversation for a while, thinking that they might bring up bowling and she could chime in with a narrative about Monica's husband and his bowlology diagrams or whatever they were. But then she looked down at her placemat, and her mind wandered back over to the topic of tracing on-line voices; there was *something* about that, something she'd been meaning to ponder. . . .

Gus laughed out loud at something Morris said, shooting a tiny projectile of pancake matter across the table and breaking her train of thought. He wiped at his eyes with his fingertips, then picked up his napkin and dabbed a little spot of syrup from the corner of his mouth. Somehow, he'd managed to get syrup in his mustache as well, and several hairs were clumped together and at a crazy angle away from his face, like a midget cowlick. Still chortling, he said to Finley, "Whew! Sorry about that, Finley!" After a few more moments of mirth, he finally recovered himself and said, "Why don't we get on with your story—I don't even remember where you left off—"

"You were telling us about getting the guy's original voice, I think," said Morris. "The question marks in your little chart there."

Finley moved her empty plate to one side—seemed like she was always clearing a place for something—and opened the logbook again.

"Um, yeah. . . . Well, first thing yesterday I went back to Redman's transcripts, and then dove into the ones for the two New York victims'. I wanted to confirm that they'd *all* met him as 'John Alden,' same as Tracy did."

"Wait a minute, Finley," Morris interrupted her. "Gus tells me that *you've* exchanged messages with this Alden character, too? You want to talk about that a little first, for the benefit of my feeble little manager's brain?"

Hmm. This wasn't where she'd planned to introduce everything that she'd learned about Alden. But maybe she could satisfy Morris with some trivia. . . . She related the story about Monday night at McGarrity's, being reminded of "The Courtship of Miles Standish," but stopped at just about the point where she left the pub. "You with me so far?" she asked, and Morris, though frowning a little, nodded. Good; that would hold him even though he still didn't get the point yet. (Of course not, she hadn't, after all, *made* the point yet, but was just stringing him along.)

"So anyhow, I found an Alden in 'Joanna' Redman's conversations on a technical BBS a couple of days before 'Mary Ellen' showed up on Eat&Drink; it was ironic because if Alden had found her on FOTOBOARD he would have come across *John* Redman, too, in which case he'd never have gone to Philadelphia.

Then, finally," she continued, pointing back down at the chart on her placemat, "I found this 'Renee' pretty fast in the second victim's messages. They met on a cooking BBS, in June. A week after meeting a John Alden on a different board." She pointed to the word "Cooking" on the chart.

"Cooking—like the whatzis, Eat&Drink thing that Redman was on?" Gus asked.

"Yeah! And that makes sense, doesn't it? I mean, the killer is only going to get on boards whose subjects he understands at least a little; people don't usually tap in to boards or even normal conversations where they've got no interest or skills at all."

"Ah!" Morris said. "So then, did Bristol also subscribe to a cooking BBS?"

"That would've made it nice and symmetrical, right? But nope. She was the hardest one of all to figure out."

"She 'was'?" said Morris. "You mean you got it?"

"No, no Click yet. Or not there, any way." She smiled what she hoped was an enigmatic smile, radiating inscrutability. "But I think I might've found how the guy met her. And I think I might even know his real name."

Why not build up the suspense even further? First, she flagged a waitress down. "Could I have another cup of tea, please?" The waitress nodded and started to move on, but Finley stopped her again. "Excuse me, I'm sorry, where are the rest rooms here?" Rising from her seat, she told them, "Be back in a few minutes, boys. You go back to talking about hockey pucks or whatever it was." They were both grinning, though in Morris's case the grin was a little belied by his florid complexion. He looked threateningly volcanic.

"So," she said brightly as she sat down a few minutes later. "Where was I?"

"You were in the bathroom," Gus said, all amiability, "laughing your butt off."

"Ha ha! Yes, all right. The first victim's messages. Like I was saying, she was the hardest of all, not just because I didn't really know who I was looking for but because she subscribed to more boards than any of the others." She checked her logbook. "Let's see . . . yes, there was a law BBS, and one like Tracy's Party Zone, only called 'PartyLine' instead, and there was one for people who play tennis and other racquet sports and one for, um, disgruntled Roman Catholics, one for China-doll collectors, a technical BBS—"

"Yeah, yeah," Morris interrupted her impatiently, "we already know all that from when you checked her phone bills, remember? Get to the point!"

"—and one for people who like to read, called 'The Bookshelf.' And I think I found him there."

"You *found* him?" the two men chorused.

"Well, not exactly. Almost. She exchanged messages with a guy on The Bookshelf BBS up till a few days before she was killed. The last thing they discussed was about arranging to meet on that night, the night she was killed; he did the same thing with the second victim and with Tracy, remember?"

Morris's hand dropped like a brick onto the table. He tried, and failed, to keep his voice light. "What was his name, damn it, Finley!"

She really was enjoying this immensely. "Just hang on, Morris. His name on all The Bookshelf messages was William Andrews, also known as Bill."

"All right! So then we just have to—"

"Morris. Relax, I'm not done yet. This Andrews guy, the first thing I *would* have thought, just like you, was, well, that's our man. But there was something odd about this Andrews guy's last message to her, and also about the first. His last message to her was about getting together with her that night, like I said. But everybody else kept sending her messages for a little while after she was dead—they didn't know she was dead, see? But this Andrews guy never bothered posting any more messages to her, as if he *did* know. So, 'Aha!' I thought. But it was his first message, almost six months ago, that really caught my eye."

She stopped to sip at her tea, counting—slowly—to five. "He was sort of rambling on—yes, Morris, just like me—introducing himself to her, that's what you usually do with a first message, and he said his very favorite American poem of all time was 'The Courtship of Miles Standish.' He said that the characters of John Alden and Miles Standish were like twin milestones at the opposite ends of the continuum of American malehood—"

"Finley," Morris said levelly, doing an Oliver Hardy slow burn, his fingers drumming on his coffee-stained placemat, "why don't you save the literary synopsis till later, I'm sure Gus let alone I myself would both like to hear about it some time," his voice rising now, "but for now would you *please get to the point!*"

"Right, sorry, Morris. Anyhow, this Andrews mentions 'The Courtship of Miles Standish' and she practically falls all over him, 'It's MY favorite poem, too!' All that sort of stuff. And then they go on from there. It sounds simple, still sounds like Andrews is the guy we want. But something bothered me about the message, like I said, but I couldn't quite put my finger on whatever it was. By this time it was pretty late last night, about eight-thirty, the last bus would be coming by the Center in like another half hour, so I packed up to go home. And it wasn't till I got on the bus that I realized what it was. She'd just had a conversation on-line with someone else on another board, just a couple days before that. It was back on PartyLine, the singles BBS, she got talking to a guy about poetry, about the 'Miles Standish' poem in particular. And after that, that guy never showed up on PartyLine again; two days later, this 'Andrews' suddenly pops up on The Bookshelf, babbling about the same poem. It was such an odd coincidence, it just stood out, you see? So first thing this morning, I was going to try to find out more about this other guy, even his whereabouts maybe. Then you two kidnapped me."

Morris said, "The *name,* Finley."

"Yes, the name—the reason that Aggie Bristol first became interested in him on PartyLine was his name there: John Alden. That's the guy I think we want. John Alden."

Morris looked incredulous. "But we already know that! The question, Finley, is this: Who is John Alden?"

This was it, the moment. "John Alden is my friend from the STACKS bulletin board, Jon Little-Olden. And I'm supposed to be his next victim. *Soon.*"

Pandemonium. The two older men couldn't get a word in edgewise past each other's voices. Other patrons in the diner were staring in their direction; their waitress approached. "Can I get you anything else?" she asked.

"Yes, I'd like another cup of tea," Finley said. "How about you gentlemen?"

"Coffee!" Morris barked, and dismissed the waitress with a flick of his hand. "All right, Finley, I know you are having fun with this but it's serious, damn it. What's the evidence for this guy you know, what's it? Little-Olden, you say? What's that, British or something."

"No. Italian." She ignored the confusion that seemed to be mounting in her boss's face, and told them about Jon's messages on Monday night to the unfortunate newcomer and to Finley herself.

"That's *it*?" Gus asked. "Gee whiz, Finley, I mean it's an interesting set of coincidences but—"

She held up a hand, silencing him, as though she were an elementary-school teacher. "What do you know about 'The Courtship of Miles Standish'? What was the name of the woman that both men loved? Anyone?"

"Well, come on—Pocahontas, right?"

"No, Morris. Wrong story. That was John Smith and John Rolfe, not Miles Standish and John Alden. Miles Standish and John Alden loved *Priscilla*." Now the two men were really quite satisfyingly lost. "When I got home last night," she went on, "first thing I did was check out an on-line encyclopedia for information about the poem and about the character. On an impulse then I looked up 'Priscilla' in my dictionary, thinking it might tell me even more about the woman in the poem. But it didn't—only covered the name as a name. And you know where the name 'Priscilla' comes from? It's Italian, the diminutive form of 'prisca,' meaning 'old.' *Little old,* get it?"

"But—"

"Morris, *please.* And when I came in this morning the first thing I did, even before I tried to visit the cafeteria, was to check first the Center's database of known aliases, and then our criminal record database. Guess what I found?" No guesses forthcoming, not that she expected any. She took a breath and then plunged on. "Jon Little Olden, no hyphen, is the alias for one Giovanni 'Hot Johnny' Priscillo, released about a year ago on a technicality from serving out his life sentence in the federal prison at Leavenworth. Leavenworth, *Kansas,* you know, where he's currently working in the public library. He'd been sentenced to life after his conviction for assault and battery and assault with a deadly weapon, and his third conviction for first-degree sexual assault. The assailant in all these crimes used a knife, a weapon which coincidentally Mr. Priscillo is especially skilled with. He should be; he's worked as a professional chef. And one final point." More doodling on the placemat. "You see? With each new victim, the time that he meets her to the time when he kills her gets shorter and shorter. He should be knocking on my apartment door any day now.

"Ahem. So now, would one of you gentlemen like to call the authorities for my protection, or should I?"

Not even a half hour later, Gus and Morris were again jammed into her cube, their heavy winter coats yet buttoned up and their hands in the pockets. They looked like a couple of elderly Soviet leaders reviewing a military parade. Finley was checking the PHONENO database, looking for a "Giovanni Priscillo," "John Priscillo," "Jon Little-Olden," and so on, in Leavenworth's area code. She found him listed as "Little Olden," living in an apartment in a development outside the town.

Morris snorted and ran a hand through his hair. "Jesus, I can't believe this. Tell you what, give me the address, Finley. I'll phone the FBI field office out there, and have somebody here do a complete background check on this Priscillo or Little-Olden or whoever the hell he is. Maybe Helen Walker, Finley?"

She smiled back at him. "Yes, I think Helen is free now."

Morris bustled off with the address, Gus staring in puzzlement after him. "Why'd *he* do that? Why not you, or me for that matter?"

"I dunno." She shrugged. "He likes to get his hands on the action every now and then. Boring at the top, I guess."

"No doubt. But listen, while we're sitting here twiddling our thumbs, I've got to tell you: this is a hell of a job you've done here, Finley. I couldn't even open my mouth half the time listening to you tell it, except to pour coffee in. But there's still one thing that bothers me—"

"I know. Whoever or whatever he is in real life," she said, "Jon Little-Olden is not a woman on-line. I don't know how to explain that, Gus. But remember that he's already impersonated a guy once before, as William Andrews. Maybe he just wanted to change the M.O. this time around, vary the routine to throw us off."

Gus looked at her, hard. "I hope you're right, kid. I'm going down to get some lunch. You want?"

But Finley wanted to stay at her desk, to start typing up her report on the two days' worth of activities. She wanted, yes, to clear her desk, figuratively as well as literally, before the Thanksgiving break. So Gus headed off to the cafeteria alone.

Finley turned back to her PC; she hadn't even looked at the event list yet this morning. The wakeup message today was:

" 'It's a poor sort of memory that only works backwards,' the Queen remarked. —Lewis Carroll."

. . . What was it that she'd been thinking about in the diner, looking down at her placemat—? Backward, forward. . . . That was it, if you could trace the killer's voices backward, you should also be able to predict his *next* voice, assuming he'd been a woman. "Joanna" Redman's on-line voice had been maternal; correct; solicitous and polite—

Gus burst into her cubicle. "Hey, Jesus, Finley, guess what Morris just found out? Your little old buddy Little-Olden's on a plane up in the air even as we speak, right at this moment. Headed into Newark. You couldn't have timed it closer, young lady!"

She grinned and gave him a thumbs-up sign. "So they'll be waiting for him when he lands . . . ?"

"You got it. And that reminds me, I gotta tell him, Morris can drop your shadow, too."

"My shadow? Are you kidding me? You mean Morris was already protecting me?"

"Hey, CIAC watches out for its prize resources! Again, *great* job, Finley." He shook her hand. "Now have a good *long* weekend; you deserve it!" he said, and waved a hand, and then he was gone.

People come and go so quickly here, Toto; we're not in Kansas. And neither is Hot Johnny Little-Olden. With a grin and another shrug Finley turned back to her computer.

The tail end of the event list was still on the screen, but she didn't scroll back through it. She brought up onto her screen the word-processing software she used here at the Center. She wanted to get this damned report written, she wanted to get out the door and get home, damn it. To get ready, as Gus had said, for the long weekend.

Chapter Twenty

Only six o'clock Wednesday night, Warren and family not even there yet, and Finley was already feeling a little set upon. Her nemesis: a nylon-netted solid-frozen boulder of poultry.

She'd literally run from the bus and dashed straight into her kitchen. Now on the table, still unread, was a scattering of mail from the last couple of days; a couple of free-sample newspapers, too, some ploy by the local paper to acquire new subscribers. And there in the stainless-steel sink, like a science-fair project demonstrating the effects of liquid nitrogen, lay the turkey.

Great, good start, Finley; you got it out of the freezer on your own. Now what? Now . . . yes, now you run cold water over it, a Thanksgiving tradition even if you can't quite think right now what its purpose might be . . . and while the cold water is doing whatever it does, there's time to check your on-line mail; your brother will never sit still for that once he gets here. Unimaginable. . . .

Fifteen messages total, it appeared, spread across the three boards she frequented. Most of them were little more than holiday greetings and announcements that so-and-so would be out of town and hence off-line for the duration of the weekend. No time now, nor need, to answer these chitchat messages.

There was one message from Flokati:

> . . . Yes Finley very good, compare between turkey carving and autopsy. Perhaps not carving, yes, but time before turkey even put into oven when cook search inside and re-

move turkey organs. Too bad human body organs not come in plastic bag like turkey, much more neatly for surgeon, you see? No mystery however!

Hmm. Was she supposed to eviscerate the turkey *now*? But *how*? It was still frozen rock-hard, and she couldn't even pry the thing open yet let alone get a hand inside. Well, postpone another decision; Nancy would know what to do.

On ABLE, there were a couple of general information-posting or -seeking messages addressed to "ALL"; one from the anonymous "Visitor" with the friend who probably had Meniere's disease, thanking Bob Melendez, her Earwig friend, for his explanation. But there was nothing from Jane or her other friends there. Ditto, pretty much, on STACKS—including, happily, no further messages from Jon Little-Olden or Alden or Priscillo or whatever his name was. One person, a stranger who (he said) had been lurking on the board for a while without openly participating, reading messages but contributing nothing, and who therefore knew that Finley was some sort of on-line specialist, asked her if she knew anything about how to locate an individual's phone number through some on-line resource. Finley gave him the information she had in her directory about a couple of public databases of listed phone numbers; she told him about PHONENO, too, but explained that it wasn't available to the public, and sent the message off.

And, whew! Barely had she had a chance to log out, to change into fresh jeans and a shirt and to drag a brush through her hair, when the doorbell rang. Warren must have insisted on leaving Tree-of-Life plenty early and then driven like a madman to get here by now, and so he had—on the theory, he explained without apparent irony, that "there are an awful lot of crazy people on the road, right?"

The three of them trooped in laden with luggage and grocery bags and stuffed animals . . . and a small, flat package, wrapped in orange and yellow construction paper, the edges of which had been sealed, unmistakably, by inexpert four-year-old fingers wielding a roll of masking tape. "It's for—*Stupid!*" Terri giggled.

"Can he see it now, or does he have to wait till Thanksgiving?"

"No! Now, now!"

Finley carefully unwrapped the package. Inside was Stupid's Thanksgiving surprise: a plastic turkey with a multicolored cuttle-bone tail. Finley erupted into giggles of her own. "Oh, Terri, it's, it's—"

"Put it in his cage, Aunt Finley!"

Finley wasn't sure about that—would the plastic be safe for Stupid?—but Nancy explained, "The pet shop *promised* her it would be all right, Finley. Terri was very concerned about that, weren't you, honey?"

"Yes! And the pet-shop man asked me who it was for! And I *said* it, Aunt Finley, I said, 'He's Stupid!'" She collapsed backward, laughing, onto Finley's sofa.

"She's a little wound up from the ride, did you notice?" Warren said.

"I noticed!"

But Terri's gift to Stupid was rewarded with a resounding lack of gratitude on the parakeet's part. He went berserk when Finley fastened it to the inside of his cage—screeching, fluttering his wings madly and aggressively, crashing into the cage's wire walls, screeching some more, setting the little wire swing a-dance, screeching. . . .

Terri touched Finley's leg. "Aunt Finley! Stupid likes it, doesn't he?"

"Oh, uh, yes, I'm *sure* he does," said Finley as she placed the bird cage into her bedroom closet and shut the door. The screech-ing continued, muffled but unabated. "But maybe in a little bit, when it's time for him to go to sleep, we should take it out, though, you know? Just like Mommy has to put your toys away when you go to bed?"

Warren rolled his eyes, but his relief was visible; Nancy just grinned and winked at her. Maybe the next couple of days wouldn't be bad, after all.

On Thursday, when Monica and Bob came to the door a little after lunch, Bob was bearing before him a huge, bulbous and appar-ently heavy object of some sort, wrapped in aluminum foil and sitting in a roasting pan. There was the huge central Something, and two roughly cylindrical Somethings placed one on each side . . . my God, it looked like a turkey, they wouldn't have brought a turkey, would they? And this one seemed to be some gigantic mutant strain of turkey, silicone-injected maybe, it was *enormous*. . . .

But—whew! and ha, ha!—it wasn't a turkey. Finley had forbidden them to bring food, so they'd hit on this alternative: a bowling ball for her in its own tote bag, and a pair of bowling shoes, disguised as a turkey. Clever!

Clever, yes, and probably expensive enough that Finley should be embarrassed about it. But it unfortunately raised the day's energy level perceptibly. When the adults chuckled admiringly over the "bird," Terri—not quite getting the joke but wanting to join in—burst into screamingly too-loud, too-crazy laughter, which of course punctured everyone else's good humor. Then she attached herself to Monica, who in all innocence leaned over and asked, "Have you met your Aunt Finley's parakeet yet?"

"Aunt Finley!" Terri cried. "Aunt Finley, where's Stupid's toy?!?" From his cage, his head tilted to one side, Stupid chirped, "Uh-oh, uh-oh. . . ."

Bearing Bob's and her own coats, Monica accompanied Finley to the bedroom, where Finley picked up the turkey-cuttlebone from the bureau. "Couldn't be helped," she replied to Monica's apology, "she would have remembered it sooner or later anyway."

Stupid's response was predictable: phobic, screeching mania, erupting even before Finley approached the cage, as soon as he laid his beady suspicious eyes on what she held in her hands. She moved the cuttlebone behind her back, and Stupid quieted; she brought it around before her, and he lost control again. And finally, when she opened the cage door and turned her back for what she was sure was only a split second, Stupid took decisive action.

"Aunt Finley!" Terri cried, "Aunt Finley, he got *away!*"

Aaargh. . . . Well, at least he'd shut up now, she thought and finished twisting the cuttlebone's mounting prongs into place.

The other adults had already repaired, in cowardice, to the kitchen. "You sure it will be okay?" Warren asked. "I mean, just letting a bird fly around the kitchen while we make dinner and eat?"

"Do you mean," Finley asked him in return, "will he c, r, a, p in the mashed potatoes? No, I don't think that'll be a problem, I think he'll try to stay out of reach."

"What about feathers, can't you get salmonella or someth—"

"*Warren.* Relax. Listen, I'll set up some games on the computer. . . ."

He was not comfortable with that, not at all. But Terri latched onto the idea at once, forgetting all about the parakeet, and in the interest of peace he agreed to sit in the bedroom with Terri while she played with the PC. "What do I do now, Daddy?" she'd ask, and then Warren would grumble and get up off the bed where he was reading one of the free-sample newspapers, go over to the PC and press one of the keys, and return to his reading. The computer emitted sufficient buzzes and squeaks to lure Stupid to a perch on the bedroom curtain rod, where he tried to strike up a conversation with it. Finley closed the bedroom door, shutting in all three potential sources of anxiety, and returned to the kitchen.

"Well," Monica said, gesturing at the stove, "at least old Stupid won't be out here to see what's been done to his cousin!"

Taking advantage of the lull which followed, Bob asked Finley if she'd had a chance to look at the new ball yet. Monica objected, "Bob! Haven't you seen—"

"No, Monica, it's all right," Finley said. She retrieved the tote bag and shoes from the living room. The shoes, it turned out once she'd removed all the aluminum foil, were plain old royal blue. Not her taste, to be sure, but she'd never wear them anyway, except in a bowling alley (if there). The ball was pretty hideous, neon blue in color, marbled with black and crimson streaks, and aglitter with what looked like sequins embedded in its surface. Pelagian, she thought, and hid a grin. "Er, gee," she said, "this was really very sweet of you guys—"

"No problem!" said Bob, heartily. "We wanted to get you a ball that would stand out!"

Stand out, she thought. It does that, all right, it would stand out anywhere except, maybe, at a Las Vegas stage show. . . . She put the ball back into its tote, and lugged it all to her bedroom closet, where she placed it on the floor. Terri, Warren, and Stupid were all engrossed in their separate preoccupations; not even the parakeet acknowledged her intrusion.

* * *

The balance of Thanksgiving day proceeded largely without incident. No word from Gus about Jon Little-Olden or whatever, although Finley couldn't help wondering from time to time what sort of results his interrogation might actually be producing. Terri returned again and again to the PC, with each session the annoyance in her father's eyes rising perceptibly. For his part, Stupid avoided even getting near his cage as long as the Thanksgiving cuttlebone was in place; but later—after the dishes had been washed, after Monica and Bob had left, while Nancy was getting Terri ready for bed—when Finley removed the invader from his cage, he flew, with only the slightest of it's-about-time chirping comments, back inside.

"Can he play with it again before we leave tomorrow?" Terri asked, her voice slurring over into slumber.

"We'll see, honey," Finley said, and kissed her good night.

But the first priority on Friday, Nancy and Finley had already agreed, was *shopping*. A couple of maternity-apparel outlets were within "only about fifteen miles of here," Nancy had learned through whatever mothers-to-be network carried such news. Nothing at all like them in Lancaster let alone Tree-of-Life, she added, and she wanted to take advantage of their proximity now, while she still could. But it was the craziest shopping day of the year, and certainly among the three or four worst for traffic as well, and what was supposed to be a little fifteen-mile jaunt turned into an all-day excursion. Finley was grateful (guiltily so) that she didn't own a car, so Nancy had to drive, but she was nonetheless exhausted by the time they got back to the apartment. Warren said, "Where the heck have you two *been*?"—practically tapping his toes with impatience. He loaded all his family's gear into the car within five minutes.

Finally, they were all standing in the living room.

"Aunt Finley," Terri cried, "the computer, one more time, *please*?"

Stooping to address her niece, Finley looked nervously, once, over in Warren's direction. The dark clouds she saw gathering in his face did not reassure her that the moment would pass easily. "Well, gee, honey, don't you think you need to leave pretty soon? Your Daddy has a long way to drive—"

"*Please*, Aunt Finley? Just for a *minute*?"

"Terri, I—"

Warren interrupted. "Yes, Aunt Finley, why don't you take her to the computer now? Why don't you show her one more time how much more fun a computer can be than a flesh-and-blood playmate?"

"Oh, come on, Warren, she just wants to play a game—"

"And while you're at it, how about this? How about if you show her how much *smarter* a computer is than a plain old human being, a human being with a plain old everyday job, a *cop,* say?" Nancy reached a hand tentatively in Warren's direction at this point, murmuring, "Warren, honey, come on, why don't we all just get in the car," but he shrugged her off. "Oh, *yeah,* that'd be a *good* lesson for her to learn, wouldn't it? And here's an even better one, why not show her how much smarter a federal employee is than a local? A woman is than a man? For that matter, a, a *kid* than an adult—?"

Finley couldn't believe this. What did he think he was doing? But the look in his eyes told her that he wasn't really thinking anything just then; the words, the questions were just tumbling out of his mouth straight from his heart, his blood, his bones, bypassing his brain altogether. "Warren, I just—"

"No, Finley, not really, you don't 'just' do anything, do you? Everything is significant, isn't that what they teach you? Everything means more than it is, everything adds up and the whole is always greater than the sum of its parts, nothing is *simple,* is it, Finley?" His eyes seemed to be popping from their sockets, the veins in his neck standing out, and while he wasn't yelling, exactly, his voice strained as though for both a higher octave and a higher truth. Terri was cowering behind Finley, her thumb in her mouth, staring down at her tiny shoes. Warren was oblivious to it all. "But some things *are* simple, have you forgotten? I've been at the same desk for more than *fifteen* years, Finley, nothing ambiguous there, is there, Finley? One of the oldest guys in the department now; all the younger ones—even the *women,* for Christ's sake, the *girls*—they almost all outrank me, that's pretty clear isn't it, sister? I told Nancy when we took you in, I don't like this, I said, something doesn't feel right about this, and I was right, wasn't I? I don't even have a sister anymore, I have a, a, an ex-tenant, a weirdo with a microchip where her brain should be—"

Finley cut him off before he could turn this last into a question. "Just a minute!" she shouted. "Maybe you can get away with talking like this at your house but this is *mine*—!" Nancy had led Terri to the sofa, where they were both pretending to be absorbed in a picture magazine whose captions Nancy was whispering into her daughter's ear. "And for your information, *brother,* when you're a guest you don't—"

"Don't *what*? Don't tell the hostess how much I enjoyed sleeping in the same apartment with a goddamn box of metal and plastic and glass that's stolen my job, my sister, that's about to steal my *daughter*?" And not wanting nor waiting for a reply, as usual, he turned and thundered out through the front door, which slammed, loudly, behind him. Stupid screeched like a cockatoo in reply.

Nancy stood up at the sofa. "I, Finley, I think I need to go get him."

"Get him? Where's he going?"

"He, well, he gets like this sometimes and then he just suddenly *goes*. Walking, running, whatever. And ends up in a bar as often as not. I can't let him do that if we're going to drive home today."

And then she was out the door as well, leaving Terri and Finley to share a silence which—yes, Warren—was far more significant than the little girl could possibly understand.

Chapter Twenty-One

She watched through the windows, over the shoulder of the blond-haired niece now on her lap. The dwindling agitated forms of her brother and his wife had already passed out of sight, somewhere out there in the gathering darkness. Why was he such a, a, an *asshole* sometimes? Only with an effort of will was Finley able to keep the angry moisture in her eyes from brimming over and spilling down her cheeks.

"Will my mommy and my daddy come back soon, Aunt Finley?"

Finley sniffled. "Oh, yeah, well, in a little while, sure—"

"Then can we play with Stupid now?" Terri's eyes seemed to sparkle now with significantly more hope than had accompanied the previous question.

The computer forgotten. Wonderful news, if a little late. But play with Stupid? Jeez. Finley wanted to give the bird a break; the "playing" he'd suffered already over the last forty-eight hours had probably permanently scarred his dim peeping little parakeet's psyche. "Uh, gee, well, honey, I don't—"

"Please? Oh *please* Aunt Finley?"

She thought for a moment more. Outside in the now-full darkness, impersonal headlights and streetlights were all she could see through the reflections in the window. Please, Warren, don't drag this out; please get back soon. "Tell you what, Terri. We'll let Stupid out of his cage to fly around for a while, okay? You can sing and talk to him, that's all right, but we'll leave his, his *toy* right where it is for now, don't want to get him too excited, do we?"

Stupid chattered skeptically when Finley opened the cage door.

"You want me to *what?*" he seemed to be saying. *"Again?"* But he climbed aboard Terri's finger willingly enough, and when she withdrew it from the cage he rode along right up until she cried, "Aunt Finley, lookit, he likes me, Stupid likes me—" And then he was off the finger and flapping around the apartment, ricocheting from curtain rod to curtain rod, a blurry, deranged, green-and-yellow bullet. "Chee-rup!" he said, over and over, translated loosely perhaps as, "Hey, not bad, I can get used to this . . . !"

Finley rolled her eyes and went outside to retrieve the day's mail while the two of them were preoccupied. It really was quite dark outside, dark and cold, with not even the limited warmth of reflected moonlight for comfort, and as she reached up into the mailbox she thought she saw out of the corner of one eye a shadowy form slipping around the end of the building. Trick of the light. Residue of her paranoia, no doubt, thank God that was over with, life on-line and off- was complicated enough without it, her hands were still shaking from the stupid scene with her stupid brother. . . .

"Ha ha!" Terri shrieked. "Lookit! He's on the bookcase, Aunt Finley, the bookcase!" Finley looked. He was, indeed, on the bookcase. She smiled wanly, thinking to herself, Come on Warren, be a jerk with me if you have to but give your daughter a break. . . . She sorted absentmindedly through the handful of mail. Bill, bill, junk mail, magazine, bill, junk, junk, another magazine and, beneath that, a 9 × 12 manila envelope. No return address. She hooked a finger under the envelope flap to tear it open —pausing once to admonish her niece, "Terri, no, I know Stupid's on the bookcase but he's a *bird,* it's not good for little girls or boys to climb on bookcases, that's right, don't climb up there, honey"— and then she had it open.

Inside was a photograph, an 8 × 10 black-and-white portrait. She knew who it was at once, of course: gray hair, glasses, mid-50s, and that endearing smile, and when she flipped it over the block printing on the back confirmed it. "I know this is vain of me but I just wanted you to have it! Love you, dear. <jane>" The printing in black felt-tip ink slanted back and to the left, and Finley was just starting to wonder about that (was Jane left-handed?) when her eye was caught by a tiny red-ink logo in the bottom right corner on the back of the photo, a slightly smudged crimson little omen which said:

J. REDMAN

STUDIO

Wha—Redman? How did Jane know *Redm—*

The truth crashed in on her mind a split second before the crash and an answering screech of avian outrage from the other side of the room. Ignoring Finley's warning, Terri had clambered up onto the base of the bookcase and knocked a pewter plate onto the wooden floor. Stupid, of course, had taken this as a challenge and was now squawking his head off. "Terri," Finley began, but her mind was reeling and repeating, over and over, not her niece's name but her friend's. Jane? Jane; Jane. It couldn't be Jane, it was *Priscillo.* . . .

"Terri, *please*—" She lifted her niece from the bookcase and was returning the plate to its shelf just as a light knock came from the door. Thank God, Warren and Nancy—

But it wasn't Warren and Nancy. It was a stranger, a man dressed all in black. Black hair, black Oxford shirt and slacks, black canvas shoes, a short black zip-up jacket and—ridiculously —sunglasses. What was this? "Yes?" The creepiest smile, too.

"Miss Finley?" He held out his right hand. "Hi, I'm John Smith, from the *Courier–News?* Circulation manager, new subscriptions. We've been delivering a sample copy—?"

"Oh, yeah, sure." Relaxing. He wants to sell me the paper.

Behind her a sudden flurry of wings and a scream from her niece. "Aunt Finley, Stupid's flying *away*!" Without thought, she grabbed Smith by the forearm, pulled him into the apartment, and slammed the door behind him just in time; the parakeet zoomed off, veering crazily to one side, and flew down the hall into the recesses of the apartment.

Finley (her mind still chanting: Jane; Jane) smiled apologetically at the newspaper salesman. "Sorry. Things are a little off-balance here at the moment." (*Jane.* . . .)

"So I see," Smith replied with a weak but sympathetic smile of his own. He was holding his forearm where Finley had grabbed it.

"Did I hurt y—"

"No no, not to worry, a, an old war wound is all. Now, about the paper—"

He was interrupted by a crash of music from the bedroom, Terri having, apparently, found the clock-radio. *"It's my party and I'll cry if I want to!"* screamed Leslie Gore.

"Look, Mister, Mister Smith," Finley said loudly, over the music, "why don't you just have a seat for a moment. I need to go tie up my parakeet and niece, won't take me a minute." (*Jane.*) The man sat on the edge of the sofa cushion, although gingerly, as though he'd really prefer to stand. He was no longer clutching his arm.

In the bedroom, the scene was chaos. Terri had obviously made the connection between knocking sounds and Stupid's loud angry cheeping. She was jumping on the bed, and each time she reached the apex of her trajectory she'd bang on the wall with a fist. Stupid, of course, perched on the curtain rod, would screech following each knock, which coincided with the instant when Terri landed full force on the mattress again with her own, "CHEEP!" *"YOU, WOULD, CRY, TOO, IF-IT-HAPPENED-TO YOUUUUU!"* yelled the radio.

Finley turned off the radio and yelled herself, "Terri, *stop* that right now!" *Please,* Warren. . . . (*Jane.*)

With another weak, brief apology to Smith—she'd definitely have to buy a subscription now—Finley fetched the bird cage from the living room. "Come on, Stupid, pretty bird, stupid bird, stupid bird, come on," she was repeating mindlessly, endlessly, while holding the cage door open, her mind chanting, endlessly itself, "Jane, Jane. . . ." Terri, mercifully, had gone off somewhere to pout.

Naturally—what else—the phone chose that moment to ring. The heck with it for now, that's what answering machines are for. . . . She continued to try cajoling the bird into the cage while aware, faintly, that from the answering machine in the other room came the tinny mechanical tones of a man's voice. Who? Not Spencer? Gus, maybe? "Come *oooonnnn,* Stupid—"

Suddenly she thought: Gus. If it was Gus on the phone she had to tell him about Jane—

She hurried back into the living room then, but Gus, or whoever, had already hung up and the answering machine tape was rewinding. Smith was standing again, across the room, by the window. "I really am sorry, Mr. Smith—"

"Well, maybe I should come back some other time. . . ."

By now, Finley had pressed the "PLAY" button in order to listen to the message. It was Gus after all: "Finley? Gus here. Listen, I just got off the phone with the Saint Louis guys. We got a few problems. No way it could be Priscillo. Number One, he's got a real alibi. Number Two, he's got *blond* hair, Finley. We're looking for a guy with black hair, remember? Straight black hair, little bit over six feet, left-handed. And that's Number Three, your buddy Priscillo is right-handed, he's even missing three fingers on his left—" She turned the volume control off altogether. No point letting this complete stranger hear the whole thing all over again.

This complete stranger. Smith had removed his sunglasses now. He was smiling, true, but his silvery-gray eyes were the color and tone of ice. One eye was encircled by a ring of bruised skin. In his left hand were the sunglasses, now moving in the direction of a black canvas fanny pack on his left hip. Ziiipp. . . . "Well, if you insist," he was saying.

This guy.

And then she heard it, The Click. And gazing into Finley's eyes at just that moment with subdued icy violence, he seemed to hear it, too, a Click of his own; his smile broadened into an outright grin, oh sweet Jesus, *this* guy, what was she going to do now—

The phone. The extension, in the bedroom, she could phone from there. . . .

"Why, why don't you just have a seat, Mister, Mister Smith?" Smith. *John Smith,* oh Jesus Christ Finley, John Alden John Smith, nothing at all to do with Priscilla or Priscillo. You screwed this one up big time and now he's right *here,* in front of you. "I, um, I need to go get my, my checkbook—" Turning her back and walking stiffly in the direction of her bedroom was one of the hardest things she had ever had to do. Jane—oh, oh *Jane.* . . .

She walked quickly through the bedroom to the other side, to the door out to the kitchen, she had to get Terri out of here, but where *was* Terri? "Terrri!" she whispered as she stepped into the kitchen. "Terri, where are you, honey?" Not in the kitchen, not under the table, so then back into the bedroom. "Terri?"

Through the hand braced against the bedroom wall, Finley felt rather than heard a sharp rap—and Stupid's answering screech. Where was Stupid now, oh *Jesus* . . . the closet. The closet door was open and the light inside was on and spilling out the door and into the bedroom. Knock *screech,* knock *screech,* they're in the *closet.* Yep, there they were. Terri was sitting on the floor, knees drawn up to her face, staring soulfully heavenward up at the para-keet perched on the sagging shelf. With the bowling shoe clutched in one hand she was hammering slowly, rhythmically, as though in a trance, on the floor: *knock.* Stupid, well maybe he did like it after all, *screech* as he did with each knock, cute very cute picture but right now they had to get *out* of there (oh *Jane*). . . .

Finley crouched down in the closet doorway and had just begun to whisper, "Terri, honey, we have to go, danger, come here to Aunt Finley, honey," and Terri had just shot her a look of seething resentment, and Finley was just reaching imploring arms in the direction of her angry niece, when the lights went out.

She whirled about in the darkness to face the bedroom door. Was that a figure there, in the doorway, a figure blending with the shadows? And then the figure, or the shadows, spoke to her.

"Finley," he said, his voice smooth, not wavering at all. (Not *mute,* oh God, oh *Jane*. . . .) "Why don't you just relax and let me take what I came here for?" What did he come here for? "Oh, I grant you," he continued, "I didn't come here to take it this time, I thought I'd be back again later, but events have a way of rushing away with us, don't they?"

Terri began to whine from behind her in the closet. "Aunt Fin-ley, turn the lights back on, Aunt Finley, who are you talking to, is that my daddy?" Her daddy. *Warren.*

She mustered her courage. "Might be best for everyone if you just, just left right now, John Smith or whatever your name is. This is my brother's daughter here. He's a police detective, got that? a policeman. And he's on his way back here now!"

No answer at first. No movement, either. Or was there? Then the shadow in the doorway *chuckled,* he *laughed* at her.

"Heh heh heh, nice try. Almost caught me there. But you never mentioned anything about a brother, Finley, and you told me ev-erything else. Heh, heh, *everything*. . . ."

Finley's eyes filled; of course she'd never said anything about a brother, she hated her brother, why would she bring someone she hated into that private little place where she went to escape with people she loved? "Oh *Jane* . . ." she sobbed aloud in a final reflexive spasm of grief for the friend she'd never meet, the friend who never existed in the first place.

He chuckled again. "Heh, that's right, Finley. Jane. Here I am. Come to Jane now." She wasn't sure but she thought she saw something glint in reflected light in the black rectangle on the far side of the room. Was he stepping through the doorway now?

What could she *do,* she'd never make it to the back door, not with Terri here in the closet—the closet. She had no other choice.

She'd need to distract him somehow. . . . She reached up, ever so carefully, and removed one hearing aid. Eyes still affixed to the black rectangle, she turned the aid's volume up, all the way up—if she could just distract him for an instant—and she tossed it, gently, with an underhand flick of her wrist, launched it whistling and warbling like a tiny magic electronic flute, through the air and in the direction of the bed.

He didn't lunge for the bed, but he did step inside the door, emerge from the blackness, and turn in the bed's direction. Finley sprang at the same instant into the closet, slammed the door, and threw the barrel bolt a split second before he reached the doorknob. The barrel bolt, yes, her landlord's blessed blessed incompetence.

But what now, ye gods, what now?

She bent to where Terri, presumably, still huddled on the floor. "Aunt Finley, what's happening, is this a game? I don't like games in the dark, Aunt Finley."

She helped Terri to her feet. "Ssshhh, I don't like games in the dark either, honey, now just move to the back of the closet. . . ." She pushed her niece behind some dry-cleaned garments still in their plastic bags. "Just be quiet for a few minutes honey and let, let Aunt Finley think. . . ."

She herself shrank deeper into the blackness of the closet, behind the clothes, pressing her back up against the closet's side wall. She could feel his footsteps as he paced back and forth, talking to himself, feel his frustration humming into her skeleton, and she could even hear, a little, snatches of what he was saying: "No good . . . *will* . . . can't *leave,* can't *stay* . . . concentrate, focus . . . *will*. . . ." The word "will" kept coming up in odd places, what was he—

That creepy Pince's nutty society or org—Then —what was this?—he was speaking to her again:

"Finley," his voice said, muffled, through the door, each syllable lodging softly in her one remaining amplified ear. "Can you hear me? No? Can you hear *this*?" BANG! "That's the sound of your death, Finley. I'm taking—" *BANG!* "—the pins out of the door hinges." *BANG!* "That's the bottom one out, Finley. . . ." With each BANG, Stupid screamed like a miniature cartoon crazy man. Terri cried, "Aunt Finley, what's that man doing, who *is* that man, I'm scared, Aunt Finley. . . ."

What could she *do,* he'd be in here in less than a minute with that blade she'd glimpsed, what could she *do*? No weapons. . . .

BANG! (Shreeeek!)

She couldn't even *see* in here except for that thin, thin slice of gray light at the bottom of the door, that slice of gray which jumped almost imperceptibly wider with each *BANG! (Shreek!)* . . . No way out and no *weapons*. . . . She thought, crazily, of the bowling ball but, God, she'd never be able to heft it high enough to *throw* it for God's sake . . . *BANG! (Shreeek!)*

"This one's putting up a bit more of a fight, Finley, but it won't take long. . . ." *BANG! (Shreek!)*

"Aunt Finley, stop pushing me you pushed my face right into a coat hanger, I don't like this, Aunt Finley, this isn't *fun* for me. . . ." And then Terri began to cry loudly, her voice melting surreally through and around Stupid's screeching and the banging from the closet door and also reaching deep down inside Finley's heart and pulling out something horrible and frightening there and then Finley was crying, too, but she couldn't afford to cry right now, get control, Finley. . . .

But— Coat hangers raining down on her niece's sobbing head, clattering to the floor. The bowling ball. . . . Down onto hands and knees then, groping along the wall. . . . *BANG! (Shreek!)*, muffled cursing from the other side of the door. . . . *Here* it is. She stood, carefully, the bowling ball tote gripped in her trembling hands, and lifted it, carefully, over her head . . . *BANG! (Shreek!)* . . . All three of them in the closet still crying loudly and screeching and pray to God they keep doing so, have to cover the noise so he won't suspect. . . .

And all the while as she cried, her voice straining up and out with as much gasping breath as she could muster, her arms were reaching up as well, shaking, reaching up and ever so carefully placing the bowling ball just *so* at the leading edge of that sagging shelf. *Creeeak,* the shelf went, and Finley felt its tormented groan through her arms and shoulders, hoped he wouldn't be able to hear it, too, through the answering screams of the world's dumbest parakeet. . . .

Smith had indeed stopped working at the upper pin when she began crying, but as she finally paused for breath and backed again into the closet's recesses, pushing Terri further back, he said, "I'm afraid that—" *BANG! (Shreeeek!)* "—I really will have to speed things up now, Finley. . . ." A final *BANG!* (and a final *Shreek!)* but the pin held, then she could see the gray light at the bottom of the door spreading in a narrow but widening line up the hinged side—*he was pulling the door off the top hinge!*

She began to wail now, involuntarily, nothing at all to do with covering up any sounds. She had no illusions about the bowling ball, it was no higher than his face, she didn't plan to drop it onto his head, it was just a distraction, a little diversion to give her the split second she'd need for the real thing . . . *rrrrriiippp* went the door frame each time he pulled at it, God help her, let the blessed shelf hold till the right moment, sobbing, Terri whining incomprehensibly now, Finley herself groping with her hands through the clothes on the rack, please let this work. . . .

With a final rip and a crash, the molding around the closet door gave way. When she paused to suck in her breath, Finley thought she could hear, as if coming from another town or part of the country, the sound of someone banging on the apartment door itself. Or maybe her ears were simply still ringing from the banging on the closet hinges. But yes! There was a voice from the hall outside the apartment, from that other part of the country, the real world, a voice tagged with a question mark at the end of every sentence. *"Finley?"* said the voice. *"Terri?"*

Time stopped for a moment in the closet. Then, "Yes," came that other nearer voice as his shadow moved to fill the doorway. "I will probably get caught this time. So," and he chuckled, unnervingly, "so why bother going through with this? *For no reason at all, Finley, for no reason at all."* He stepped into the doorway then, came *into the closet with them,* and stepped forward. She stopped sobbing, caught her breath, *made* herself stop crying, in order to concentrate, even Terri and Stupid were hushed and still now as though breathless at the moment's drama, *good;* she would need to time this— "Love you, dear," he added, and *laughed,* and in spite of her resolve Finley felt this time a *scream* rising in her throat as he took another step forward, his black form outlined now like a nightmare in the flickering light filtering in from behind him through the bedroom window, and she was still screaming when she yanked down, *hard,* on the handful of clothes in her left hand and that goddamned shelf at last gave way and came crashing down and startled the bejeezus out of all of them there in the closet, and she was still screaming when she pulled back her right arm, swathed in a pair of jeans, and then thrust with her every last uttermost breath, the uncoiled coat hanger gripped tightly in her right fist aimed, as nearly as she could tell, for his startled face. She was still screaming a few minutes later, not at the thin trickle of her own blood leaking through the narrow slash in her forearm but screaming, so it would seem to her ever after, in concert with this man's scream dying even now, dying with his last breath, the coat hanger cork-screwed through one eye and beyond, the coat hanger ever more weakly, spasmodically gripped by both of his gloved hands, Finley and he joined, shuddering, brought terribly together in sound and pinned neatly, at last as at first as always, at opposite ends of a length of wire.

Terri's crying was completely uncontrollable now, but through it Finley could hear the word "Daddy" repeated over and over. She herself was shuddering and crying and gasping, and she wasn't sure afterward but it seemed that in every gasp sounded the single word "jane," repeatedly. Then there was a crash from the living room, and then the crazy oblique scattering white light of a flashlight, and the sound of a querulous voice shouting terri-fied questions about her name. She almost believed she had never in her life heard a voice so sweet.

Chapter Twenty-Two

"You all right, Finley?" Morris's voice brought her gently but unequivocally back to the here and now. The now was Monday afternoon, three days later; the here, on a train headed from New York City back to New Brunswick, Finley sitting in a seat by herself, facing the one occupied by Morris and Gus. The three of them had come into the city today to be escorted by New York police detectives through the apartment of this, this Smith person.

"Hmm? Yes, sorry, Morris. Daydreaming, I guess."

Gus leaned forward across the small space separating their seats. "So your brother's a cop," he said. "You never even mentioned a brother before this."

She shook her head. No, she'd never mentioned a brother before. Not to Gus. Nor to Jane. . . .

Nancy had caught up with Warren a couple blocks from Finley's apartment; after walking together for a few minutes more, they'd stopped for a single drink, just a beer, at McGarrity's of all places. She'd eventually managed to calm him down and then they'd strolled briskly arm in arm, shivering in the cold night air, back to Finley's apartment. To chaos; to horror. After banging on the apartment door for several minutes without reply, realizing in consequence that something must be seriously wrong, Warren had gone to his car and charged back to the apartment, armed with a pistol which he kept in his glove compartment and a flashlight. And then he'd broken in and found them, still huddled in the back of the closet, not daring to step over the form lying prone on the floor.

The rest of Friday night and Saturday morning had been a blur, would probably always be a blur for her. The black-clad thing in the closet had eventually been removed, of course; to the extent she remembered anything else, it was all the gentle questions to which she'd replied, numbly, from police, all the insistent questioning glances from her neighbors and the Falcos. In fact, the only one with no questions for a change had been Warren, something deep in his being sufficiently shocked by what he'd seen to drive him to declaratives. "Never seen anything like this," he kept repeating, "never." And, "I got here too *late,*" which, oddly, seemed to have rattled him more than anything.

And in the motel room Friday night—all of them having agreed that there was no way they'd get to sleep in the apartment—with Stupid chirping sleepily and finally silent from beneath his Garfield cage cover, with Nancy holding Terri in one bed, rocking her back and forth, crooning to her, then Warren had leaned across to Finley and almost whispered, in tones almost too quiet for her to hear, "You'll come back to Tree-of-Life with us for a couple days. I'll bring you back Sunday night if you want, or you can stay longer, Sis." She had accepted the decision with gratitude, and unable to speak for a moment had merely touched him on the wrist, nodded quickly, and blinked back a sudden hot moisture in her eyes.

But once she'd talked to Gus and learned of this planned excursion into the city, she did indeed want to return on Sunday. She wanted to see the guy's apartment. Like he had seen hers, *almost* like he had seen hers.

But there was little of interest to see. The weights, the knives mounted on the wall (one niche conspicuously empty), the kooky framed "Pelagian Creed," the all-black wardrobe, even the PC—there was nothing there that had for Finley the slightest connection, the slightest bit of intellectual or emotional resonance. Nothing there said to her, You knew this person. Certainly nothing said to her, "Jane lived here," and at the memory of that awful vacuum Finley's throat once again constricted. . . .

There were the file folders of photographs of Redman's models, of course, from which three photos were missing. Somewhere out there, as with Finley, two young women were staring puzzled at the screens of their computers, each of them puzzled that the dear friend whose picture she'd just received should have disappeared so suddenly and so finally. . . .

From Smith's apartment they had headed downtown, to the Pelagius Institute. Pince had already been interrogated by the New York police (who had satisfied themselves that he had nothing to do with Smith's activities), but Morris and Gus wanted to meet him for themselves. As small as he was, he seemed to have shrunken since the first time Finley saw him, and at the same time grown if possible even grayer. He seemed vague, confounded, and, well, not so sure of himself. Frightened, almost. His parakeet was gone, and the door to the paint-bombed meeting room was padlocked.

". . . one weird son of a bitch," Gus was saying now of Pince. Then he nudged Morris in the ribs, gestured at Finley, and said, "*She* told us that. Hell of a cop there, Morris."

"Tell me about it," said Morris. "If I know her she'll never let me forget it. Every year at appraisal time it'll be, 'Remember the time I cracked the Smith project?' and 'When can I become an agent, Morris?' And I'll tell her not now, damn it, but she'll pretend like she didn't hear me."

Finley smiled at the teasing. She knew deep in her heart that she hadn't cracked anything; indeed, *it* had almost killed *her*. And on the other hand Morris was right—she suspected that she'd never ever ever forget this project, certainly not for a long time to come.

But she wasn't really attending to the banter of the two men. She was twisting a tissue in her hands, repeatedly, shredding it, and staring out the window. If you asked her what she was staring at, she'd smile a little, a little bit embarrassed, and reply, "Oh— nothing." But she wasn't staring at nothing. The train had pulled out of the Newark station some twenty minutes ago, was threading its noisome way through a maze of New Jersey suburbs, crossing backyards with a roar and soaring in a pavement-shaking clatter over Main Streets. And Finley was staring at the telephone poles zipping past the train in synch with the click-clack of the rails, staring at the wires draped like an exotic black necklace from pole to pole to pole, at the mysterious boxes and connectors into and out of which the wires ran, and she was thinking about and *hearing* the tumult of voices they carried. Foreign voices, some were, and some familiar, and some friendly but indistinct; anxious voices, as well as voices resonating with confidence; excitable voices and calm. Voices you would never hear at all, and voices you would never hear again, and voices you would hear, over and over and over, till the day you died.

She shivered a little and tore the last scrap of tissue in two; disposed of it in the trash receptacle sunken into the wall of the car; and then, finally, turned back to the real world.